Margaret Yorke lives in Buckinghamshire. She is a past chair-man of the Crime Writers' Association and her outstanding contribution to the genre has been recently recognised by the award of the 1999 CWA Cartier Diamond Dagger.

Margaret Yorke

False Pretences

WARNER BOOKS

A *Warner* Book

First published in Great Britain in 1998
by Little, Brown and Company

This edition published by Warner Books in 1999

A CIP catalogue record for this book
is available from the British Library.

ISBN 0 7515 2323 2

Typeset by Palimpsest Book Production Limited
Polmont, Stirlingshire

Printed and bound in Great Britain by
Clays Ltd, St Ives plc

Warner Books
A Division of
Little, Brown and Company (UK) Limited
Brettenham House
Lancaster Place
London WC2E 7EN

False Pretences

1

She wanted to scream. The desire to do so came over her at intervals when she was not fully occupied with something that took all her concentration, and she felt that if only she could indulge it, could go to some huge open empty space and fill the silence with her own pain, there would be relief. For it was pain. She must acknowledge that.

Why? Why did she have this urge? Was it a common desire? Could it be a symptom of extreme frustration? Was it the same impulse that drove young men to become vandals? Did everyone have a tendency to violence, only masked by a veneer of civilised self-control? What would happen if she gave way to her compulsion? Suppose she came downstairs one morning, as usual, and put on the kettle for breakfast, then bellowed at the top of her voice? There would be no words: only a banshee wail, a sound like 'Eeeee—' going on and on. She'd turn red, as actors do at moments of high drama, their blood pressure rising, one must assume, a professional hazard, no doubt. But she was not an actress, or not in a professional sense, only in the way that everyone, she now supposed, must be in order to cope with their lives, and if she gave way the verdict would be that she had broken down at last.

Perhaps she had, or was about to, but why now, after so long? And perhaps no one would respond: if anyone heard, they would think the noise came from the radio or television, not from someone's troubled soul, any more than help could be expected if you were attacked. People minded their own business, did not get involved, respected privacy, and expected the same in return. In the end, you were alone, and it was terrifying. No wonder young people formed groups and went round in gangs. Yet solitude was an agreeable state, and peaceful, a condition where fear was absent, but it left you vulnerable to your thoughts. Surrounded by others, keeping active, anxieties could be held at bay.

Alone now, driving along, she tried a small scream in the car, gripping the wheel, staring at the road ahead, not wanting to put anyone else at risk, not even herself. No one would hear; if they did, they might think it was her radio. But the scream, thus uttered, was muted; she maintained control, and what she wanted to do was to lose it.

Isabel slowed down, nearing the West Country town that was her destination. It was a bright, cold day, with occasional flurries of snow, and she had driven nearly a hundred miles from the once rural, but now commuter, almost suburban village where she lived. No one knew where she was: when she left the house, Douglas, who daily caught an early train to London, had already gone; she had stuck a Post-it note to the fridge warning him that she might be late and if so, would telephone. He would think she had gone to the shop, as usual on a Tuesday. Since their marriage, she had never done anything unexpected until now. Even opening Gifts Galore with Joanna had been well discussed in advance. However, when Douglas learned the facts, he would agree that she had a responsibility in this matter and could not walk away from Emily's predicament, which required her physical presence.

The police station was not difficult to find. She'd been given directions on the telephone and, having managed not to make a mistake in the one-way system in the unfamiliar town, drove in between tall iron gates to where there were several parking slots for visitors.

She had never been inside a police station before, and she had not seen Emily since she was a small child with fair, curly hair. What would she be like now? And what had she been doing to get herself arrested? Assault and disorderly conduct, the solicitor's secretary had said on the telephone. Emily had not been granted bail, but Isabel's intervention might make a difference, and anyway, Emily needed her, for her mother was dead and it seemed that there was no one else.

There was a father somewhere, but no one had heard from him for years. After he left her, Emily's mother had gone to Spain where she married a man who was a musician; she had lived with him until her death from an unspecified illness some years ago. Isabel had learned about this from a letter Emily sent her which stated the stark fact. Isabel had written to her at her mother's address, but had had no reply. For a while she had felt that she should try to trace Emily; later, she forgot about her, until yesterday when the telephone call sharply reminded her.

Shock was her first reaction. What had Emily been doing? Surely by now she was pursuing some career, might even be married? Neither activity precluded either assault or disorderly conduct, which Isabel assumed meant, in this case, getting drunk and being rowdy in a public place. What could she do about it, even when she learned the details? The deed was done, and Emily had been arrested. Various reasons for saying this was not her business had entered her mind as she heard herself tell the telephone voice that she would come next day, arriving as early as she could. It was impossible to drive down that night, she stated firmly. This would have meant giving Douglas an explanation, which even now she had avoided. It would have made scant difference, said the woman on the telephone, for before she could arrive, Emily would be tucked up in her cell and, it was to be hoped, asleep, in preparation for her appearance before the magistrates the next day. Time enough tomorrow, the solicitor had said. And now tomorrow was today.

I am not responsible for Emily, Isabel told herself, locking the car. I am not a relative, nor an aunt, only a godmother, because I was her mother's friend.

What am I going to find, she wondered, walking through the police station doors, hesitating, seeing there were several other people waiting for attention. She took her turn behind a woman reporting a lost dog and a man who was required to produce his driving licence and proof of car insurance. By the time her turn came, she was in a trance, almost forgetting the reason for her visit.

Once this was established, she was led to the regions beyond the front office, and into a small room. There, a few minutes later, she met Emily again.

She would never have recognised her friend's daughter: where was the attractive child with the mass of fair curls whom Isabel remembered from when the families were neighbours more than twenty years ago? Now she saw, shambling into the room, an ill-dressed, overweight young woman with a shaven head, haggard and exhausted, who could have been any age but was, in fact, twenty-three. What could have happened to her to bring her to this state? Isabel was horrified.

'Emily,' she said, and 'well—' her voice trailing off, for it wasn't well, at all.

'They asked me who I'd like informed,' said Emily. Her voice was flat and slurred. 'I couldn't think of anyone.'

But you had two brothers, Isabel thought: and, somewhere, perhaps, a father. And a stepfather. Where were they?

'Well, you remembered my address,' Isabel answered brusquely. 'What's been happening to you, Emily?'

A woman police officer had brought them cups of strong milky tea. Emily gulped at hers while Isabel, trying not to notice the noisy slurping, sipped her own. The same officer had told Isabel that Emily had been arrested while demonstrating against the construction of a new road; she had been living in a tent on the site, and when ejected, had, allegedly, become disruptive and violent, throwing stones and, eventually, hitting a security guard on the face with a sturdy stick.

'I had to do it,' Emily said now. 'They took away my home. I'd lived on the site for months. I'd got friends.' She swallowed, and then said, 'They took my tent away. That's theft.'

'But where's your real home?' Isabel asked.

'I hadn't got one. Just the tent,' said Emily.

'But after your mother died – what happened then?' Surely there had been some money?

Emily shrugged. 'I wasn't living with her,' she said. 'Things didn't work out. I shared a flat with people, but I had to leave.'

She'd written about her mother's death from Spain; presumably she'd simply been there for the funeral. Isabel was silent. Had she really understood? Emily seemed to be saying that she had feared to lose her only home, a tent, and had aggressively defended it.

'Didn't you realise you were committing a criminal offence?' she asked.

'I had a bed last night, didn't I?' said Emily, and she grinned a strange, wild grin which made Isabel's flesh creep. 'Where else was I to go?'

And what was Isabel to do now? Emily was due to appear before the magistrates that afternoon. Unless bailed, she would probably be sent to prison. That had been made quite clear to Isabel before she even met the girl. Or woman. Emily's manner and accent were those of a teenage drop-out, but that was not what she was – well, a drop-out, maybe, but no teenager.

'What made you take up this protest?' Isabel asked, and Emily launched into a rehearsed discourse about the environment, much of which made perfect sense but it was recited almost parrot-fashion. 'I'd my friends, too, you see,' she added.

What friends, wondered Isabel, and where were they now? None seemed to be supporting her. Perhaps they were occupying other cells in the police station. She would have to go to court and see what happened there.

If Emily were to be allowed bail, she, Isabel, would have to guarantee it, and she might have to take Emily home with her, unless the magistrates forbade her to leave the area. Perhaps they would.

Clutching at this possibility, Isabel made ready to attend the hearing.

If he'd known of her existence, he'd have sent her presents at Christmas and on her birthday, even though he had never seen her. But no one told him she'd been born.

Hadn't he a right to her? She was his daughter. He found

out about her when she was four and he came back to England. On a whim, he had returned to the village where Alice, her mother, lived with her elderly parents. He'd been sorry for her when he discovered what her situation was. She was born in her parents' middle age; her father, starting with very little capital, had anticipated the potential of plastic containers for perishable foods, and had built up a thriving business which he had sold soon after his sixtieth birthday, making a small fortune. After this, he had undertaken the chairmanship of another company. His wife, who had once been his secretary, had done his paperwork at home, and other tasks arising from charities they supported. As they grew older and Alice finished her education at Northtown High School, they saw no need for her to go to university but sent her to a secretarial college, requiring her to live at home and take care of them. She had dutifully complied, while working in a museum, mainly in the stacks, maintaining and repairing artefacts and pictures kept in store. He had met her in a pub one evening. Alice often went there, seeking social contact, he discovered.

She'd been an easy conquest. At the time, he was not long out of prison, unemployed and not looking very hard for work. He'd picked her up. She was sitting at a tiny table on her own, drinking vodka. Of course, it didn't smell on the breath. Her parents mustn't know she drank.

After he had met her on several consecutive evenings in the pub, he'd learned that Alice's father wanted some decorating and repair work done in the house, and he had volunteered for it. An appointment was made for him to estimate, and when he met her parents, he implied that he could oblige them as he was waiting to go abroad to a new position; he had no ties or other obligations.

The size of the rather ugly Victorian house was a surprise.

There was money here, lots of it, and the unmarried daughter was the only heir.

He made a good job of redecorating the high-ceilinged rooms; he had done plenty of casual work in his wavering career and the task was well within his powers. He told Alice that he had sold up everything and was living in lodgings, and it was not many days before she persuaded her parents to offer him the flat above the stables, so that while he did the work, he was on the spot. She still left the house daily for her own job but now she did not need the pub, for there was purpose in her return home.

She did not fall in love with Godfrey, but for a brief period she experienced lust. Without difficulty, he seduced her in his stable flat, pinning her down on the thin mattress where he slept dreamlessly each night. The narrow bedstead was iron, like a prison bed. This was where the gardener-cum-chauffeur her parents had once employed had lived. Now, an elderly man came twice a week to keep the weeds at bay, and each season a schoolboy did the mowing.

There were corners of the garden which Alice tended. She liked flowers and grew sweetpeas and roses, blocks of cornflowers and larkspur. Godfrey found this quite an endearing trait: one that he could tolerate.

He'd tell her the job abroad had fallen through. Then he'd marry her and be quids in for ever.

His plan failed.

The old man had thrown him out.

Not physically: he was too frail for that, but he had sent for Godfrey, who was still living in the flat although the work he had contracted for was finished. He had been paid a weekly sum, in cash; the paint, paper, and other materials he had used had been billed direct so that Godfrey had not been able to work a racket on charging those up profitably. Even so, he was living free, and soon, he calculated, he would be the couple's son-in-law.

'It's time for you to leave,' the old man said. 'You have done the work to my satisfaction and there's an end to it. I will give you a reference if you need one, but I'm sure you're anxious to get another post abroad, are you not? Since that was your plan when you first came here as my daughter's friend.'

'Well – er – I haven't yet applied elsewhere,' he said.

'No, I thought as much,' the old man said. 'You expected to remain here, did you not? Expected to make a fool of my silly daughter and stay permanently. I knew what was in your mind as soon as you moved into the flat,' he added, and as Godfrey instantly denied such plans, he held up a hand, like a policeman halting traffic. 'Don't waste your breath on excuses. I've met men like you before and I've protected my daughter from fortune hunters. She gets not a penny if she marries without my consent.'

'She's of age.' Godfrey thought she must be thirty.

'The condition applies, whatever her age,' her father said. 'And to protect her after that, everything is left in trust.'

This was a shock, but even so, there would be the house, the benefits. And the boredom. That was inevitable; she was tedious already.

'I shall give you a thousand pounds in cash on condition that you depart before my daughter returns from the museum, that you leave her no message, and that you undertake not to contact her again,' said the old man.

Godfrey did it. A thousand pounds now was easy money after six weeks' free board and lodging, with pay and with some sexual gratification on the side. It took him to Toronto, where he got married and stayed until his wife, who ran her own letting agency, threw him out. After that he had several tries at business, but each venture was a failure. Eventually, when a scheme inviting subscriptions to a non-existent magazine was exposed, he fled back to Britain with his profits before he could be arrested. In the plane, he thought about the house in Fordswick once again, and about the girl who'd been so hot for him. And about the money.

Was she still there? Had she married, with or without the old man's approval? Were the old parents dead?

If nothing better turned up, he might go there and find out.

Life is a journey punctuated with crossroads and side turnings. One wrong decision and the traveller may find there is no space for going back, though there may be an opportunity, further ahead, to take a lane leading away from the false trail he has been pursuing. Perhaps it will convey him, by a longer route, to the destination which was his aim, but perhaps it will lead him to a dead end or along confusing byways until he has lost his way completely. The choice may not always be his; life can throw obstacles into his path – a fallen tree, a mandatory alternative route – and he must look for signs to guide him in the right direction.

Alice's choice had been to use Godfrey as a means to change her own monotonous existence and escape the bondage to her parents which ordained her life. She had never before met a man who showed any lasting interest in her. She had lost touch with her few school friends, and did not win new ones at the secretarial college. Alice was not someone people remembered or sought out. Her colleagues at work found her quiet, dull, and dependable; as her duties at the museum lay behind the scenes, she rarely came in contact with the public, so her social skills did not improve. When she and Godfrey met, she was on the prowl, desperately seeking someone who would rescue her. She had even considered responding to a lonely hearts advertisement in the press, but many required use of a telephone, and she could not have strangers calling her at home; nor could she suddenly start receiving unexplained letters. It was even difficult to go out at night, though sometimes she did manage a concert or a film, alone, but pretending to her parents that she was meeting Mary, a friend she had invented. Mary provided an alibi for her meetings with Godfrey, before he moved in.

Quite soon, she realised that he was not going to rescue her in the sense that she required. He did the work he was engaged to carry out, and effectively, but there was no talk of seeking another job overseas, or anywhere else, come to that, and it became clear that her parents did not like or trust him. Her father minutely inspected the bills from the builders' merchants, questioning everything, and any hopes Godfrey had of buying surplus materials and selling them on the side were soon proved to be in vain. Her mother did not appreciate his manner, though Godfrey was extremely polite to her; he overdid it, Alice thought.

She did not care for the sex. At first it was exciting, in an alarming way, because it was a new experience, and she hoped it would improve with practice; after all, it was supposed to be what life was all about. But Godfrey was rough and impatient, so that her eager anticipation turned to reluctant dread. She had finally stopped slipping out at night after they had spent one Sunday afternoon in the stable flat. Lying beside her, sweating, sated, and smoking a cigarette, which she hated and which he always did after sex, he led the conversation round to the possibility of his staying on, doing the flat up to make it more comfortable, buying a large bed. She saw what was in his mind and knew she could not go along with any thought of marriage. He had said he could get a job locally, or travel daily up to London. The next thing would be his asking her father to find a post for him.

For all she knew, he might already have a wife. He had told her nothing more about himself and never mentioned any family. If she asked about his childhood he changed the subject. Perhaps he was an orphan, had been in care, she thought, and was not far off the mark.

She did not discover that she was pregnant until after he had gone away, suddenly departing without warning. Then she made her one bold stand. This, at least, she could accomplish: produce a child and bring it up, and now she was glad that Godfrey was not there to have a part in it.

Her parents spoke of their shame and disappointment. She endured a long sermon from her father about unscrupulous men wanting to ensnare wealthy wives, and another from her mother who wondered how she could have been so stupid.

'If you had to behave like that, couldn't you have been more careful?' she demanded. 'The doctor would have prescribed a contraceptive without question.'

But how could Alice go to the health centre, where she was known, with such a request?

Belatedly, it occurred to her that Godfrey must have thought that she had done so. Hadn't he even realised that she was a virgin? Surely it was obvious. They did still exist, after all; she was sure there were others as old as she was.

When her little daughter was born, the joy she felt was

unimaginable. This small, perfect creature was her own creation, and she did not have to share her with another soul. What was surprising was her parents' response. At first grim with disapproval, and going nowhere near the hospital, both were captivated by the baby as she turned from a tiny infant into a rounded, chubby little individual who would smile and gurgle. For the first time in her life, Alice knew true happiness.

So that when Rowena was four, and he returned, her heart turned over in dismay.

2

Isabel knew she should warn Douglas that she would be late arriving home and would have Emily with her, but it was not an easy call to make. She decided to ring before he came back himself, and leave a message on the answerphone, thus avoiding explanations at this point.

Douglas liked people to be conventional. Their own two sons had not openly rebelled in any major way; Matthew was now a systems analyst while Toby was in his final year at Southampton, reading law. When he saw Emily, Douglas would have a shock, just as she had done, but she couldn't simply give the girl some money and tell her to check into a guest-house until her next court hearing, for the terms of her bail were that she resided with Isabel in the meantime. Besides, it would be so cruel. How could she abandon this poor, bewildered girl? And what had brought her to this state?

Driving home with her, Isabel was aware of how the girl – or woman: she was no girl – smelled. It was a mix of odours: sweat, and other body smells. Isabel had even contemplated renting a hotel room and insisting she have a bath, then buying her some clothes before she took her home, but this was a grown woman, not a child; she could not so humiliate her. And besides, she must be deeply wretched to be in such a plight.

She seemed, however, to be untroubled, sitting beside Isabel in the car. She had said nothing since they left the court, merely smiled and climbed meekly into it, her shabby hold-all in the rear.

'I expect you're hungry,' said Isabel. 'We'll get on to the motorway, and then we'll stop at a service station.' Maybe, in the washroom, she could persuade Emily to use what facilities there were, but until she put on fresh clothes, nothing much could be done about the smell. Isabel felt like Professor Higgins in *Pygmalion*, confronted by Eliza. She concentrated on driving, watching the signs, anxious not to take the wrong turning, avoiding conversation. Just as she was thinking she would play the tape loaded into her car stereo, Emily began a soft humming: hymn tunes, Isabel recognised with amazement, one after another until eventually they ceased and, glancing sideways, she saw that her passenger had fallen asleep.

After that, Isabel drove faster, putting the miles behind her, anxious to get back to safe, familiar territory, planning how she would run a deep, hot bath, offer a shampoo for those cropped locks, produce a nightdress, postpone further plans until the morning.

She would have to talk to Douglas as soon as they were alone. She must explain. But how to begin? Her message on the answerphone had been elliptical, to say the least.

'I may be very late,' she had said. 'Midnight, or even later. I can't explain now, but don't worry, and don't wait up.'

Would he? She did not know. Sometimes she wondered if they knew one another at all, these days. They never quarrelled. If they disagreed about anything, the matter was dropped, and usually, where decisions had to be made, if differing views prevailed, a compromise was reached. This must be how most marriages which lasted evolved. Douglas would not be pleased to see Emily; she was hardly an attractive guest, though cleaning her up would improve her, and Emily herself could scarcely object when Isabel proposed such action. Gaol, after all, was the alternative.

Isabel concentrated on driving through the darkness of the night. It was very cold; she hoped it would not snow again. Emily slept on, and the miles rolled by. Useless to fret about how best to explain: Douglas would consider any godmotherly duties were long since discharged and that she was foolish to have become involved, but he would not refuse to have the girl in the house, though after seeing her, he might want to lock up the silver and Isabel's few pieces of jewellery.

Isabel had no idea about how Emily had spent the years since her mother's death. Her thoughts kept returning to the girl's physical squalor; it was difficult to avoid reflecting on it, since the stale smells from her body and her clothes were increasing in the warmth of the car. She opened the window to admit a current of fresh air, but at last she had to stop. As the signs for a service area appeared, she pulled into the inside lane, preparing to turn off the motorway.

Emily did not stir as the car slowed down and Isabel looked for a parking slot close to the buildings. Even when they stopped, and Isabel turned the engine off, she slept on. What to do? Though she could buy coffee and sandwiches to take away, Isabel could not lock the girl in the car while she did so, and in any case, she must make her visit the washrooms.

She put a hand on Emily's wrist which, in its tangled, dirty woollen sweater, protruded from her felted khaki coat, and shook her.

'Wake up, Emily,' she said, and repeated, 'Emily – wake up.'

She had to keep on shaking her and speaking to her loudly before at last she roused Emily, who appeared confused. She seemed to have forgotten what had happened to her, and who Isabel was. Isabel was growing impatient as she tried to explain where they were and why they had stopped. However, once she understood, Emily obediently clambered out of the car and set off towards the building which housed the caféteria and the toilets.

Isabel, locking the car, caught up with her, ready to guide her inside, but it seemed that she knew her way about, heading straight for the sign pointing to the female facilities.

'I've been here before,' she said brightly. 'I stopped here on the way down to the site. Stayed the night. It was warm and dry.'

It would be, Isabel supposed. She was pleased to see that when she emerged from the cubicle, Emily made an effort to wash her face as well as her hands. Isabel combed her own hair and touched up her face, as an example more than anything, for who would notice at this time of night? It made her feel better, though, and she brightened as they went into the caféteria. It would work out. Somehow she would reclaim Emily and return her to mainstream life.

They both had sausages and chips, with tea for Emily and coffee for Isabel. The place was almost deserted at this hour, but there were a few individuals lingering at tables, hoping to sit the night out, Isabel supposed. You could, she thought: you could sleep in your vehicle, if you had one.

'When you were here before, were you with friends?' she asked, sitting opposite Emily at a table near the wall.

'No. I had a lift. I met the friends later,' Emily said. 'At the site. It was great.'

'Where had you come from?'

'London.'

'Oh?'

But Emily did not want to tell her any more. She was tucking into the sausages and chips as if she had not eaten for a month. Perhaps she hadn't, or not properly, thought Isabel, though no doubt the police had been obliged to feed her while she was in custody. She was so fat. She hadn't starved while in her tent or up the tree, which, it seemed, had for a time been her perch.

Isabel was also appreciating her meal. She had already driven nearly three hundred miles today and still had over sixty to go. It wouldn't do to fall asleep at the wheel.

Emily ate a piece of apple pie while Isabel drank a second cup of coffee, hoping it would keep her awake for the rest of the journey. The meal had revived the younger woman and she began singing again as they drove on: still hymns. Isabel did not ask her about her choice of music. Perhaps the Salvation Army had been earlier rescuers.

Was she an obsessive conservationist or a straightforward drop-out?

'We're nearly home,' Isabel said at last. The persistent humming and the constant repetition of *Abide With Me*, always a rather depressing air, which Emily had settled on for some miles, was getting on her nerves. When they turned into the driveway of the house to which Isabel and Douglas had moved from London three years ago, lights were on downstairs, but Douglas had gone up to bed. Isabel unlocked the front door, ushering her companion inside and whispering to her to be as quiet as possible. If he were asleep, she would be spared an explanation till the morning and then there would not be much time before he had to leave for the station: indeed, he might depart without discovering, until his return in the evening, that they had a guest.

But it was not to be. He, despite her reassuring message, was anxious because this unexplained absence was so unlike Isabel, and was listening for her. In his green towelling robe, he appeared at the top of the stairs while she and Emily were still in the hall.

'Who – what – ?' he began, descending, a magisterial figure, bare-legged but wearing slippers.

'Oh Douglas, I'm sorry if we woke you,' said Isabel. 'You remember Emily Frost, don't you?' She spoke brightly, in what her sons called her hostess voice.

Douglas, nourishing his resentment at not knowing why Isabel had behaved so unpredictably, had tried to keep awake, but had finally dropped off, and was now in the fuddled state of one who has woken suddenly. He had been genuinely concerned because it was a bitterly cold night, and wherever Isabel had gone, it was no weather for her to be out driving on her own. He did not remember Emily, and what he saw now standing in his hall was an obese figure of indeterminate sex, wearing a greatcoat which must have come from army surplus over baggy tracksuit trousers and filthy trainers. The round head was cropped so short that it looked almost bald. A small gilt horse dangled from a single earring, and shadowed eyes stared at him out of a pallid face.

Isabel saw his total mystification. She, after all, had at least known whom she was going to see when she set off that morning, even though the reality was so astonishing.

'She was only a child when we last saw her,' she said, and even to herself she sounded like a reassuring nurse. 'I've brought her here because she has no home at the moment,' Isabel continued. 'You go back to bed and I'll explain in the morning.' Or, if you insist, as soon as I've dealt with Emily, she added mentally.

Douglas, for once outmanoeuvred, turned without a word and did as she suggested. Both of them were sure that he would not go to sleep.

Emily was giggling like a child. Isabel wondered if she had taken some drug; those capacious pockets could contain all sorts of things, but there hadn't been much chance for her to delve into them without Isabel's noticing, and surely the police would have searched them thoroughly, confiscating anything suspicious? Perhaps it was just reaction; Emily, at least, was rested, having slept for most of the journey.

'Come along,' said Isabel, leading the way upstairs.

The house, built about fifteen years ago, had two bathrooms, which was a relief, as Emily could be kept out of theirs. Isabel opened the door of the second one and said she would find some towels.

'You should have a bath before you go to bed, Emily,' she said firmly. 'I'm sure you didn't have the chance of one while you were in custody.'

'I don't know when I did last have one,' Emily said sunnily. 'Or a shower. It wasn't top priority, where I've been.' She seemed to bear no resentment at the implied criticism of her personal hygiene.

'No – I thought not,' said Isabel. 'Perhaps you'd undress in the bathroom and leave your clothes there. We'll see about them in the morning.'

'Oh, they're all right,' said Emily.

'Have you any spare underclothes?' asked Isabel.

'Yeah – but not washed. They're in here.' Emily indicated her shabby rucksack. Isabel assumed it contained all her possessions.

There was no chance that any of Isabel's underclothes would fit Emily.

'Take them out and leave them with those you're wearing outside the bathroom door, and I'll put the washing machine on now,' said Isabel. 'Here's your room,' she added, opening a door across the landing. 'The bed's made up.' She always kept the spare room ready for an unheralded guest. She wondered when Emily had last slept in a bed.

She fetched two big, soft towels and put them in the bathroom, where Emily was slowly undoing her enormous khaki coat. 'It might be a good idea to wash your hair,' Isabel suggested. 'There's some shampoo in the cupboard.' Drying those wisps, which though barely visible could still be host to nits, would be no problem. She reached up and took it down, and a bottle of bath essence, some of which she poured generously into the tub. Then she went into the spare bedroom, drew the curtains, and turned down the bed. The duvet cover was a new one, printed in a pale impressionistic flower design. It was pretty, as was the room. Would Emily appreciate it, or would she rather be back in her field?

It didn't really matter. Isabel was exhausted, but she knew she was beyond sleep herself, and she still had to give Douglas some account of why she had brought this unwashed young woman home with her. She could postpone the moment by bustling about, ensuring the welfare of her guest, although scurrying was not her style.

On the landing, Emily's heap of discarded garments grew as she shed what she had on, casting them, as instructed, outside the bathroom door on top of those which were in her bag. As a matter of sheer curiosity, Isabel would have liked to know when she had last removed them, but the answer might be too dispiriting. When the pile had stopped mounting and the door had closed, she carried them all down to the kitchen and put the lighter clothing – tracksuit, a single shrunken felted vest, and some knickers – in the machine. There was no bra. The thick sweater would have to be washed separately. The dreadful coat was beyond reclamation; she did not want to leave it in the house lest it was host to parasites, so she stuffed it straight into a bin bag and put it out with the rubbish. Some other coat must be found for Emily.

What was she going to do about her own work tomorrow – or rather, later on today? She knew Joanna could not go in again as she had an appointment in Birmingham to see some manufacturers, but she couldn't abandon Emily with scarcely any clothes. Perhaps one of Douglas's old anoraks would tide her over.

Returning to the house, she put the kettle on. A hot drink might settle her, she reflected, and perhaps Emily would like one, too. Leaving it to switch itself off, she went upstairs. Sounds of splashing came from the bathroom, but luckily no singing. Isabel decided to get undressed herself; she would like a bath, too, after her long, exhausting day, and perhaps it would clear away the aura of Emily's smells which seemed to linger in her nostrils.

In the bedroom, Douglas was sitting up in bed, his steel-rimmed glasses on his nose, aggressively reading a life of William Gladstone. He had been plodding through the book for weeks. What would Gladstone, saviour of prostitutes, make of Emily, wondered Isabel, who had also wondered about Gladstone's motivation.

Douglas put a marker in the page, closed the book, took off his spectacles, and spoke.

'Well? Are you going to explain?' he asked.

'Of course, but not now. I must make sure she's in bed

and has all she needs,' said Isabel. 'I'm going to have some camomile tea. Would you like anything?'

He didn't care for herbal teas, or Horlicks, or any of the other comforting brews she sometimes drank. Outwardly calm, Isabel was often unable to still her restless mind, which churned away at night, magnifying legitimate worries and inventing needless others.

'No,' he said, and added, 'Thank you.'

He had a right to be annoyed about the disturbance to their routine which she had introduced.

'I'm sorry, Douglas, but I couldn't leave her with nowhere to go,' she said. 'Do try to go back to sleep. I won't be long, and I'll be as quiet as I can.' A postmortem, after all this, would be hard to bear.

She left him to it, and went to run her own bath. The house, which should have been tranquil at this hour, was riven with muted sounds – her own bath running, Emily's, in the other bathroom, now draining away, and, downstairs, the washing-machine trundling her clothes around.

Isabel had put out her largest, loosest nightdress for Emily. If it ripped, too bad. She went downstairs and brewed the camomile tea. Emily would like this, she was sure: it went with her recent life style. She squeezed lemon into it, spooned some honey into Emily's but not her own, and took the mugs upstairs.

Emily was now in bed. The pleasant fragrance of Morny's French Fern – the talcum powder in the second bathroom – emanated from her. This was a big improvement on her previous emissions.

'Thanks, Isabel,' Emily said. 'You've been great.'

Her eyes suddenly filled and her cheeks reddened but Isabel was too tired to cope with tears now.

'Let's leave all that until we've had some sleep,' she said. 'Don't hurry up in the morning. Douglas leaves early – he'll probably be gone before you wake up.'

Emily nodded. Blinking, she accepted the mug Isabel handed her.

'Goodnight,' Isabel said, and left her to it, hastening to the bathroom.

Some contests you have to win, and she won hers, that night. Despite his resolution, Douglas had dropped off, with Gladstone on the floor and his glasses on his nose. Isabel managed to rescue them without his waking.

3

When Emily woke up the next morning, she had no clothes to wear.

It was early. Her watch, beside her on the night table, said six o'clock. It was a practical watch which also revealed the date, and had an in-built alarm; Daisy, another conservationist, had stolen it one day when they were in town collecting Daisy's benefit. Daisy, who had helped Emily before, had lifted several watches while Emily, to cause a distraction, asked the assistant about a stereo player. They'd got away with it; Daisy had kept one watch for herself, given another to Emily, and sold the rest.

They had slept a lot at first, while they were in the trees, but latterly the teams sent to rout them out had woken them at dawn and they had had to be alert to dodge pursuit along their rope walkways. Emily had soon moved into a tent. Some had burrowed underground and dug caverns where they waited to be flushed out like vermin. Emily couldn't have done that; it was too claustrophobic. Now, although she had sunk into bed grateful for its warm, womb-like welcome, with the soft pillow beneath her unaccustomed head and the duvet over her, she felt suddenly oppressed. She pushed back the bedding and stood up, rested after her sleep in the car and from the night, and went to the window, pulling back the curtains. It was going to be a fine day; the rising sun spread a golden glow beyond the trees at the end of the garden. She wondered what they were: a few leaves clung to them. They were not sturdy oaks, like those which had been felled around her on the site. The central heating had not yet come on and she shivered, dressed in just the thin cotton nightgown Isabel had provided. She looked around the room, then opened the fitted wardrobe which ran along one wall. Hanging in it was a man's tweed jacket. Emily put it on, and, bare-footed, went downstairs to explore the lower part of the house.

Douglas, coming into the kitchen later for his breakfast, found her sitting at the table eating cornflakes, which were piled high in a bowl. A steaming mug of instant coffee was beside her.

'Hullo,' she said, as he came in. 'Thank you for letting me stay. Shall I make you some coffee?'

Angry words had been springing to Douglas's lips as he entered the room and saw the strange young woman he had encountered in the small hours of the morning ensconced as if she owned the place, but her greeting briefly disarmed him.

'I can manage, thank you,' he replied, refilling the kettle before pouring out the muesli which would not promote cholesterol in his system.

'It's lovely, having electricity,' Emily said, brightly. 'I'd forgotten its convenience.'

'Had you, indeed?' said Douglas. 'Where have you been living, then? In a tree?'

'Oh, that's so funny,' Emily chortled, almost choking on her cornflakes. She beamed at him. 'Hasn't Isabel explained?'

'Not yet,' said Douglas grimly. 'You both arrived too late. Suppose you do it now?' He put two slices of wholemeal bread into the toaster, and set his coffee cup, with its individual filled filter, on the table, then sat facing her.

Emily, who had spent weeks confronting police officers and security guards, not to mention sheriff's men, was not intimidated by this tall, thin man with, she had to admit to herself, rather a cross expression, and angry brown eyes beneath thick, dark brows. She would tell him what he wanted to know while he ate his breakfast. She had finished hers, unless she were to have a second bowlful of cornflakes; they were so crisp and delicious; you couldn't keep such stuff dry, sleeping out.

'It's like this,' she said, and was about to tell him when he looked at his watch.

'There's no time now,' he said. He hadn't yet fed his tropical fish, kept in a tank in his study. 'I'll hear about it later. I have a train to catch.'

Emily was glad of the reprieve. She felt he might not like her story.

Douglas, a conventional man, a senior civil servant who lived by rules, had shuddered at the sight of this goddaughter of Isabel's, now wearing his old sports jacket. Where had she sprung from? Isabel, an only child, had no nieces or nephews; he did not remember her acquiring responsibility for any godchildren, but she could be secretive and might have kept it to herself. Dimly, he remembered a wedding they had been to, many years ago, when a school friend of hers had married a painter. Was this the product of that union? The glimpse he had had of her last night from his position on the upstairs landing had been far from reassuring; indeed, had it not been for Isabel's sketchy introduction, he would have been confused as to the gender of the visitor. She looked anything but trustworthy, and even in his jacket resembled those shiftless folk who lived off the taxpayer, vagabond scroungers who evaded honest work. Casting an anxious glance around his kitchen, he prepared to leave the house. Isabel would have some explaining to do when he came home this evening.

Upstairs, awake, but unaware of Emily's presence in the kitchen, Isabel stayed in bed until she heard him leave. By the time he returned, she would have dealt with the day, done something about Emily's clothing, and decided how best to present the *fait accompli* to him.

She had to go to work. The success of the gift shop she and Joanna had opened several years ago depended on their cooperation and the dovetailing of any extra helpers they engaged. They sold framed prints, small items of porcelain and pottery, basketwork, novelties, and greetings cards. Their trade fluctuated, but with Christmas over, it had slackened off.

'I have to go out,' she told Emily, who was reading the paper in the kitchen when Isabel came downstairs. She explained about the shop.

'Can't I help?' asked Emily.

'Well—' Isabel hesitated. The alternative was to leave the girl here on her own, with the television, surely a novelty after her outdoor life, to amuse her, and there were plenty of books in the house. What would she do with her if she took her to the shop? For one thing, it was very small, and Emily was large, though as yet not revealed as clumsy. 'We need to sort you out some clothes. I've washed what you had on yesterday. You could do with a few new things.' Probably the best plan was to take her into Northtown, give her some money and send her shopping, but meanwhile she would need covering. Nothing of Isabel's would fit her, but Douglas had a tracksuit which he wore when cycling. Not being one for squash or working out, he bicycled for exercise. That, and one of his old raincoats, would do for now.

They would have to hurry. Isabel wound into action, giving Emily the tracksuit trousers, a green sweater of Toby's and an old anorak. She rescued Douglas's sports jacket, one he was very fond of, and replaced it in the wardrobe. They left together, the girl, now clean, fresh-faced and looking healthy, passable enough, and Isabel in her charcoal pleated skirt and big sweater, wearing a scarlet jacket for the journey.

Emily sat beside her in the car, as excited as a child, her mood very different from the day before. She seemed to have cast her problems from her.

'I've been nowhere for ages,' she said. 'Just the fields. Mind you, I like them. I like nature.'

So do I, thought Isabel, but not in the raw, not tooth and claw.

They entered the outskirts of Northtown, where Gifts Galore was situated among a row of shops which included a unisex hairdresser's, a delicatessen, a florist, a record shop, a travel agent and a chip shop. Isabel parked in a side street, and as they walked towards the shops, Emily looked about her with interest. To her, this edge of town shopping area seemed very lively. The delicatessen was busy, even at this hour; it had built up a reputation and proved that small, specialised shops could hold their own against the supermarkets.

'Their bread and pâté are famous,' Isabel told Emily, seeing the girl glance at the window. 'People come from miles away to shop there, and some spill over on to us, which is good.'

'Cross fertilisation,' Emily remarked.

'Exactly.'

They reached the shop, and Isabel opened the door.

'Be careful, Emily,' she warned. 'Much of our stock is breakable.'

'I am quite large these days,' said Emily. 'A cow in a china shop, eh?'

'I wouldn't have said that.' Isabel was dismayed. The girl must be self-conscious about her weight, but she was still smiling in her sunny way. She seemed to have a lively wit and a happy disposition, which was lucky if she was to be their guest for any length of time.

'I put weight on, living as we did,' said Emily. 'Some people got thin, but I didn't.'

Isabel did not answer. She had picked up the post from the mat inside the door and was leading the way through to the small back area where she hung up her coat. There was a small sink, a kettle, and outside, in the tiny back yard, a lavatory. Isabel indicated all this to Emily, then suggested that she might take a walk around the neighbourhood, see what it offered, and perhaps look for a few things to wear at one of the charity shops, which would open soon.

'You can tell me what you've seen and how much it costs, and we can decide about it later, but you'll need pants and socks, or tights,' she said. 'It's a bus ride into the centre of town to Marks and Spencer. They stay open later than we do – we'll go down there after I've locked the shop and kit you up.'

'Don't bother,' said Emily. 'My own stuff's fine. I'll be going back to my friends once my case has been heard. Or when I get out of gaol, if they send me there. I'll find my mates soon enough. There are always sites for us. Besides, I haven't any money.'

'My treat,' said Isabel. 'I'm your godmother, remember?'

Isabel had some sympathy with Emily's views, but not with

her methods, though she saw that it solved the problem of finding friends and a purpose without doing anything to earn one's keep.

Any sermonising would have to wait. She handed Emily a five pound note.

'Have some coffee and a walk around,' she suggested.

When Emily returned, she brought Isabel a bunch of carnations, on which she had spent quite a large proportion of the money. She'd also bought herself a red woollen cap at the charity shop.

Isabel had put the flowers in water in the back area of the shop. She bit back reflections on their having been bought with her money: after all, she had given it to Emily as one gives a child a tip, and the gesture was generous. She's a nice girl, Isabel decided, despite her onslaught on the forces of the Crown, but what am I to do with her until her case is heard? And what is Douglas going to say?

Douglas had not wanted her to put money she had inherited from her mother into the business with Joanna. Such ventures were almost always risky, but they had researched their prospects and had concluded that if they catered for a middle-of-the-road clientele, not so exclusive that they priced themselves out of the market, they had every chance of success. On some days, they both came in, particularly at busy times or when there was extra work, like stocktaking, and they divided appointments with suppliers and with their accountant. They worked alternate Saturdays, with a schoolgirl assistant. Apart from the rent, their outgoings were not high. Far less capital was tied up in stock than if they had opened a bookshop, which they had rather fancied doing, but decided against because there would be competition from an established one, part of a chain in the centre of the town. After nearly two years they were making an increasing profit. Isabel's investment had been justified and she had gained satisfaction from establishing her independence. Douglas had tolerated her return to work; before they married, she was a legal secretary and she had wanted to find a similar position when the boys were growing up, but by then her secretarial skills were outdated. At that time, lacking the incentive to retrain, she had taken a part-time job in a language school. She could tackle a retraining course now, but she no longer had that sort of ambition; it was better to be her own boss.

'I'm fat, but I'm not clumsy,' Emily told her, during the afternoon. They had had sandwiches for lunch; Isabel had sent her to the delicatessen to buy them. 'I could dust the shelves, if you like.'

Isabel agreed. She must trust Emily. If all went well, perhaps she could be left at home tomorrow, given cleaning tasks to perform and be paid at their successful conclusion. Isabel did employ a cleaner, but she missed smears and dust because she would not wear her glasses at work, and there were always outstanding chores to be done. Having Emily to stay was going to prove expensive, but at least she could be useful. Presumably she could sign on for unemployment benefit, even find a temporary job. Douglas, however, had yet to be told the facts, and Isabel did not look forward to the interview they must have. He would be condemnatory. Right was right, and wrong was wrong, in his view; he claimed to be a man of integrity, and he was, but he was also intolerant and he did not take kindly to having his opinions challenged.

'God has spoken,' Toby, their second son, would sometimes

say, irreverently, after one of his pronouncements, knowing argument to be in vain.

Now she wished that Toby were here, so that she could tell him about Emily and laugh about it, get his opinion on what to do about her, and receive, as she knew she would, his support for her rescue operation.

Douglas would probably say she should have left the girl to reap the consequences of her actions.

I loved Douglas once, Isabel thought, watching anxiously as Emily, standing on a small stool, took china articles from the top shelf and handed them to her to pile neatly in a corner so that the shelf could be wiped down. I'm not sure I even like him now, she concluded, passing up a dampened duster.

Theirs was, she knew, regarded by friends as a successful marriage. Yet if it was, why did she so often have this urge to scream?

She had it now, turning away so that she could not see Emily, so precariously perched.

Emily's declaration that she was not clumsy turned out to be accurate. She stepped ponderously on and off a stool, dusting carefully, and nothing was broken though she adopted her own scheme, rearranging the layout of the objects on the shelves. Isabel forbore to comment: as when a child is peacefully occupied doing no harm, so was Emily. When customers came in, the small shop seemed crowded as each one squeezed past this new assistant, and after school finished, youngsters buying birthday presents or just browsing filled the narrow aisles between the shelves; this was an almost daily event, and Isabel, as half-past three approached, warned Emily and told her to put the stool away.

It was Emily who saw a girl pick up a small china figurine and pocket it. As she had earlier dusted and replaced it on the shelf, she had noticed and remembered the price, written on a tiny adhesive label on its base.

'That'll be five pounds twenty-five,' she told the girl.

'What will?' the girl, now examining a sachet of pot-pourri, enquired.

'That doll you just put in your pocket,' Emily said, and stepped forward to confront the schoolgirl, who had blushed but looked defiant, thrusting her hands into the pockets of her coat.

'I don't know what you mean,' the girl blustered, while her two companions stared at her, giggled, and then, as a diversion, picked up other items to inspect.

'Give it here,' said Emily, holding out her hand. 'If you do, and either hand it back or pay, Mrs Vernon won't call the police. If they come, they'll search you and they'll find it, and no receipt. She's going to do it now. Aren't you, Mrs Vernon?' she added loudly, and moved to block the doorway.

Isabel was watching this scene, amazed. She had not noticed the girl's sleight of hand, but there were frequent instances of shoplifting, when small items disappeared. On cue, she reached out and lifted the receiver.

The culprit pulled the small figure of a shepherdess from her pocket and put it in Emily's now outstretched hand.

'You can have it if you pay for it,' Emily said sweetly.

'Can't afford it, can I?' muttered the girl.

'I'm happy to have you look round,' said Isabel, thinking it was time she joined the conversation. 'But shoplifters will be prosecuted and there will be a notice up to that effect next week.'

'I'd like this, if you don't mind,' said one of the other girls, in a tone of high sarcasm. She had selected a china box with a rosebud lid; its price was eight pounds and she proffered a ten-pound note.

'Of course,' said Isabel, and made a business of wrapping the box in tissue and putting it in a Gifts Galore bag. She gave the girl her change, with a till receipt, and they trooped out. Emily was now by the door, ready to hold it open, and she spoke to the third girl.

'I'll just have that little bear you picked up, please,' she said.

The girl looked at her, an eyeball challenge, and then she followed her friend's action, pulling a small brown furry bear from her pocket and almost hurling it at Emily.

'It's like Cell Block H in here,' she growled, following her friends outside.

'Whatever did she mean?' asked Emily.

'Some television programme, I think,' said Isabel faintly. The girls had found Emily as threatening as a prison officer. 'Thank you, Emily,' she added. 'You were sharp to spot what they were up to.'

'Been there, done that, haven't I?' said Emily.

And would again, if necessary, but she would not get caught. Not if she could help it.

Isabel refused to believe what she had just heard.

Isabel and Emily reached home before Douglas. He was usually back by half-past seven, tired and feeling martyred as the trains were so crowded. Modern, linked coaches with sliding doors now ran on the line he used, but the seats were narrow, with inadequate leg room, and he often complained that he felt like a battery hen must, compressed into a tiny space.

Douglas had decided that they should leave London when Toby, their second son, had finished school and was having a gap year before university. Douglas wanted to put down roots well before he retired, in preparation for what he described as the third age of their lives. Isabel had been willing to comply with this plan, though it had meant giving up her job, which had fitted in with the boys' school terms. Douglas had retained his working colleagues; she had lost hers, and had moved away from the friends and neighbours she had known for years. At first she had been busy. Douglas, a keen amateur carpenter and handyman, had done some renovation, and directed the labours of the plumber and electrician. Isabel had been busy, too, with new curtains to make and carpets to order and have fitted. Toby, between a stint in France to improve his knowledge of the language and a trip to Canada, had helped Douglas with the painting and decorating, and had cleaned up the garden, which had been neglected in the final months before the previous owners left.

It wasn't an old, attractive house, full of charm and atmosphere, which disappointed Isabel.

'They harbour woodworm, dry rot and damp,' Douglas had pronounced. 'Something solid is a better plan.'

Thus it was that they had acquired Elm Lodge, so named because there had once been elm trees in a field between two older, larger houses. The owner of one of these had sold the land for building during the eighties boom – permission was granted because it was in-filling, not expansion beyond the village boundaries – and a developer had cut down the trees and put up seven new houses, all slightly different.

It was practical. Isabel had admitted that, and now it was very comfortable. The house was well built, and the garden was not so large that tending it would be a burden. It swiftly became one of Douglas's major interests. No sooner had he carried out one plan than he thought of an improvement, moving trellises, building small dividing walls, and putting in a pond. The actual cultivation of plants appealed to him less than rearranging what had previously been laid out. Isabel had given him a greenhouse for Christmas; he had spent the holiday period happily assembling it.

When she married him, Douglas had seemed to offer security, Isabel reflected, and he had provided it. What she had failed to notice was that he was dull, and, even as a young man, set in his ways.

Driving home with Emily, this was in her mind. The girl's appearance – both her person and her presence – must have been a shock to him. The guest – the cuckoo in the nest – must now cooperate with how they lived. Douglas worked very hard; it wasn't fair to burden him with added worries. After closing Gifts Galore, they had driven into town to Marks and Spencer, still open, and there, on her account, she had bought Emily a minimum wardrobe of a very large sweater – Toby's was rather tight – and two polos from the men's department, some underwear and leggings. There seemed to be no slacks big enough, but they found some men's jogging trousers that would fit.

'It's very good of you,' Emily said, carrying the green plastic bags to the car.

'Godmothers do this sort of thing,' said Isabel. She had feared Emily might seek to economise by demonstrating her shoplifting guile in the store; here detection, she was sure – and hoped – was very probable. A serious talk must, at some point, be held, wherein Emily's past conduct and her future would be discussed. Had she trained for anything? Had she ever worked? Isabel rebuked herself for not keeping in touch, but after all she was of age; Isabel was not responsible for her.

Except that now she was.

'I'll tell Douglas about your court appearance when the moment is right,' she warned. 'You say very little. I'll explain that you had been turned out of where you were living, and had nowhere else to go.'

'Well, it's the truth, isn't it?' said Emily. She spoke cheerfully.

'Yes, it is,' Isabel allowed. 'But I don't think he'll like it when he knows the details. And I don't, either,' she added. 'I respect your opinions, even if I don't agree with them, but I can't condone the behaviour that led to your arrest.'

'What does Douglas do?' Emily enquired. 'I've forgotten.'

'He's a civil servant in the department of transport,' Isabel replied.

'Is he really? He's making all these roads, then. He's the enemy,' said Emily, but calmly, not in threatening tones.

Isabel slowed down for the turning that led to Fordswick. Why couldn't he have been in health, or even the treasury, she thought crossly. She did not answer Emily.

While Douglas was out of the house, he ceased to think about the inappropriate guest at Elm Lodge. His day was occupied with meetings and discussions, consultations about plans and statistics and other affairs of state; there was no time in it for considering domestic matters. Returning home, having secured his usual seat in his usual compartment in his usual train, he read the evening paper and then dozed for ten minutes or so, as he always did, awaking refreshed and ready to confront the next challenge life would offer him: his return to domesticity. He and Isabel had evolved a calm mode of existence; they spent few hours together, even at weekends, for she had taken up golf, while he preferred to work in the garden. He had designed what he considered was an attractive plot, made to seem more spacious than it was, with corners, arbours, and a dell where there was a small pond which local cats had stripped of goldfish. Neither cared for confrontations, and with their adult sons now seldom at home, they peaceably went their separate ways.

Holidays were a problem, because to go away together meant that they were in each other's company around the clock, but last year, and the year before, they had gone on cruises, and this year were contemplating a cultural tour of Italy, which was Isabel's suggestion. They would be with a group of like-minded people, she had explained. Douglas had the brochures in his brief case, to study when he had a moment to spare.

He had a few minutes now, sitting in the train, and after satisfying himself as to the cleanliness of his compartment – he travelled first class only on official business, feeling it part of his duty to observe how effective were the railways, even though his local line had now been privatised – pulled them out. Florence, he saw, and Padua, were included in the itinerary Isabel had marked with a pink Post-it sticker. Venice would be pleasant, he decided, remembering a trip there in his youth. For years they had gone to France, staying in farmhouses and cottages near activities appropriate for the ages of the boys; later, when there was more money, they had taken their teenage sons skiing, with occasional trips, between times, to Scotland for themselves as the boys had begun to make plans of their own. Isabel and Douglas had taken their first cruise after stressful holidays touring with the car, sampling the Dordogne one year and Provence the next. Once they grew accustomed to the routine, both had enjoyed it because there were other people they could talk to.

Studying the cabin prices and the dates for the trip which took in Venice, Douglas suddenly remembered the uncouth young woman who had arrived during the night, and had been eating the cornflakes which Isabel kept for Toby, who sometimes came home unexpectedly. She was Isabel's goddaughter, and she had been wearing his tweed jacket. He deserved an explanation, and Isabel must give him one.

But he seemed to have no opportunity to demand it. When he reached home, Isabel was preoccupied with dinner preparations and during the meal she was unusually talkative. There was chicken, done in a wine sauce and garnished with grapes. Emily ate heartily. The night before, when she arrived, Douglas had not been close enough to catch her unwashed aroma; now, he saw an overweight young woman with a cropped head, no longer wearing his jacket but a new green sweater and a pair of black leggings. He considered it indecent garb, just as he regarded the tiny skirts young women wore as much too brief; the sight of stick-like legs in black tights aroused lascivious feelings in him which he deplored, whilst at the same time relishing the lustful thoughts they provoked.

Isabel, pointing out the carnations which Emily had given her, now in a vase on a deep window sill, related the defeat of the shoplifters, hoping that this would reveal their guest in a favourable light, but beyond a grunt, Douglas made no comment. Emily did not sit silent, or subdued. She chatted about the charms of Northtown, its park and river walk which she had discovered on her exploratory trip, not mentioning the later shopping expedition. She mentioned a road-widening scheme she had noticed, and a busy flyover, and was about to embark on a proselytising speech when Isabel intervened to point out that the traffic now flowed more smoothly at the rush hour, with fewer snarl-ups of stationary cars emitting fumes.

'Isabel said you had lost your home.' Douglas had laid down his knife and fork, his plate clean except for a neatly stripped chicken thigh-bone. He bent his stern gaze on Emily. He had thick, bushy eyebrows, very straight, and large brown eyes. There was the shadow of the day's stubble around his jaw; Emily found it strange that men lost the hair on their heads while retaining vigorous facial growth. What about their body hair, she wondered, and began to giggle, stifling her mirth with her table napkin. She had been amazed when she saw the table laid so formally for just the three of them: in the dining-room, with cut glass and real silver. Isabel had laughed.

'Bit different from your arboreal life style,' she had remarked.

'You're right,' Emily had agreed. She thought such elegance was quaintly fascinating.

'Emily's mother died,' Isabel now reminded Douglas. 'She remarried and moved to Spain, and then she died.'

'Oh – I'm sorry, Emily,' Douglas said, after patting his lips with his napkin. He smiled kindly at her. 'I'm glad we could take you in, while you settle your affairs.'

Neither of his companions made any attempt to correct his assumption that this demise was recent, and the immediate cause of Emily's need for shelter.

'Tell me about your fish,' said Emily, inspired. And, successfully diverted, he did. At length.

4

When he returned to England, Godfrey had spent some of his fraudulently acquired money on a camper van which solved his accommodation and mobility problems, and he had made it snug, with a sleeping bag, radio, and even a small battery-powered television. A gas heater provided warmth. For a while he had moved about the country, doing casual work as a packer, and later with an office-cleaning company in Essex. He'd hoped to find scope there for a scam, but had failed, and the job was deadly dull, the ritual duties being carried out in the evening after the various businesses were closed. It was during a tedious hour, while he was wielding an electric polisher in a lengthy corridor, that he had remembered Alice and her wealthy parents.

He decided to pay her a visit, find out how she was placed these days, and so, collecting his pay at the end of the week, he set off for Fordswick in his van.

It was a bitter January day, with the sky grey and the air raw and chill. Maybe Alice still worked in Northtown museum, prowling the pubs in the evening as she had been doing when they met. He'd stroll round before he went to Fordswick.

Parking in a residential street, he set off towards the centre, and entered the museum – admission was free – wandering round galleries where ancient statues were displayed, and others where paintings and artefacts were on show. He liked some of the pictures; you could imagine a life going on beyond the scene depicted: an open gate leading to a building where people lived – who? And a portrait of a Victorian citizen, his watch chain spread across his stomach, a knowing look in his button-black eyes. Bet he'd done a shifty deal or two, thought Godfrey. He'd been quite keen on art himself, while at school, and had once had a job painting scenery for a film company, but that was long ago. The company had collapsed and he had moved from job to job, and from woman to woman, never settling. Maybe he could start to paint again, he thought, but there was no money in the artistic sort of painting, though there might be in the decorating variety.

He didn't ask for Alice. Her work had gone on behind the scenes. If he'd bothered to talk to her about it, he might have been quite interested in what she did, he thought now; perhaps they could have done a line, between them, in reproducing Old Masters. The notion amused him, and he bought two postcards, one of the Victorian gentleman he had admired, and another of a moorland landscape.

He didn't see Alice anywhere around. If he had, he'd have greeted her warmly, for she would certainly be pleased to see him.

It was still daylight when he reached Fordswick, and he drew into the parking area by the recreation ground where there was a public lavatory. It might be locked at night to keep vandals out, but while it was open, he could fill his water cans. He was unlikely to be immediately challenged here, he thought, though if he stayed more than twenty-four hours, someone might get curious.

Godfrey used the facilities, collected his water, locked the van, and left on foot, walking over the football pitch and down an alley which led to the main road running through the village. In his absence, little seemed to have changed, though there were traffic calming measures near the few shops and the pub, a chicane narrowing the approach on either side. He'd met it, driving in, but as no traffic had been coming the other way, had not been delayed. He didn't like these new obstructions; if you were in a hurry, you might not see them and that could cause an accident.

Alice, if she still worked in Northtown, would not be home yet, even if she no longer toured the pubs, but he had wanted to reach Fordswick before the light went. He needed to get his bearings, have a look around. He walked towards the square where, centrally placed in this straggling village which straddled a river, were several shops, and saw that there had been some recent building. Two small closes opened off the main street, each containing three or four good-sized houses. They'd be pricey, for couples earning well. What about youngsters, newly-weds? What were they supposed to do? Did no one think of catering for them? Godfrey had been married more than once.

He'd nearly married Alice, and if he had, it would have worked out materially, but her parents would have been around, even though there was plenty of space at Ford House. They'd have expected him to be the handyman, to fetch and carry, be subservient, and he could not have endured that. Godfrey liked to control those around him, though when it was politic, he could briefly play a humbler role. Reaching the handsome wrought-iron gates, he saw that they were closed. Formerly, they were always left open, held back by iron bars which hooked into sockets on the posts. This must be a sign of the times, an intruder-defeating tactic. He peered through; there was still frost lingering beneath the trees, and all the plants were hibernating, with no spring growth, not even an early snowdrop, visible from where he stood.

But there was something new. To the right of the short drive, on the lawn, there was a child's swing.

His first thought was that the old couple had died, Alice had sold up and moved on, and a new young family was now living here. She had found her freedom, but where had she gone? He could go up to the door, ring the bell, and ask about the previous owners. The new occupants might have an address for Alice. Maybe she had married. After all, if her parents were dead and she had inherited their money, she would have been able to find a husband fairly easily, even if she'd had to do it through an agency. He thought about it, standing there, then turned away. This needed more consideration.

Godfrey walked back along the street and turned towards the newsagent's shop, which was in the middle of the terraced row which included the post office and general store, and a butcher's. He picked up an *Express* from the rack and approached the counter to pay for it. When he had briefly lived in Fordswick, he had come here every day and was known to the newsagent and his wife. Now, a younger man stood behind the counter, a stranger.

Godfrey decided not to ask any questions. He did not want to draw attention to himself, to be remembered later. Fordswick was a thriving village with many residents travelling some distance to work. Few of the original rural families were left; farms were mechanised and there was no community of agricultural workers in tied cottages, as there must have been until – when? the Sixties? Godfrey was not sure, but he remembered staying on a farm when he was a child, seeing cows milked by hand and even a horse pulling a plough. He bought a bottle of milk, a sliced loaf and some cheese in the general store. He'd return to his camper van and read the paper. Later, he might wash the van, which was dusty.

Sitting on a bench in the children's playground, some distance from the car park where he had left his van, was a woman on her own.

Godfrey walked towards her, glancing sideways at her. She was watching two small children on the swings, one being pushed by its mother; the second mother, whose child was older and could propel itself, leaned against the upright, chatting to her friend. Several children were using the slide, a shallow one which ended in a bed of bark. Other women were supervising them. The seated woman, Godfrey saw, was plump, with a red woollen cap pulled over her head. Sturdy limbs in track-suit trousers, ending in shabby trainers, were stretched out in front of her. She was eating a Mars bar. Godfrey sat down at the further end of the bench, and watched the children too.

'One of those yours?' he asked her.

'No,' she said, and took another bite of her Mars.

Silence fell. The children went on swinging or sliding, and the mothers conscientiously observed them, fielded them, encouraged them.

'Want some Mars?' asked Emily eventually, pulling another from her pocket. Down on the site, everything had been shared, people were your friends, and she had no hang-up about speaking to men sitting on a bench watching young children. It never occurred to her that he might have paedophilic tendencies.

'Thanks,' said Godfrey, accepting the chunk she broke off and handed to him.

They munched together, silently. One of the mothers bundled two children into a twin pushchair and gathered several others round her, a few on harnesses, calling farewells to the remaining women, who were also collecting their children. It was too cold to stay out long.

'She's got a lot of kids,' said Godfrey.

'She's a child minder,' Emily replied. 'She looks after them while their mothers are at work.'

'How do you know that? Is she a friend of yours?'

'No. She came into the shop when I was buying the Mars,' said Emily. 'I asked her how she came to have so many, and she told me. I was asking the shopman about some work. There are cards in the window, people wanting cleaners and selling things.'

'Oh?'

Emily was lonely. She was missing the camaraderie of the protest site, the company of her former friends – those not arrested would have moved elsewhere by now – the sense of purpose they had had even when they were concentrating on basic survival. She had spent two nights beneath Isabel's sound roof, in the warm and comfortable spare-room bed and today she had decided against going to Gifts Galore, saying she wanted to explore Fordswick but intending to find some way of earning money. After Isabel left that morning, Emily had thoroughly cleaned the kitchen, the drawing-room, and the dining-room, and had lightly dusted Douglas's study, spending some time gazing at the tank of tropical fish which stood against one wall. Each fish seemed concerned only with itself as they swam at varying speeds among the fronds of greenery which turned their aquarium into a feathery jungle. She had not liked to venture into Isabel and Douglas's bedroom, or their own bathroom, as that might be an invasion of their privacy. Feeling stuffy after being indoors for so long, she had set out to discover what Fordswick had to offer, calling first at the shop. She had been sitting on the bench for some time before Godfrey arrived.

In her months spent living rough, Emily had learned to look after herself and her meagre possessions. She did not trust everyone she met, but she saw no threat in Godfrey, who was, as he now told her, like herself, a stranger to the village.

'There's a job going at a big house here,' said Emily. 'Ford House, it's called. They want someone to do cleaning and help with a four-year-old child.'

'Oh?'

Because it was Ford House, Godfrey was interested; this was the child who used the swing.

'Lives with her grandparents,' Emily continued.

'Oh?' said Godfrey again. He thought he was immune to emotion, but now he felt a spasm in the area where he supposed his heart to be.

'No dad. He bunked off,' said Emily. 'It's the same old story, isn't it? They just don't want to know. Heard she was on the way and left the mother.'

'How do you know this?' Godfrey asked.

'That woman told me,' said Emily. 'The child minder.'

'Do you know the name?'

'What's it to you?' asked Emily. 'It's me that'd be applying, not you.' She giggled. 'But you could, too. It's sex discrimination, if they don't consider you just because you're a man.'

Godfrey, slowly absorbing the fact of her revelation, ignored this observation, which could be true.

'But do you?' he insisted. 'Do you know who lives at Ford House?'

'They're called Watkinson,' said Emily. 'The grandparents are Mr and Mrs Watkinson.'

'And their daughter's this kid's mother?' Godfrey said. His blood was pounding. Alice had had a child – his child – and, far from deserting her, as had been alleged, he had never known that she was pregnant. 'Did she die? The mother?' He'd almost used her name, biting it back, just in time. Even this ungainly, naive girl might wonder how he knew it.

'I don't know,' said Emily.

Godfrey could scarcely believe what she had told him.

'You should think about that job,' he said. He looked at her. She didn't, at first glance, inspire great confidence, but if she applied, in person at the house, even without getting the position, she could carry out a preliminary investigation, for now that he knew he had a child the whole scenario had changed. He had rights, hadn't he? And what had happened to Alice? If she wasn't dead, had she married someone and abandoned this kid? 'The grandparents must be pretty old,' he added.

'Not necessarily,' said Emily. 'Grandparents can be quite young.' Some had demonstrated on the site, coming for an occasional token few hours, bringing a grandchild or two they were minding while its own parents were at work, and saying that in their day they had marched to ban the bomb. They seemed to find protesting quite exciting. She stood up, which was an effort with her bulk. 'I'd better be going,' she said.

Godfrey asked her where she lived.

'I'm staying with my godmother,' she said. 'Just for now.' How long would she be in Fordswick? To keep her out of prison, Isabel might have to be responsible for her throughout a possible suspended sentence. 'She lives at Elm Lodge. It's at the other end of the village, about a hundred yards past The Stick and Monkey.'

This pub, formerly The Rising Sun, had been taken over by new owners who, wanting to jazz up its image, had renamed it. It was no great distance from Ford House, in the old part of the village which had grown around a ford across a stream, now bridged.

Godfrey decided not to push his luck by moving too fast with this possible link to the past, who was also a source of information. 'I'll be here for a bit,' said Godfrey, not describing his abode. 'See you around.'

'Oh – right,' said Emily, pleased. She'd found a friend – not young, but not as old as Douglas and Isabel, and he had time to talk to her. It was gratifying. A curious sensation came across her, a vague stirring of forgotten feelings.

You never knew what was waiting round the corner.

5

Isabel, briefly tempted to invent a history for Emily that would be acceptable to Douglas, soon discarded the idea, for to wander from the truth was to embark on a web of deceit which might cause still more difficulties. However, his assumption that Emily had recently suffered a bereavement had brought a temporary reprieve. Ultimately, he would have to know the truth.

She could not imagine how Emily had existed in the trees, where she said she had lived for some time. Isabel knew there were rope walkways and platforms but even so, how did she move about among the branches? Why hadn't she lost weight on the meagre diet which surely must have been all the demonstrators could produce?

Arriving home on Thursday, she had found the house tidy, the kitchen spotless, and vegetables prepared for dinner.

'Would you like some tea?' were Emily's first words. 'Or coffee?'

They both had coffee, Emily ladling sugar into hers, and Isabel asked her how they had managed to feed themselves on the site.

'Surely you have to apply for jobs now, don't you? Show

you're available for work and have tried to get a job before you can draw benefit?' Hadn't the law recently been changed?

'People give you stuff,' said Emily. 'Some supporters are well off. There are university dons and lawyers and all sorts of people who agree with our aims and even if they can't stay, they come for a few days, and they give us money, and sometimes even cook. We had a lot of meals prepared for us. It's amazing.'

It was. Emily thought Douglas would care for no part of this tale, though he must be aware of the facts, since his department was concerned with building the new road. Indeed, when he saw television news clips about the protests, with the often grubby demonstrators grinning, and the cleaner ones articulately holding forth on camera, he turned white with anger. Isabel, appreciating both sides of the argument, nevertheless felt the law must be upheld and those in towns spared traffic bottlenecks and the attendant fumes. The cost of protecting the site to let work proceed was vast, and was an avoidable expense if people would only stay at home and let it go ahead. She could see, though, that the protestors had now found a cause to believe in, and a purpose to lives which for many may have been drab, aimless and empty before they took it up. Of course it was exciting to burrow underground and defy hundreds of security guards, police and trained rescuers; of course there was a thrill in defying authority. And they were getting plenty of fresh air. But when Isabel was Emily's age, she was already married, with one son, and pregnant with another. She had had responsibilities. She sighed. Had she missed out on youth?

Not really. She'd been to university, enjoyed her freedom; now, in middle age, she was refashioning her life.

'You'll miss your friends,' she said.

'Yes,' admitted Emily. 'But I'll find them again. There's always another road planned, somewhere, and they'll be there.'

The ones who don't get sent to prison, she thought. 'I'm trying not to think about it, it's so great here, but I wonder what sort of sentence I can expect.'

Isabel wondered the same thing. With luck a suspended one, as the solicitor had hoped, and maybe a fine.

Douglas was not going to let them off the hook a second time. He must know where he stood, in regard to the duration of Emily's visit.

Over dinner, a time for conversation, he tackled her. She had had a further twenty-four hours in which to mourn, and must face facts.

'What are your plans, Emily?' he asked. 'Are your mother's solicitors advising you?'

'I'm having legal aid, yes,' said Emily warily.

Isabel, arriving home, had praised her domestic labours, but as she prepared the meal, she had said that Douglas must be told something of her predicament.

'Otherwise you're here under false pretences,' she pointed out. 'He thinks your mother died recently.'

'I know. Wasn't it funny?' said Emily cheerfully. 'You didn't put him right.'

'No. Well, it wasn't a good time,' said Isabel weakly. 'He won't be pleased when he knows why you're really here. Not that we wouldn't have welcomed you after Ginnie died,' she added hastily. 'Were you living with her then?' There was no reason why she should have been; she was an adult woman.

'No,' said Emily. 'She hadn't been ill,' she added. 'It was sudden. A virus.'

So Emily had not been summoned to look after her. Isabel remembered a letter from Ginnie which revealed that her husband and Emily had not got on as she grew older. It was years ago. As godmother, she should have done something about Emily at the time, even if it had been only to write to her, but Ginnie, a poor correspondent, had not referred to it again, so Isabel, relieved, had decided that the situation must have improved. She'd scarcely given the girl a thought since then, she realised, with guilt. Now, faced with Emily's plight, she must make up for past neglect.

'Emily had not been living with her mother for some time before she died,' she told Douglas, helping him to apple crumble, which he liked. So did Emily; she'd looked gleeful when Isabel began putting it together, saying she hadn't had it since her childhood. It wasn't exactly what one thought of as a Spanish dish, Isabel had answered, tipping healthy low-fat yoghurt into a bowl and explaining that they had cream only when there were guests.

'Where have you been living, Emily?' Douglas asked.

Which of Isabel's friends had gone to Spain? Douglas himself had no close friends: colleagues, yes, but no intimates. Women went in for that sort of thing more than men; they seemed to enjoy clustering together and forging bonds, like hearty men who played team games. He was not one of those.

'I was in a flat,' Emily said. She had finished her crumble. Would Isabel offer her a second helping? She paused, but no one spoke. 'Then I left,' she said.

'You weren't working?' It was a statement. Douglas had laid down his spoon and fork and now stared at her across the table. 'You were turned out of your flat.'

'I had no job,' said Emily. She could not meet his penetrating gaze, steady beneath the well-defined eyebrows.

'What had you been doing?'

'Oh – this and that,' said Emily.

'Nothing structured?'

'Not exactly. No,' said Emily, and, afraid of further questions, decided she must reveal some of the truth. 'I had these friends. We believe in protecting the countryside,' she said. 'I became a conservationist.'

Isabel could endure no more of this.

'Emily was at that road-building protest,' she said. 'She'd been living there with the demonstrators.'

'I see.' Douglas dabbed his lips with his napkin. 'So that's how you came to be without a home. You were evicted from the site.' He remembered asking her, sarcastically, if she had been living in a tree. It seemed she had, in fact as well as metaphorically.

'Yes, and as I didn't know what to do or where to go, I thought of Isabel,' said Emily.

'You didn't move on to the next demonstration with your fellow campaigners, all costing the taxpayer a great deal of money in benefits besides the astronomical expense of enforcing security?'

'No.' Emily now looked him in the eye. Why should she bow down before this dictator? 'I will, though, eventually. When I'm really free. Isabel rescued me from being sent to prison,' she declared, staring at him defiantly.

'You'd been arrested?' Douglas's voice rose in shock.

'Yes. And I'd do it all again,' said Emily.

Isabel, quailing, had to admire her courage.

'Unfortunately there was a bit of a scuffle. That's why she was arrested,' she said.

'You've acted as her surety for bail,' Douglas stated.

Isabel nodded.

'I couldn't let her go to prison,' she told him, her tone imploring. 'I simply couldn't, Douglas.'

'What was she charged with?' Douglas asked.

'I'm here. I can speak for myself,' said Emily, angrily. 'Assault and criminal damage, if you want to know,' she told him.

'It was unintentional,' Isabel hurriedly intervened. Douglas's formerly pale face was now flushed; his blood pressure must be soaring.

'It wasn't,' said Emily. 'We were fighting for our homes.' She forgot to mention the environment.

'If you'd paid your rent, you'd have your home,' said Douglas. 'One made of bricks and mortar.' His tone was scornful, almost sneering.

'Douglas, Emily knows she shouldn't have been violent, but she didn't really hurt anyone, and feelings were running high.' Isabel felt that she was on shaky ground. Adult women shouldn't be wielding sticks aggressively, as it seemed Emily had done.

'You say she didn't really hurt anyone. How unreal was the injury?' Douglas was glowering now.

Isabel had seen the photographs. A security guard's helmet had been dislodged, his face had been cut and blood had poured down his cheek, but could anyone prove that Emily was responsible? Someone else might have struck the blow that wounded him. There would probably be film shots of the incident, she supposed; the media had had a fine time recording every possible incident.

'People were hurt,' she said. 'Not seriously, but other protestors were involved, not just Emily.'

'Isabel, you must see that harbouring her here, a known violent individual, could be damaging to me. To my career.' He said it as if it were spelt out in capitals.

'I thought British citizens were presumed innocent until

proved guilty,' said Isabel. 'And it isn't going to be for long. She has to appear in court again quite soon.' She would not even contemplate what might happen after that.

'How could my being here affect your career?' demanded Emily, before he could ask the precise date of the hearing, then answered her own question. 'Oh – because you work in the ministry of transport, I suppose.'

'I am a government servant,' said Douglas repressively. 'It's my responsibility to see that the law is enforced.'

'And my presence in your house is contaminating it, is it?' Emily's colour, too, was high. 'Well, I'd better go, then.' She stood up and turned to face Isabel. 'At least you made me welcome,' she said.

'Sit down,' said Douglas sharply. 'We haven't talked this through yet.'

Isabel laid a hand on Emily's arm. The flesh beneath the sweater was surprisingly firm: not just flab, but muscle, too.

'Cool down,' she said. 'If you leave, you'll be breaking your bail terms and liable to go to prison.'

'God!' Douglas rolled his eyes to heaven. 'Prison,' he said.

'You won't be going there, Douglas, and you're not the subject of an enquiry. This isn't a sleazy scandal affecting you, and you're not the minister, just one of his underlings. Suppose Matthew or Toby had been involved in something like this, and we weren't there to back them up when it went too far. Wouldn't you be grateful if someone else did?' Matthew had demonstrated, though not violently, about university lecturers' pay. Perhaps Douglas did not know about that.

'It's not a true analogy,' said Douglas.

'I think it is,' said Isabel, who was surprising herself by the stand she was making. 'I am Emily's guarantor, not you, and she has already justified my confidence by picking up two would-be shoplifters yesterday in Gifts Galore, and today she has cleaned the house, most thoroughly. She helped prepare the dinner, too. She'll earn her keep.'

'The first sign of trouble and you're out,' said Douglas warningly, his gaze bent fiercely on the visitor. 'And if you're locked up, perhaps it will teach you a lesson.' He rose to his feet. 'I'll have my coffee in the study, please, Isabel,' he said frostily, and left the room.

Emily, realising that for the moment she was safe, was now calmer.

'He's a chauvinist,' she said.

'Yes,' said Isabel. 'He is. And he won't change now.'

Douglas spent the evening in his study, working on various papers, and occasionally gazing at his fish; he never tired of watching the soothing spectacle of their ceaseless swimming. Eventually he heard Isabel go up to bed. Bringing Emily here without obtaining his consent, or even informing him of her intentions, was an act of rebellion, and Douglas was not only angry: he was seriously alarmed. He had always found her dependable, trustworthy and biddable, but now, by her defiance, she had shocked him. It was a betrayal. She had known he would not allow the girl, in these circumstances, to enter his house, and so she had not asked his permission. If he were to turn Emily out, force her back into police custody, the press would soon discover what had happened, and though Douglas, in rank, was nowhere near the minister, nevertheless he was senior enough for his apparent heartlessness to provoke, by association, considerable embarrassment.

On the other hand, the fact that he was sheltering one of

the demonstrators who had caused so much trouble could also be a source of departmental difficulty.

What should he do? Douglas's mind thrashed around as various plans and their probable consequences came and went inside his troubled head. He was accustomed to formulating schemes and predictions, but when policies were being decided, emotions were not factors taken into account. Unexpected actions were upsetting; Douglas liked to know in advance where he would be and what he would be doing at any given time, and though emergencies had a way of upsetting even the most carefully worked-out schedules, those domestic in origin were usually avoidable.

Isabel, though aware of his disapproval, had not apologised. Douglas decided to speak to her upstairs in the privacy of their bedroom, discover more about the gravity of Emily's offence and her likely punishment; he'd better lose no time in doing so, or she would feign sleep, as he had suspected her of doing on previous occasions when he wished to discuss some serious matter with her. He could, however, wake her up.

This time, it was not necessary. She was sitting in front of her dressing-table, brushing her straight brown hair which, ever since they met, she had worn below the ears; recently, however, she had had it cut short, almost in a shingle, and he found it disconcerting. She looked younger, sharper, and Toby had enthused about it; Douglas, by refraining from comment, had succeeded in making his disapproval clear.

'How long is she staying?' he demanded, entering the room.

Their eyes met in the mirror, and Isabel swung round to face him, still holding the hairbrush.

'While she's on remand, at least,' she said. 'That's just over two weeks. When her case is heard she may get a suspended sentence, or possibly community service.' She did not mention that the hearing could be postponed if any of those charged with Emily failed to turn up. Delays could prolong the outcome for a long time. 'It's unlikely that a domiciliary order will be imposed,' she went on. 'She's not a juvenile.'

'She looks like one, and has acted like one,' Douglas said.

'She's acting from her convictions, which you don't share, of necessity,' said Isabel. 'And I don't approve of what it's alleged she did, however strongly she feels about damage to the environment.'

'You don't share her convictions either,' Douglas told her, frowning. He laid his hands on her shoulders, his grip tightening. He could feel the fragile bones beneath his hands.

'I regret the ravaging of the countryside and the cutting down of trees,' said Isabel. 'And I respect Emily's right to her own opinions. But I know regeneration can occur, given a chance,' she added.

'Don't digress, Isabel,' said Douglas. 'This young woman is of age and you are not responsible for her.'

'I have a moral duty to help her through this bad patch,' said Isabel. 'Her mother was my friend.'

'Hmph. And a pretty feckless friend, traipsing off to Spain,' said Douglas, as though Ginnie had gone off to some unexplored jungle.

'She's dead, Douglas.' Once again, Isabel reminded him of this. 'She died about four years ago, as you know. If she hadn't, maybe Emily wouldn't have fallen in with these conservationists. She must have grieved for her. She must miss her. Surely you can see that?' Even you, she felt like saying.

'Who was her mother, anyway?' Douglas was asking.

'You must remember the Frosts,' said Isabel. He couldn't have forgotten. 'They were our neighbours in Dulwich – well, not next door, but along the road. We went to dinner there, and they came to us.' That was in the dreadful days of competitive dinner parties at which Douglas wanted her to impress their guests. She had eventually realised that such occasions were sometimes created because the various couples could not endure too many evenings spent together without dilution; then there had to be the return matches. Since they moved to Fordswick, this practice had been discontinued and it was Isabel, now, who would have liked, occasionally, to revive it. Douglas, however, proclaimed himself too tired after his week's commuting.

She and Ginnie did not go back as far as he had assumed; they had met one day when Isabel had retrieved the Frosts' dog – a terrier of mixed parentage – which had escaped from their garden and sped away towards the main road at the end of their street. She'd recognised it, having seen Ginnie pass, taking her two small sons to school. With Matthew toddling beside her, Isabel had returned the dog, whose address was on his collar, and had found Ginnie in tears in the kitchen, furious at being pregnant again, and feeling very sick. Isabel, pregnant herself with Toby, but fit, had dried her tears, suggested drinking weak Bovril with a dry biscuit, and become, almost by default, Ginnie's friend. Controlled by Douglas and subservient at home, she was able to exert some power over Ginnie, who, though the elder by at least ten years, responded to her warmth and sympathy, and settled down to accept her unwanted pregnancy, of which Emily was the result. Later, the two women took Toby and Emily for walks in their prams. It had seemed natural for Ginnie to invite Isabel to be Emily's godmother, but as the child had never been baptised, it was an honorary, unofficial appointment; one, however, that was no less binding.

After Emily was born, Ginnie had blossomed, and her

marriage, shaky during the pregnancy, had recovered, or so it had seemed. Isabel, lonely within her own, had envied the Frosts' apparent harmony, so that it was all the more shocking when Ginnie's husband, Ralph, took off, abandoning his family and leaving debts. The house, heavily mortgaged, had been sold. Ginnie had taken the children to her parents' home in Scotland, and Isabel had not seen her since, though for a while they had kept in touch by post. She had moved to Spain when Emily was about five, having met her Spanish second husband on a holiday. It had seemed somewhat hasty and impetuous.

'I don't remember her at all,' said Douglas impatiently.

'It was a long time ago,' said Isabel. 'She and Ralph split up when the children were quite young. I wasn't a good godmother. I didn't keep in touch.' She'd sent presents – games, books, and later banknotes which could be changed into Spanish currency, but eventually, when letters of thanks ceased to arrive, she had stopped sending further gifts.

'He must have had good cause to go,' was Douglas's verdict. 'She was feckless, I suppose.' He had a dim recollection of Isabel spending too much time with some local family.

'Douglas, he didn't just leave his family. He left debts as well,' said Isabel.

'Oh,' said Douglas, who certainly did not approve of such irresponsible behaviour. But perhaps the woman, Ginnie, was extravagant, running up vast bills. He said so.

'Douglas, that's most unfair. You say you don't remember her, so how can you make such an assertion?'

Ginnie had suspected that Ralph had found someone else.

'A young woman without stretch marks,' she'd said bitterly.

Isabel had not thought it was so straightforward. She had remembered Ginnie's dismay when she was expecting Emily;

much of her distress had been because Ralph was angry, though when Emily was born, at first he had been delighted with his little daughter, who was a pretty child. He had seemed emotionally volatile; at the time, Isabel had thought this might be better than Douglas's apparent lack of feeling; later, she was less certain. At least Douglas was predictable.

'It's deplorable, whatever the true circumstance,' said Douglas now. 'Very unfortunate.'

Ginnie had called her supposed supplanter 'The Bimbo', but when her existence was revealed she turned out to be nothing of the sort. She was a thin, dark woman whose Italian father was a shoe manufacturer; he gave Ralph a job in his company, but after a year or two that alliance ceased and the couple parted. Isabel had heard no more about him and she did not know what had happened to Emily's two brothers, both considerably older than their sister. Emily, when Isabel asked her about them, had been vague, saying they were both working overseas and she did not know their addresses.

Douglas's hands still grasped her shoulders. Isabel hid a sigh. She hoped Ginnie's Spanish romance had led her into wonderland, making all that led up to it, and what followed, worthwhile. Submitting now was the easiest way to avoid further awkward discussion.

6

That night, Godfrey strolled past Elm Lodge, where his new acquaintance, whose name he did not know, was living with her godmother. It was a substantial fairly modern house, he discerned, assessing it by the others around it in the short road. He could see slivers of light at an upstairs curtained window but the rest of the house was in darkness. He contemplated moving nearer to take a better look, but decided not to risk barking dogs or security lights. Godfrey was not planning burglary at the moment, though who could tell what he might have to do in the future? His funds were limited; more must come from somewhere and easy money, not hard grind, appealed, but he was not keen on breaking and entering, which could be hazardous and messy.

He sauntered back to his van. The night was cold; a little snow had fallen earlier and all the houses he passed were closed and shuttered. He had spent the evening in The Stick and Monkey, where he had had several beers and a large helping of lasagne and mixed vegetables. The pub was very different from how he remembered it when it was The Rising Sun. Then it had had a lounge bar, but most of the locals had used the snug, where a log fire had blazed. The food, at that time, had been simple – sandwiches and ploughman's at midday, steak or sausages, or fish, with peas and chips in the evenings. The menu this evening was more exotic; he could have had warm duck salad or Dover sole, among many other choices. The place was busy, and the car park was full. There were couples in their late thirties and forties but no young or elderly people; previously, there would have been a good mix in the evenings, most of the customers being from the village. It had gone up-market with a vengeance, and was expensive. No doubt the former patrons now went to The Bull, at the other end of the village; he'd try it out tomorrow night.

He was very hungry, and followed his lasagne with sticky toffee pudding, which was surprisingly good and not the nursery dish he had been expecting. He had had a shock today, so no wonder he was hungry; suddenly discovering that you are a father would be a jolt for anyone.

Godfrey liked pulling off scams and when he could work them, aimed to live by them. Successful deceit gave him a thrill, and he enjoyed devising tricks to extort or exact money from his victims. People were so gullible. He'd done the door-to-door selling routine, taking deposits for non-existent garden furniture and even conservatories; he'd once worked briefly for a construction firm and could do the technical patter which convinced some potential buyers. He would measure up, type a bill and obtain a deposit, then disappear. He had worked in department stores and retail outlets, where there were opportunities for pilfering goods which later he could sell off. It was after a spell in prison, when he was caught in possession of stolen property, that he had first come to Northtown and met Alice. Here, in Fordswick, he had had a fantasy of becoming, in effect, lord of the manor, master of the substantial estate that must eventually come to Alice, only to be routed by an astute old man who had met people like him before. Now he had a real chance of realising that earlier dream, for he was the father of the child who played on the swing at Ford House. Even though he was not married to her mother, he must have rights, be entitled to access. What did the law say about that? Plenty of unmarried couples had children and shared their parenting. Surely he was as much entitled to the child as its mother?

He'd agree to a blood test to establish paternity. If it wasn't his kid, then he'd no interest in it, but it was unlikely that Alice had found someone else on the rebound; that fat girl in the red hat had said it was four years old, which would be about right. Godfrey did not want the responsibility of caring for the child, only what was his due. That meant an acknowledged role in the household. Alice would be happy to see him again, he decided. After all, she hadn't thrown him out; her father had done that, and she might have been heartbroken after he left. He'd thought it probable that the old geezer had turned up his toes by now, but the fat girl had mentioned both Mr and Mrs Watkinson; she, if handled cleverly enough, could be his agent and spy. He'd seek her out in the morning and coax her to apply for the job.

He'd try legal means, at first, to obtain what was his due, which he didn't define except in vague terms of indefinite financial gain and a comfortable roof – he could still marry Alice and make the child legitimate, if such things mattered to anyone. What he really desired was something akin to a lottery win: a fortune obtained without effort, so that he could live in luxury without wondering where the next week's rent was coming from. A gambling win might do it for him, or a big haul for a one-off heist.

Or, if simpler methods failed, a ransom.

*　　*　　*

Alice Watkinson left Ford House every weekday morning at twenty to seven to catch the London train.

After Rowena's birth, she had not returned to the museum. Though no one had made sarcastic or wounding comments when her pregnancy became obvious – indeed, there had been some kindly interest – she feared criticism and curiosity and had snubbed friendly overtures. It was her father who, when the child was three years old, suggested she should return to work and should consider seeking a better position. She had experience, and could depend on a good reference from the Northtown museum, which she had left of her own volition.

'There's no need for you to stay at home,' he told her, contradicting the edict imposed earlier by her parents. Too late, they had realised that through boredom and lack of opportunity, she had been vulnerable to Godfrey, and was literally seduced by him.

'Your mother adores Rowena,' he had stated, with truth. 'The child won't miss you, and she'll be well cared for. She likes her nursery school. You've more time now.'

'But you've always wanted me to be here,' Alice had said. 'What about the cooking? I've always done most of it.' And most of the cleaning, too, though there was a woman coming in once a week.

'We can pay for more help,' her father had said. 'We were wrong to keep you here,' he added. 'I'm sorry, my dear.'

Alice wearily remembered her invented friend, Mary, who had enabled her to escape the confines of home. To account for why Mary did not come to visit after Rowena's birth, she had told her parents that Mary had been offered an excellent job in London. Very rarely, Alice had travelled to London, ostensibly to see Mary. She had gone to an exhibition or visited a museum on these excursions. Now, her father suggested Mary might know of an opening in London for her. It would enlarge her horizons, he declared. Mary proved unable to find her a job; however, she secured one for herself after plucking up courage to write to her former boss, asking if he knew of anything suitable outside Northtown. So it was that she found a post at a London gallery, and began catching the train from the small station five miles from Fordswick. Her father bought her a third-hand Fiat Uno to drive there; she'd find it useful, also, he said, to take Rowena around as she grew older.

This sudden kindness and generosity, coming almost too late, made Alice want to weep, but she blinked back her tears, which were partly of anguish, because if it had been displayed sooner, she might not be in her present plight: an unmarried mother ashamed of the circumstances of her child's birth.

But she did not wish her child away. She hated leaving Rowena, who was the centre of her life and gave it meaning. At first she felt as though her heart was being plucked from her body when she started her job, and daily the train journey back could not pass fast enough for her. She would run to the Fiat, and be one of the first to drive out of the station car park, hurrying home in time to put Rowena to bed and read her a story.

Most mornings, on the station platform, she saw Douglas Vernon, who usually caught the same train. She knew who he was and that he lived at Elm Lodge, for she had done door-to-door charity collections for years. They never spoke at the station. He would be reading *The Times* while he waited, standing exactly opposite the spot where his preferred compartment would halt. Normally, she caught an earlier train home than he did. So it went on, until Godfrey returned.

*   *   *

Back in his camper van after his nocturnal stroll, Godfrey drank several cans of beer.

The public lavatory in the corner of the recreation ground was now, as he had anticipated, locked up. Whoever had secured it would have seen his van, so it may have been just as well that it was unoccupied at the time, Godfrey reflected, urinating against a convenient chestnut tree.

The beer had made him maudlin. Along the road, less than half a mile away, his child – his daughter – that fat female had said it was a girl – lay sleeping, unaware that her father was close at hand.

A child needs a father.

A father has a right to his child. To his daughter.

He would insist on having what was his. He'd go up to Ford House and demand to see her. Alice would recognise him at once if she were there, but was she? Was she still skivvying round after her parents? Why did they need someone to look after the child if her mother was there? Had she left home at last?

Alice must have gone. Or died.

Wrapped in his sleeping-bag, Godfrey worked himself into a mood of sentimental self-pity, imagining himself as an old man, Lear-like, being ministered to by a fair young girl who was his daughter. He'd every right to claim her, particularly if Alice had, for whatever reason, gone away.

He fell asleep imagining that he was wandering through sunlit fields, holding the hand of a pretty, blonde child who skipped along beside him, wearing a flowered dress.

In the morning he woke slowly, with a hangover. The van's windows were fogged up with condensation, but gradually he became aware of a face staring inquisitively through the windscreen, and closed his eyes again. When he opened them once more, the watcher had gone, and Godfrey, emerging, found that the lavatory was now unlocked; the face probably belonged to whoever had opened it up. Perhaps he was employed by the council. Half-fuddled though he still was, Godfrey knew that if the van stayed here, questions would soon be asked, and the police might be informed. They could check its ownership, and if so, would find it unregistered, for though the dealer he had bought it from might have recorded the sale, Godfrey had not registered his purchase. He had no fixed address, which to him was a good enough reason but would not satisfy the police. In any case, he did not want to be traceable.

He'd have to move, find another spot, but he need not go far. Soon he'd be back at Ford House, comfortably installed, with the van parked in one of the vacant garages. The Watkinsons must accept the father of their grandchild. Head throbbing, he crawled from the van and went across to the toilet block. No one else was about, but later some children cut across the recreation ground on their way to catch the school bus. Godfrey washed, filled his water can and, back in the van, made a mug of strong black instant coffee. After drinking it, he felt marginally more alert, and had shed the emotional mood of the night before.

What next?

Last night, he had planned to demand to see his child, but now he realised that it would be foolish to act in haste. His earlier plan of using the fat girl to discover the position at Ford House – who was in charge of the child, and what had happened to Alice – was the wiser one. He knew where she was living. She'd probably respond favourably if he were to call round, but what if someone else answered the door? He couldn't ask for her by name because he didn't know it, and that would look bad. Even so, he felt there was no choice, unless he loitered about in the hope that she would emerge.

He shaved with the remains of the hot water; he liked to be neat, his moustache brushed, his sideburns trimmed. Then he moved the van, parking it near the church and locking it, and walked down the road to Elm Lodge. The house looked reassuringly solid, its windows closed against the weather, various plants, now leafless, tethered to the brick walls; roses and such, he supposed, correctly. Though it was slightly warmer, the ground was hard after frost in the night. If there were no answer when he rang, Godfrey could walk all round and look through the windows. His feet would leave no marks on the gravelled paths.

But the door was opened, and Emily stood revealed, minus the red woollen cap she had worn when they met. Her shorn head startled him and he knew that it would not endear her to Mrs Watkinson. Rallying, he spoke.

'Ah – I've found you,' he said. 'Do you know, you never told me your name?'

Emily had recognised him instantly.

'It's Emily,' she said. 'What's yours?'

'Graham,' he told her, suddenly deciding on an invented one he sometimes used. If she applied for the job at Ford House, as he intended, he did not want her blabbing about him by the name he had adopted when he lived there.

'Well, come in, Graham,' Emily said, welcomingly. 'Would you like some coffee?'

He would, and he'd like the warmth of the house, which he felt lapping comfortably round him as he entered.

'Nice,' he said.

'Yeah. Good, isn't it?' Emily beamed. 'It's all right,' she added, as she looked about him. 'They're out.'

She was pleased to see him. Isabel had suggested she might like to spend the day at Gifts Galore, but Emily had said there was the chance of a job in the village and she planned to apply. Isabel had wanted to know what it was, and where, and Emily, deciding to be vague, had said it was cleaning work and she would have to find out more from the newsagent's, where she had heard it mentioned the day before.

Isabel had thought this a positive plan, and Emily had already proved she was good at cleaning. It could be more satisfactory than taking her into the shop, where there would seldom be enough for her to do, and earning something towards her keep would improve her self-respect. Douglas would not be able to call her a scrounger and it might count in her favour when her case was heard.

Emily had more sense than to show Godfrey/Graham round the house, but she enjoyed entertaining him in the kitchen. After his second cup of coffee and a shortbread biscuit, he asked her if she was going after the job at Ford House, and she said that she was.

'Good,' he approved. 'At worst, they can only turn you down.'

'But I might get it,' she said. 'That would be brilliant.'

After the sudden collapse of her previous effective arrange-ments, Muriel Watkinson had assured Alice she would manage until she found someone to help her with Rowena and the housework. The cleaner who had come once a week had broken her leg and would be out of action for months, and the younger woman who had helped with Rowena had left the village after her own marriage broke up. However, Muriel insisted that there was no need for Alice to take time off from her job, much less leave it; the little girl was fond of her grandmother and enjoyed the nursery school she went to every morning. Soon she would be starting primary school and then things would be easier. Until they found another cleaner, Alice could do the housework at weekends.

During the past year, Muriel had become very lame and was due for a hip replacement; she took Rowena to and from nursery school by car. She did not want to upset Alice's routine and was determined not to have her operation until she had found someone capable to look after Rowena, the house, and her husband, who had had a slight stroke in the summer. He had recovered well, but could walk only short distances. They had considered employing full-time resident help, but were reluctant to do this if they could engage someone from the village, or two people, dovetailing their duties. A housekeeper-cum-nanny could live in the stable flat, where Rowena's father had spent far too long and where, no doubt, the child had been conceived – an act neither grandparent cared to contemplate – and so remain separate from the family when off duty, but it would have to be done up – decorated, made more comfortable. Muriel had thought Robert's expulsion of Godfrey too extreme, an opinion strengthened when Alice, who, when he left, seemed heartbroken, told them she was pregnant. Muriel had been angry; in her opinion, children were better born within wedlock than outside it, and perhaps Godfrey had been Alice's only chance of finding a husband. As time went on, however, she agreed that such a marriage could have been a serious mistake, and when Alice went back to work, she approved. Too late, her parents recognised that by keeping her at home like a Victorian daughter, they had unreasonably curtailed her life and inhibited her development.

But if she had really wanted wider experience, wouldn't she have struck out and obtained it? Defied them and gone?

Muriel knew that Alice lacked the confidence to rebel; perhaps she needed the excuse of her parents to avoid challenge. All the more reason, now, to make sure she stayed at the gallery despite the fatigue incurred by travelling in crowded trains.

Muriel had rung an agency in Northtown which at the moment had no one on its books wanting to care for a child. They specialised in supplying women to look after elderly people or convalescents. Alice said she would contact an au pair agency, and meanwhile Muriel had put the card in the shop in case anyone local was seeking a job.

On Friday morning, driving back from dropping Rowena, parking the car outside the house, for she would need it to fetch the child later, Muriel Watkinson clasped her hands on the steering wheel, laid her head on them, and, like Isabel, suppressed her almost overwhelming urge to scream.

7

Emily walked up the drive to Ford House, past the swing which Godfrey had seen the previous day. She saw the grey Honda Accord parked on the gravel sweep near the front door.

Godfrey had urged her to go back to the newsagent's to check the advertisement, which gave a telephone number for applicants to ring. They had collected the van from where he had left it and driven up to the square together. He had waited outside in the van while she consulted the card in the shop window and then telephoned from the public call box. She'd told Mrs Watkinson that she was visiting her godmother, Mrs Vernon, and might only require a temporary position as she didn't know how long she would be staying, but at the moment she had no plans to move on. Mrs Watkinson had suggested she should come round that morning, and Emily had agreed.

Replacing the telephone, encouraged by the caller's clarity, Muriel Wilkinson let the thought of the stable flat run through her mind again as she built up a fantasy in which the applicant – the only one there had been – proved perfect and wanted to stay when the Vernons' hospitality came to an end. The actual sight of Emily Frost, when she arrived, was a let-down. The young woman wore baggy trousers, a shapeless anorak, and had a red woollen hat on her head. Godfrey was relieved to see the hat. As he dropped her at the gate, he managed not to warn Emily that the Watkinsons were a conventional pair. He said that he would wait for her near the newsagent's, to hear how the interview had gone. Not wanting to be seen from the house, he drove off at once.

Muriel told herself that appearances could be misleading, not caring for the single earring depending from Emily's left ear. Why not wear a pair? However, the young woman smiled pleasantly and looked Muriel in the eye as they talked.

'I like children and I can clean,' she said. 'I've been helping my godmother.'

She'd said children, not kids; Muriel approved of that.

'You said you were only visiting,' she probed.

'My mother died,' said Emily, implying, as she had done before, that she had been living at home.

'Oh – I'm sorry.' Muriel knew that Douglas Vernon worked in some government department in London. Any goddaughter of his wife's should be a suitable person to engage. 'Have you references from past employers?' she asked.

'No – she – my mother – lived in Spain, you see. I haven't worked for a while,' said Emily. 'Tell me about your granddaughter.'

So she learned that Rowena – named, on a whim of her mother's, after the character in *Ivanhoe* – lacked a father and that Alice, her mother, worked in a London art gallery. Muriel's own physical fragility was obvious, and she explained about Robert's stroke.

'He's improving,' she said. 'But he can't get about much. Not like he did. He can't drive now.'

She ran through the duties Emily would have to undertake, and took her with her to collect Rowena from her nursery school. The little girl was too young to sit in the front of the car but clambered into the rear and strapped herself in.

She had a beautiful name, but she was a plain, sallow child who wore glasses and had straight dark hair tethered into a single plait.

Emily loved her at once.

Rowena babbled away to her grandmother about her activities during the morning. They'd done pretend shopping, and played various games. Mrs Watkinson had told her, 'This is Emily,' and Rowena, in a curiously old-fashioned but charming way, held out her hand to shake Emily's. Without its being discussed, somehow or other Emily stayed to lunch – shepherd's pie, which Mrs Watkinson had put in the oven before they left. They ate in the kitchen, a large, rather bleak north-facing room which was kept warm by the big old Aga.

Mrs Watkinson turned to Rowena.

'Emily will bring Grandfather in,' she said. 'Will you show her the way, Rowena?'

'Course. Come on.' Rowena seized Emily's hand and led her through the house to a ground-floor room, once Robert's study and now doubling as his bedroom. The old man was sitting by the window in a wing armchair, looking out over the desolate garden. A winter-flowering viburnum made a pale splash against a far wall but otherwise it was a sombre outlook.

Emily smiled at him, sunnily.

'Hullo,' she said. 'I'm Emily. Are you ready for your lunch?'

'She's engaged you, then? My wife?' said Robert Watkinson.

'I suppose so,' said Emily. 'Anyway, I'm still here. Let me help you,' and with a skill that surprised him, she helped him into the wheelchair parked beside him, and propelled him through to the kitchen where Rowena was helping her grandmother lay the table, which was now covered with a yellow-and-white checked cloth.

'Aren't you going to take your hat off, Emily?' said Mrs Watkinson. Emily had removed her jacket, revealing her new sweater which she wore over a polo and her men's jogging pants. The outfit was far from chic but, being new, was spotless.

'Oh – right.' Emily swept it from her head, her earring swaying, and her stubbled pate was revealed.

Both Watkinsons stared, then recovered themselves.

'I see why you wear your hat,' said Robert, with a slight smile. 'I'm bald. It's chilly, with no hair, in this weather.'

'Have you been ill? Did it all drop out?' asked Rowena. A child at her nursery school had lost his hair through chemotherapy, and she did not find Emily's hair style strange.

'No. I like it like this,' said Emily, not offended. 'Saves trouble.'

'You don't have to brush it,' giggled Rowena. 'Or plait it,' she added.

'No,' agreed Emily. 'Come along now, Rowena. Let's get you settled.'

She was very good with the child, who had clearly taken to her. Without its being seriously discussed, Emily's appointment seemed to be confirmed. She stayed till three o'clock, after washing up. While Rowena played with her Lego, she did the ironing. Both of them were perfectly content.

Mrs Watkinson, able to put her feet up and even doze after lunch, thought it was probably too good to be true, but as Emily left, they agreed a rate of pay and a week's trial. She would begin work on Monday.

'I'd better ring Mrs Vernon,' Muriel told her husband later.

'And what about Alice? Perhaps she should see Emily. Approve her, and so on,' said Robert Watkinson.

'If she wants to, she can go and see her over the weekend,' she said, deciding not to ring up the godmother after all.

Godfrey had almost given Emily up for lost. He was sitting in the camper, now parked within sight of the gates of Ford House, when she emerged, and he roared up behind her, stopping and motioning her to get in.

'Well?' he demanded. 'You've been there for hours. I thought they'd kidnapped you.'

'Did you? You are silly,' said Emily. 'I stayed to lunch. We went to collect the little girl from her nursery school. It's not near the shops.'

Godfrey, reading his newspaper, had not seen the Honda leave the house and turn in the opposite direction from where he was waiting.

'And?' he said.

'And what?'

'And did you get the job?'

'I start properly on Monday,' said Emily. 'I'm to be there at a quarter to nine to take her to nursery school, and then help in the house, and fetch her again, and stay till half-past three. If Mr Watkinson has to see the doctor or anything like that – he's an invalid and sometimes has appointments – I'm to stay till they get back. And Mrs Watkinson's as lame as a duck, poor old thing. She's to have her hip done. They're too old to have all the hassle of Rowena.'

'Rowena?'

'The little girl. Their granddaughter,' said Emily. 'She's great. I didn't meet the mother. Don't suppose I will. She works in London. Goes by train each day, leaving early. So does Douglas.'

'Who's Douglas?'

'Douglas Vernon. Where I live. Isabel's husband.' said Emily.

'You've not done badly,' Godfrey said, approvingly. Considering he had heard only the day before that he had a daughter, neither had he. Now he had to decide what to do with his knowledge.

'The father,' he said. 'What about Rowena's father?'

'He wasn't mentioned, except to say that she hasn't got one,' Emily replied. 'That childminder person said he'd just gone off and left her. Left the mother. I expect they don't like to talk about it. She was lucky, though, that they stood by her. Didn't turn her out. People still do that. Can you believe it?'

Godfrey could. Why should grandparents have the bother and expense of raising another family?

'Sounds as if this lot can well afford to help,' he said.

'Maybe so. And though she doesn't let on, the old girl's dotty about the child,' said Emily. 'But she just can't cope. Maybe she'll be able to manage after her operation.'

'How long do you mean to stay?' Godfrey asked her.

Emily shrugged.

'Can't say,' she said. 'It depends.'

'On what?'

'On how long Isabel will put me up, I suppose,' said Emily. She did not want to tell Godfrey about her forthcoming appearance in court.

'If you're a hit with these people – these Watkinsons – you might move in,' he suggested. But he didn't plan to hang around long himself. He'd soon decide what to do about the child.

On reflection, he didn't really want the kid. That had been the drink, weakening him. He wanted, however, to assert his rights. Legally, he must have some, even though he hadn't married Alice. At the very least, he could make the grandparents pay him, once again, to stay away. It sounded as if they were both in poor shape; when they were dead, only Alice would remain to keep him from his daughter. Then she'd pay, too, one way or another.

'She's such a nice little girl,' Emily was saying.

Women were so sentimental. Godfrey suppressed a sigh.

'I'll meet you on Monday. Then you can introduce us,' was his answer.

He'd disappear over the weekend, go somewhere more exciting – London, say, or Birmingham – find some woman, have a bit of fun. Pity this girl Emily was so unappealing; she'd be willing enough, he guessed. She couldn't get many offers, and here she was, on the spot.

Emily was disappointed when he said he'd be seeing friends over the weekend, but at the same time, she was relieved. She wasn't keen on revealing her new friendship to Isabel; she knew for certain that neither she nor Douglas would approve of him.

Why not, though? He was all right. He didn't seem to want anything from her, and he hadn't mocked her for being fat.

It didn't occur to her to wonder why he bothered with her.

Alice Watkinson came to Elm House the following morning, which was Saturday.

Her mother had explained that she had engaged Emily Frost, goddaughter of Mrs Vernon, as a temporary mother's – or in this case, grandmother's – help. Alice, wary after her experience with Godfrey, had mentioned references, and her mother had replied that the girl's connection with Mrs Vernon was a recommendation in itself. Alice, however, wanted to see Emily for herself and had called on her way back from the weekly major supermarket shopping trip that she did early every Saturday. Rowena had accompanied her and was now in the car, strapped in her seat looking at a book as Alice rang the doorbell.

Douglas opened the door.

'Oh – er – Mr Vernon.' Alice was disconcerted. She had expected either Isabel or Emily to answer her ring.

'Yes?'

Douglas, wearing his half glasses, the *Financial Times* held in one hand, peered at her enquiringly. She looked vaguely familiar, but he could not place her.

Alice, knowing herself to be unmemorable, understood his difficulty.

'Alice Watkinson, from Ford House,' she said.

'Yes?' Douglas repeated, frowning.

'It's about your niece. Goddaughter. Emily. May I speak to her, please?'

What had the girl done now? Flung stones at poor old Watkinson when he was out in his wheelchair? Douglas sighed.

'Is there a problem?' he enquired.

'Oh no, not at all. That is,' Alice hesitated. 'She's probably explained that my mother has engaged her to help with Rowena. My daughter. While I'm at work. I go to London, like you,' she reminded him. 'I've seen you at the station.'

So that was why she was familiar: a dreary figure in a long black coat and an all-enfolding hat, waiting on the platform.

'Ah yes – yes, of course,' he said. 'Well, you'd better

come in,' he told her, standing back so that she could do so.

'Rowena's in the car. She's quite happy,' Alice said, enquiringly, and Douglas correctly interpreted her remark as hoping the child would be asked in, too, but he did not respond.

'Good,' he said, and called out, 'Isabel. Emily. You have a visitor.'

She wasn't married. This woman, Alice, was yet another single mother. Douglas approved of none of them, whether they lived in apparent harmony with a long-term partner or were the feckless variety always swopping round. Though no one had suggested that Alice was feckless, except in getting pregnant in the first place, and she was not a drain on the state, as she worked and had supportive parents, she was not exempt from censure. Isabel must deal with her. He knew nothing about this job which Emily had, it seemed, secured. She had not thought fit to tell him about it, though maybe Isabel had been informed, but perhaps she had been merely amusing herself by applying for it. The Watkinsons must have been desperate if they had engaged her, and was it proper for them to employ someone who was waiting to be tried for a criminal offence? Isabel must discover the facts; let her be the one to interview Alice Watkinson and apprise her of the true position. Meanwhile, he wanted to return to his newspaper. He called again, more irritably this time, and when Isabel appeared from the kitchen, he walked off without any explanation.

Isabel knew Alice slightly. She must have come to say they'd changed their minds about employing Emily at Ford House, and who could blame them?

'Hullo,' she said, and waited to hear the worst.

But it was Emily whom Alice wished to see. She told herself that this encounter was no more difficult than one she might face in the gallery, where, though she was usually in the office, sometimes she dealt with clients. She spoke firmly.

'My mother interviewed Emily yesterday about helping with my daughter and in the house. May I speak to her?' she said.

'Oh – of course,' said Isabel.

'As she'll have charge of my daughter, I want to see her for myself,' Alice explained. 'Not just to rely on my mother's judgement. But please don't take that personally,' she added, her pale face flushing.

So she hadn't decided not to engage Emily after all. Isabel, surprised when Emily told her about the job, had felt that it was an ideal temporary occupation, for Emily could come to no harm while with the Watkinsons, an exemplary family apart from Alice's modern approach to motherhood. And Emily, relating the tale of her afternoon at Ford House, though with no reference to Godfrey and his encouragement, had been enthusiastic; she had revealed sympathy for the old couple in their fragile state, and seemed drawn to the little girl.

'Of course you must see her yourself,' said Isabel. 'Come into the drawing-room and I'll fetch her. She's making a cake,' she added.

Alice thought this sounded promising.

'I won't stay long. Rowena's in the car,' she said.

'Your daughter? Oh, do bring her in,' said Isabel. 'I'll make some coffee, and what would Rowena like? Fruit juice?'

She was nice. She was kind. Alice felt a glow as she went outside to undo Rowena's harness. The goddaughter must, by association, be the same.

Her mother, never one for lengthy expositions, had not described the new employee. Alice had asked her age and learned that she was twenty-three. She bustled Rowena into the house where Isabel was hovering hospitably in the doorway, waiting to shepherd Alice and the child, who was carrying her book, into the large drawing-room with its big bow window overlooking the garden. It seemed light and airy after Ford House, where the curtains and furnishings were dark and practical. Here, Isabel had chosen pale colours; the walls were a light apricot, and the room seemed warm and welcoming.

'Make yourselves comfortable,' said Isabel. 'I'll ask Emily to bring in the coffee and orange juice, and leave you together.'

She went away. What a pleasant person, Alice thought; so friendly. She settled herself and Rowena on the sofa, and looked round the room. A bowl planted with daffodils, now almost flowering, stood on the deep window ledge, and on a table there was a tall vase of forsythia which, brought into the warm house, had come into bloom. Alice hoped there was no cat; she and Rowena were both allergic to them and got asthma from even touching a chair or cushion where one had sat.

Very quickly, Emily appeared, carrying a tray. Alice's coffee was in a pretty pottery mug, and Rowena's fruit juice in a plastic mug.

'Hi,' she said. 'I'm Emily.'

Her mother might have warned her, Alice thought, as she beheld the large, tank-like young woman in her vast sweater and baggy trousers, but of course she hadn't known that Alice planned to see the girl. Emily's cropped head was bare; a fuzz of fair hair was just visible. She set the tray on a coffee table, put Alice's cup down in front of her and offered her sugar, which Alice declined, and then turned to Rowena, who had slid off the sofa and approached her, a finger in her mouth, peering at her, smiling.

'Do you like orange juice, Rowena?' asked Emily. 'Well

then, sit down on this little stool, look, and you can have some. And a biscuit, if your mum says so.' She pulled forward a small footstool and placed it beside the large armchair in which she planned to sit.

Rowena took quick little steps towards her and sat down. Emily gave her the mug and lowered herself into the chair, watching as Rowena drank. After a few sips, she took the mug away.

'More in a minute,' she said, and offered Alice the biscuits, which were custard creams.

'I won't, thank you, but Rowena, you may, if you'd like one,' said Alice. She was impressed because Rowena had, as her mother had declared, so obviously taken a liking to Emily.

Rowena took her biscuit and nibbled it, scattering some crumbs, and Emily said not to worry, she'd sweep them up before Douglas saw them.

Alice ignored this comment.

'You really want to work for us?' she asked her.

'I do. I want to pay my way here,' said Emily, and then added, 'I didn't say this to your mother, but I got into a little trouble down in Somerset recently.'

'Oh dear.' Alice sighed. There had to be a snag. 'What sort of trouble?'

'I was protesting about the new road,' Emily confessed. 'Things got a bit out of hand and some of us were arrested. It was meant to be a peaceful protest,' she explained. 'Isabel stood bail for me. I won't let her down, or you, but maybe you won't want me, now.'

Alice had seen the rowdy protestors on television. Chaos had been caused by really very few of them. The various sheriff's officers involved had been so patient. Did it matter that this girl had been among the troublemakers? Both sides had valid points to make, and many of the demonstrators seemed more mischievous than malicious.

'We need help badly,' she said. 'You've seen my parents. They've been wonderful over Rowena. You don't need to know the story,' she added. 'But I made a mistake, too, one with more lasting consequences than yours, I'd say. If my parents and Rowena are happy about it, then I will be satisfied. At least it gives us time to look for someone else if this doesn't work out in the long term. You'll be fined, I suppose? And you'll need to go to court?'

'That's about it,' said Emily.

'I'm owed some holiday. I can take time off. Do you know when it is?'

Emily told her, and Alice nodded.

'We'll know by then if it's going to work out,' she said. 'On both sides, I mean.'

'Isabel and Douglas won't want me stopping on,' said Emily anxiously.

'We can probably work something out,' said Alice, not thinking of the stable flat at all, but of the rooms on the top floor of the house, where many years ago a housekeeper had slept, and the nanny who had looked after her when she was a child. With her parents getting frail, live-in help would be essential if Alice were to keep on her job, which she was determined she would do, for through it, she was asserting herself at last. She had lived in her parents' shadow all her life, and she would always see that they were cared for, but she need not perform every task herself if she could find someone reliable to help her.

Reassured, at least for the short term, she and Rowena left. Isabel heard them as they moved towards the door and came to say goodbye. All three were smiling. Isabel, alone, looked anxious.

'It's all right, Mrs Vernon,' Alice said. 'Emily's been quite frank with me but it's best my parents don't know the details. We'll see how things work out.' She paused, and then added, 'She is your goddaughter. That's worth a lot.'

'You'd better not let me down, Emily,' said Isabel, when the door had closed behind the visitors.

'Oh, my God,' was Douglas's verdict. Still, it solved the problem of what to do with Emily while she waited for the hearing, and the Watkinsons must look after themselves. The old man, after all, had been in business all his life.

It didn't occur to him that all three, and the child, were vulnerable.

8

Emily felt dazed.

A week ago, in bitter weather, she had been living in a tent on doomed and threatened land. Warmth had come from camp fires, on which the demonstrators burnt wood from trees slaughtered by the developers' chainsaws. Wooding – collecting boughs and branches – was exhilarating, moving, with companions, over the frost-hard ground, laughing, often singing. There was friendship and anonymity: no one was curious about another person; you told what you wanted known, and several people used nicknames to hide their real identities, calling themselves after cartoon characters or animals or by any other designation which caught their fancy. You could lose your true self here, as she had done for months. She had managed to blank out what had really caused her to seek refuge among the protestors.

More comfortably placed sympathisers eased the lot of the grubby, unwashed groups by bringing food and money, but they could not lay on lavatories or running water. Soon such details ceased to matter and Emily, like most of them, lived for the moment, high on the thrill of the attention they attracted. Those not originally convinced of the value of the cause soon persuaded themselves that they were dedicated, and not simply pursuing the campaign to give direction to hitherto unfocused lives. For many, it was a happier, healthier existence than they had ever known.

Emily missed her undemanding friends. You were never lonely on the site, for just as you looked out for others, so they watched your back, and anyone who did drugs or sex acted of their own free will, not because they were pressured. Sometimes she had longed for a bath and clean clothes, and when rare chances came to wash either herself or her clothing she seized them eagerly. She had not looked far ahead. Other more dedicated characters planned for when surrender was inevitable and a new operation must be mounted – perhaps an airport extension or an industrial complex. If she had not been arrested, she would have moved on when they did. Maybe she would find them again when this episode was over, but meanwhile she must bide her time, conform to any rules imposed by Isabel and Douglas, cause no trouble, and pass the days as agreeably as possible. She had not expected anything like the diversion offered by the job at Ford House, nor had she anticipated meeting a man who would befriend her, as Godfrey had done. And amidst all this, she was living in conditions of comfort which, after her past privations, seemed positively hedonistic.

She mustn't let it soften her up. She must plan to return to the ecological fight, for although there were arguments on both sides, she believed in it by now. Didn't she?

Her main worry was that Isabel would start seriously searching for her brothers. Though she had spoken the truth when she said she had no addresses for them, it might not be too difficult to trace them. Then the truth of what had happened would come out. She must fend off any further questions Isabel asked.

She had liked Alice, who was justified in wanting to check her out. Emily knew her appearance was not that of the perfect nanny, but she took most people at face value and must hope that Alice did the same; if so, she would be satisfied. It was wise not to look too far beneath the surface, for who knew what secrets, best left undisturbed, might thus be exposed?

It was Isabel's Saturday off from the shop and she had been anxious about the weekend. Golf was out, not only because of Emily, who must be kept occupied and who could have walked round with her, but because it was so cold. She had decided that they should spend the morning cooking, and Emily seemed delighted; she said that when she was small, she had enjoyed helping her mother. Douglas never cooked and he seldom wandered in when she was busy in the kitchen. Today, however, he came in after Alice had driven off.

'I suppose you've lost the job now,' he said to Emily, without preamble.

'No.' Emily looked defiant.

'You didn't tell her, then?'

'Tell her what?'

'Your story. That you are an arrested person out on bail.'

'I did tell her,' said Emily, thus, but only for an instant, deflating Douglas.

'Oh – oh, did you?' he said, unable to think of how to answer this.

'She was very understanding,' said Emily. 'And after all, I'm innocent until proved guilty, aren't I?'

'Am I not,' muttered Douglas, who was a pedant.

'You're pleading guilty,' Isabel reminded her.

'I might change my mind,' said Emily, and Isabel saw the way ahead pegged with hazard signs.

'Well, anyway, it's solved their problems at Ford House for the time being,' she said bracingly. 'It'll give old Mrs Watkinson a break, at least.'

'The woman should take care of her own child,' grumbled Douglas.

'She did, at first. But maybe she doesn't want to sponge on her parents,' said Isabel. 'Or the state,' she added craftily.

Douglas thought of the cost of a railway season ticket.

'A part-time local job would have been as profitable,' he said.

'She used to work in Northtown,' said Isabel. 'Before the child was born. Maybe she needed to get away.'

'Stands to inherit a packet,' Douglas said.

'Not necessarily. The old pair might need to spend it all on nursing care,' said Isabel. 'They may not have much capital. Most of it's probably tied up in the house.'

'She's an ugly child. The little girl,' said Douglas, who had watched Alice and her daughter return to their car.

'Rowena's her name,' said Emily.

Douglas snorted. 'How ridiculous,' he said.

'It's just your opinion that she's ugly,' said Emily. 'She's a great little kid and you're intolerant, judging people by appearances.' She glared at Douglas as she spoke, and as she seemed about to say more, Isabel decided it was time to drop a saucepan with a clatter. Under cover of the noise, Douglas left the room without the verbal explosion that had seemed inevitable after Emily's remark.

'You're lucky he didn't turf you out after that,' said Isabel. 'Then you would have been in trouble.'

'Sorry,' said Emily, but she didn't look it.

'You were right, though wrong to say it,' Isabel said quietly. 'I've never had the nerve.'

'You're afraid of him,' Emily realised.

Isabel paused in what she was doing, thinking about Emily's remark. Was it true?

'I don't think so,' she replied at last. 'But I'm afraid of upsetting things – the status quo. My life's improved a lot lately, with the shop. And golf. Don't you mess things up for me now. Remember,' she added, 'I can send you off to prison just like that.'

Did she mean it? Would she do it, if provoked?

Emily did not intend to find out, but even though she resolved not to push him too far, she saw no reason why Douglas should call all the shots. One thing she had learned on the site, and that was to appreciate teamwork. You soon knew whom you could rely on, there. Looks were not a problem, either; no one was exactly in a state to go to a party at Buckingham Palace.

She settled down to concentrate on her kitchen duties. Rather as if Emily were a child who needed to be occupied, Isabel had embarked on a programme to stack the freezer with supplies. She liked to store prepared dishes in case she was too busy to cook, or something unexpected cropped up, and though the Vernons rarely ate cakes, she always kept one in reserve.

Emily enjoyed cooking and was eager to assist. She carried out Isabel's instructions, proving efficient.

'You'll be a help to Mrs Watkinson, I can see,' said Isabel. 'She may be quite surprised to find how handy you are in the kitchen and she'll certainly be pleased.' The job might work out satisfactorily for all concerned. 'Weren't you bored with camp food and tins?' A poor diet probably accounted for her weight.

'It didn't bother me,' said Emily. 'Sometimes we did get treats, when people brought us meals, and once a chef came and cooked for several days.' She sighed. 'I wouldn't mind being a chef,' she added.

'Well, you could be one, once this trouble's over,' said Isabel, pleased to discover this aspiration, which, with effort, could be fulfilled. At some point, she must discuss Emily's future with the girl. 'You could enrol for training.' Catering courses, she thought: easy to find out about. The weight problem might sort itself out, meanwhile. 'What about going for a walk?' she suggested. 'Some exercise would be good for you.'

'You mean, to get my weight down,' said Emily. 'I can't seem to do that.'

'Were you a plump little girl? I can't remember,' said Isabel. Neither of Emily's parents had been overweight; maybe it was glandular, and perhaps she should see a doctor. Isabel resolved to recommend the idea after the court hearing, if all went well. She must also discover exactly what Emily had been doing before she joined the protestors; so far, she had been evasive.

'I've got into bad habits,' Emily admitted. 'Scoffing chocolate and biscuits.'

'Yes – well, you can stop that now. There's plenty of fruit here. If you feel hungry, have an apple,' Isabel advised. 'See how much you can take off by the time you have to go to court.'

Emily didn't care to be reminded of this prospect. It might not all end happily; she might yet get sent down.

Walking for its own sake was boring. She didn't know anyone in Fordswick except the Vernons, the Watkinsons, and

Graham, as she thought of Godfrey, but he wasn't there now. She felt wistful as after lunch she obediently set out for exercise. She lumbered off down the drive, Isabel watching her departure from the window. Her rolling gait was like a sailor's. Poor girl. Would she ever get back on course?

She must, Isabel resolved, and when she had done so, Isabel's debt to Ginnie would be paid. She had told Emily about a footpath over the fields behind the church; if she took that, it would bring her out on the main road and she could make a circle back to Elm Lodge. There were stiles to cross, but she couldn't get lost; it would take her about forty minutes, Isabel estimated. She did not offer to set off later in the opposite direction and meet her; suddenly, she felt extremely tired. Weekends were often difficult.

She was quite startled, lost in thought, when Douglas appeared, dressed in his new winter cycling garb of knee-socks and cord breeches, saying he was going out for a ride. She made appropriate encouraging remarks and then, with the house to herself, she settled down in the drawing-room with a book, trying to suppress the guilt she felt at being idle. In ten minutes, she had dozed off, and was woken when the door opened and a voice said, 'Hi, Mum.'

'Toby!' Isabel sat up abruptly, dropped her detective novel and felt instant happiness as her son Toby stooped to kiss her.

'Thought I'd drop in. I'm on my way to a friend's party,' he said. 'So you're not in the shop today?'

'No. How lucky. Have you had lunch?' she asked.

'Not really,' he said. 'I'll grab something just to keep me going, shall I? What is there?'

Soon they were both sitting at the table in the kitchen, Isabel with a mug of coffee and Toby with a glass of orange juice and several slices of cold ham from the piece Isabel had cooked the night before. He piled the ham, with some cheese, on to a hunk of bread. Isabel wondered what he would have done if he hadn't called in at home for fuel: gone without, and eaten heartily this evening, she supposed. Occasionally he did appear like this, unheralded.

'Dad talking to his fish?' he asked. He'd come in quietly and his father might not have heard him.

'No. He's out on his bike,' she answered.

'In full gear?'

'Of course. A new rig-out. Helmet and all.' Douglas's helmet was bright yellow, so that he was easily visible to passing traffic.

Toby, who had gone skiing at Christmas, had not seen Douglas for some time. 'And what else is new?'

'You'll never guess.'

'What?'

He wouldn't, because probably he could scarcely remember her.

'We've got a visitor. Emily Frost. My goddaughter,' she said.

'Good heavens! From the grave?'

'That was her mother. Ginnie. She died in Spain about four years ago.'

'I remember. You were a bit upset.'

'Silly, really, when I hadn't seen her for ages and we'd lost touch,' said Isabel.

'Not at all. You were friends and you pushed Emily and me out in our push-chairs together,' said Toby. 'Ever so sweet, we must have been,' he smirked.

'Funnily enough, you were,' said Isabel. 'Two dear little things. I expect I've got some photos somewhere.'

'I wouldn't know her if I saw her,' Toby said. 'We were just little kids.'

'You will see her, unless you plan to leave at once. She's gone out for a walk. She's put on a lot of weight,' said Isabel.

'I should imagine she has. We can't have been more than four or five when we last met,' Toby said.

'No – I mean serious weight. She's got a problem. Several, in fact. That's why she's here,' said Isabel, and went on to disclose the details, mentioning the job at Ford House, and Emily's day at Gifts Galore.

'Oh dear,' said Toby when her tale was done. 'Bet Dad doesn't like any of this. Except the bit about the job. That seems a step towards redemption.'

'I hope it is. And Dad doesn't like the rest of it at all, and nor do I, but I had to scoop her up,' said his mother.

'Yes, maybe you did, but you needn't hang on to her, once this is all ironed out,' said Toby. 'Won't she go back to her drop-out friends?'

Isabel felt that if she did, Emily's future would remain uncertain and she might reappear, needing to be rescued, whenever things went wrong.

'I'll have to try to find her brothers. She doesn't seem to know where they are,' she said. 'They're abroad somewhere.'

'Good idea,' said Toby. 'What do we know about them?'

'Not much. They're called Charles and Anthony and I don't know what they do to earn a living,' said Isabel. 'I've got an idea Ginnie said one was in banking, but I may be imagining that.'

'They should be traceable,' said Toby. 'Internet or Interpol,' he suggested, grinning.

'No need to be so drastic,' said Isabel. 'She's streetwise, though. She spotted those shoplifters.'

'Yes. But set a thief, Mum,' said Toby.

'Cynic,' said his mother. But she remembered Emily's remark; he spoke more truly than he knew. 'Here comes one of them now. Emily or your father,' she warned, as they heard the front door close with a slight bang. She had left it on the latch for Emily to let herself in. Toby, in the few seconds before he met her, wondered if his mother had given her a key to the house, and told her the security code. His father had recently had an alarm system installed. If she was in with a group of hippie types, it might not be wise for her to know the code. Then the door opened and, alerted by the dark red Renault parked outside that there was a visitor, Emily came in, her face flushed, glowing from the exercise she had taken.

'Here's Toby,' Isabel informed her. 'He's changed a bit since you last met.'

And so had Emily, thought Toby. She certainly had.

'Oh, hi!' Emily shifted her weight from one foot to another, her hands clasped behind her back.

'Sorry about your mother,' Toby said.

'Yes – well, it was a while ago,' said Emily. She looked away from him and said, embarrassed, 'I expect Isabel's told you why I'm here.'

'I understand there's been a spot of bother,' Toby replied. 'I hope you get off lightly.'

'So do I,' she answered, and went on, rather defiantly, 'I'll pay my way. I've got a job. I start on Monday.'

'Mum told me. That's good,' he said.

Isabel gaped at her. There'd been no question in her mind of Emily contributing to the housekeeping.

'I'll just go and take my coat off,' said Emily, and she left the room. They heard her clumping heavily upstairs.

'Phew! I see what you mean about the weight problem,' said Toby. 'You'd think she'd lose it, swinging about among the trees.'

'Yes, you would, wouldn't you? But maybe she didn't move around much, once up there,' Isabel suggested. 'And she ended up in a tent. I suppose she filled up on cakes and stuff. She says well-wishers brought them food.'

'Perhaps she wasn't with them long,' said Toby. 'Did she tell you how long she was there?'

'No. Months, I should think. I imagined her lot had come from somewhere else – there are always demonstrations going on,' said Isabel.

'Maybe you should ask her,' Toby said.

'You're probably right. Once the case is over, we'll have to make a plan. I expect she'll be bound over to keep the peace or something,' Isabel said.

'Oh, at the very least,' said Toby.

'How do you feel about these peaceful protests?' Isabel asked him.

'So often they aren't peaceful at all,' he answered. 'So often they're hijacked by troublemakers.'

'I don't see Emily as one of those,' said Isabel. 'I think she just got swept along with the mob.'

'Well – whatever – I hope this doesn't land you with problems,' he said.

'I don't think it will. When she's got through the trial, I expect she'll want to join her friends,' said Isabel. 'Though it would be better if she pursued some more constructive plan. Meanwhile, she'll be helping out at Ford House.'

Toby, after finishing his snack, decided he must go. He was

collecting someone else on the way to the party. Isabel managed not to ask who it was. Emily had not reappeared.

'What's she doing, staying upstairs all this time?' Toby wondered, getting to his feet. 'I hope I didn't frighten her off.'

'Perhaps she's being tactful. Leaving us alone,' said Isabel.

'Well, she can't be washing her hair,' said Toby, laughing at his own wit.

Passing through the hall, he called goodbye to Emily and she shouted back. When he had driven off, she came downstairs.

'Nice guy,' was all she said.

Thrown together as small children, they had got on well together, Isabel thought. She had no memory of fights or squabbles. They were not likely to have a lot in common now.

Douglas, bicycling back, had met Toby in the road and exchanged a brief word, he astride his stationary bike, Toby leaning out of the car.

'Great, Dad,' Toby had said. 'I can see you're keeping very fit.'

They did not have much to say to one another. Making an excuse about the approach of darkness, Douglas said farewell and pedalled on. After they had parted, Toby wondered how the evening would be spent at Elm Lodge. Would there be a lively conversation? Or a game of Scrabble?

Isabel had decided how to deal with it. She told Emily they were going to the cinema, rang up to discover what was showing and the times, and asked Douglas if he would like to go with them, offering him the choice of several films.

'You go,' he said. 'I've got things to do.'

When they returned, he had gone to bed.

9

Douglas was relieved that Isabel had removed their guest for the evening. Had she not done so, he would have continued with Gladstone, as he did now, sitting in his armchair by the hearth, where a gas fire resembling real coals had replaced the open fire which had been in position when they bought the house. Douglas believed in maintaining, when possible, clean air, and at least in minimising pollution. Isabel and Emily, if in the room, would have chattered, or would have wanted to watch television, and he would have felt obliged to sit through their distracting noise rather than remove himself to his study, for he was a family man and thus must spend time with those who comprised his personal domestic unit, namely, at present, Isabel. Emily did not count as family. Depriving his wife of his company would be shirking his duties and it should never be said that Douglas Vernon was not aware of his responsibilities.

Freed from the need to act a role he had always found uncomfortable, Douglas set Gladstone down, poured himself a glass of port from the bottle left over from Christmas, and pondered the concept of the family. When he was young, the convention was that when a man could afford to marry – which implied providing a home and paying the household bills – he did so: thus, he founded a family, which would swell as children were born and would become a stronghold for those within it, each supporting the others, children obedient to their parents and wives submitting to their husbands. Isabel was a pretty girl, not rebellious, bright, but not as intellectual as Douglas considered himself to be, and having decided that she would be a suitable life partner, he had pursued her with determination. Douglas was too unadventurous to embark on sexual escapades; he wanted to confine himself and the woman of his choice within the safe walls of matrimony. His aim was not to score, but to secure. He considered himself to be a moral man, but he was also frightened of rejection. Before selecting Isabel he had wooed another girl, Yvonne Young, taking her to concerts and on the river and eventually proposing, to be refused with astonished mockery. Yvonne had said he was a prig. To save face, he lost no time in finding someone else.

He won Isabel by sheer persistence. She had had a couple of romances, neither very serious and only one of them a fully fledged affair. At some stage she must cease to be a virgin, Isabel had decided, and had passed this watershed as a rite of passage to maturity. It had been a disappointing experiment, improving very little when repeated, and both parties had agreed to part without regret or pain. Douglas had solemnly told her that he had not indulged in loose living and that he expected them to learn together on life's path. To this day, Isabel did not know if he had ever slept with anyone else; she thought he might have read some books before their wedding. Lack of sexual joy was a big disappointment to her; she knew she had missed out on something which could dominate – though possibly not wisely – many people's lives.

Douglas had told himself when he entered it that marriage

was a partnership. You made a commitment, which you kept. On the whole, his had worked out adequately; Isabel had kept her looks and she was efficient. This shop business was a tiresome distraction but it showed a modest profit and seemed harmless. His own horticultural and constructive interests, and his cycling, occupied him so that they were not in each other's pockets. Later, when retirement loomed, a bigger role in village affairs – he felt, as a government servant, he must keep out of anything remotely controversial but was on the parish council – would fill up time. Their sons were both following their own lines and Matthew was doing well; at the moment he was on a course in America. He had a girl friend, Fiona, who had been preceded by some others, and he lived in a large house in Clapham, sharing it with two male friends and three girls. People did that today, with no sexual implications. Douglas, not approving, nevertheless knew it was a financially sound arrangement and he was glad Matthew had not married early in life, saddling himself too soon with a mortgage and responsibilities. Things were different from when he was Matthew's age; young people seemed to live for the moment but if a man flitted from girl to girl, like a butterfly, settling nowhere, at what point did he resolve to stop and select one with whom to form a new family? Today, such a step was constantly postponed, and when marriages took place, many foundered.

Douglas was certain that his marriage was solid. Each partner knew their role and fulfilled it, not expecting the impossible. Matthew and Toby, with the example of their parents before them, would eventually marry wisely, and in time Isabel would enjoy being a grandmother.

Predicting this successful future, his uncertainties suppressed, Douglas returned to Gladstone while, at a small cinema in

Northtown, Isabel and Emily were transported by the delights of *Sense and Sensibility*, though Emily was disgusted by the perfidy of Willoughby. She said she had never read the book, nor any other novel by Jane Austen, which Isabel found odd. Hadn't she had to study one, at least, at school? She remembered Ginnie having a full set of the novels on her shelves. Perhaps they never reached Spain. Isabel resolved, if Emily stayed long enough, to rent the various videos and thus fill in some gaps there seemed to be in Emily's education. That would truly be a fitting godmotherly deed.

They had not talked about the years in Spain. Undressing quietly, not wanting to wake Douglas, who had gone to bed before their return and had fallen asleep over Gladstone, Isabel wondered about that period in Emily's life. She must speak excellent Spanish. That could lead to work – translating, travel, radio – there must be many openings for someone fluent in the language. She would have obtained the Spanish equivalent of GCSEs, surely? Blaming herself for not showing more interest in her protegée's past, Isabel carefully removed Douglas's half-glasses, still perched on his nose, and the book, and climbed cautiously into bed beside him. He gave a grunt, rolled over away from her, but did not wake.

Twin beds would be nice, she thought; would she ever dare suggest them? She turned her mind towards the film she had just seen. Marriage had been the sole target for young girls in those days. In her own youth, it had been the ultimate goal, but at the proper time. What was the proper time?

No wonder many people seemed to think it had outgrown its usefulness.

Emily had been enchanted by the film. It had been lovely to

look at, with beautiful scenery and gorgeous houses, and there had been some genuine affection among the families. It had been showing at an independent cinema in a side street in Northtown; Isabel, who seldom went to the cinema and had missed it when it was first released, was not enthusiastic about what was on at the multi-screen cinema on the town's outskirts and had insisted that they see it.

'You can't have had much entertainment on your site,' she'd said. 'No telly or videos.'

One youth had had a portable television, but it ran out of batteries.

'Some people made music,' Emily said. 'There was a girl who played the flute.'

Back to basics, thought Isabel. There was more merit in participation than merely plugging in to someone else's performance.

Lying in her comfortable bed, Emily reflected on her day. A lot had happened, but none of it was bad. Alice Watkinson had come to check up on her, which was fair enough, and she had passed that test. She had put Douglas down, which was something, but on the other hand, he could call her bluff and turn her out, and he could get his revenge on Isabel, which would be a pity. Then Toby had appeared. He was nice, and had been friendly, but he was sharp; he might detect lies or question things Isabel took on trust. Well, he'd gone now, and if he came again, she'd avoid him. As for the future, she couldn't look too far ahead. If she was bound over, or given a suspended sentence, she would move on. Otherwise the past would catch up with her and Isabel would discover everything.

She fell asleep, not worrying about what would happen the next day. It would pass, and on Monday she would go to Ford House.

Sunday did pass. Douglas went out on his bicycle and Isabel tackled Emily about her brothers. Why had they lost touch? At this question, Emily had turned pale, looked frightened, and said, 'They're both abroad. I told you. I don't hear from them.'

'You've had a row?' asked Isabel.

'Yes. I don't want to talk about it,' said Emily, and set her mouth firmly in a stubborn line.

Defeated, Isabel handed her *Persuasion* to read, telling her it was about fidelity. Probably she would rather have a magazine, Isabel thought, going into the kitchen to listen to the omnibus edition of *The Archers*, who had become so quarrelsome and were always moaning, except for patient Jill, who worried ceaselessly about her family. Peeling potatoes, putting together a casserole, for Douglas could return at any time, late or early, Isabel wondered why she was so hooked on the radio serial, and decided being concerned about other people's troubles and dissatisfactions, even fictional ones, took your mind off your own. Yet she had few, she told herself. Her life ran smoothly, with satisfactory sons whom she loved, and a husband on whom she could rely. Emily's presence was a minor hitch, true, and she must keep in touch after the girl left, though how could she if Emily were living in a camp? Give her a pile of stamped addressed envelopes and bid her write from time to time?

Emily went for another walk on Sunday afternoon, and Isabel, still curious about Ginnie and feeling guilty because she had allowed the friendship to lapse, began looking in her desk for any old letters she might have kept. Had Ginnie not sent photographs from Spain? When had they stopped exchanging Christmas cards?

On Isabel's part, not at all, till Ginnie's death. Every year she had sent a card to Spain – a snowy scene, to remind Ginnie of the climate she had left behind, and she had felt very sad when she learned what had happened. Surely Emily's letter giving her the news must be somewhere? Or had she destroyed it?

She came across all sorts of distractions in her search for it – early efforts by the boys, and a letter from Douglas looking forward to their wedding three weeks from the date on which he was writing. He was pompous even then, she thought, reading it, trying to remember if her heart had beaten faster as a consequence of its arrival. It contained no passionate phrases and only the mildest endearments. She tore it into countless small pieces and flung them into the wastepaper basket. So much for youthful dreams.

She found the letter eventually. In it, Emily said her mother's death some months previously had been sudden, coming as a shock, and she apologised for not giving Isabel the news sooner. She did not mention her own plans, nor her brothers, nor her Spanish stepfather. Had Isabel, replying, invited her to stay? It had been around the time of the move, so perhaps she hadn't: a serious omission.

Emily, out walking for the second consecutive afternoon, had now explored the whole of Fordswick. Today, she met others taking exercise: parents with young children in push-chairs or dragging along on foot, a few on small cycles, and older couples, some walking with arms linked, others in single file. She glanced in a friendly way at most of them but no one spoke to her. If she filled up spare time by walking, she'd lose weight. She'd put it on after all that trouble.

Subconsciously, as she walked, she began looking out for the man who had told her his name was Graham and his camper van. Would he come back? He had said he would, but why should he want to? He had no reason to return. She meant nothing to him, but if he did reappear, he was someone she already knew and who was ignorant of her brush with the law.

It had been so stupid to turn violent, and she hadn't meant to, but for a few uncontrolled minutes she had taken out her frustrations on the helmeted heads of several security officers. For this, despite her present bail, she might pay heavily, but she was not going to think about that now. She had a brief interval in which life would be simple.

She walked a fair way round the village, eventually passing Ford House, where the gates to the drive were closed. There were lights on in the house and Emily imagined the warm scene within: Alice playing with the child; the kindly grandparents in the background. In her imagination it was idyllic, whereas in reality Mr Watkinson had developed a cold and was in bed, his wife, who had been up in the night attending to him, was lying down; and Alice was in the kitchen cooking a batch of dishes to freeze for the week ahead. Rowena, meanwhile, was watching a video of Postman Pat.

There was no sign of the camper van. Emily had nurtured a frail hope that once again it would be parked in the recreation ground; now she decided that he would not return.

He telephoned that evening, however, while Douglas was upstairs having a bath. Isabel, who answered, handed Emily the cordless phone, telling her the call was for her and hiding her surprise. Who wants her, she had asked the caller, and a male voice had told her, 'Just a friend.'

Watching Emily, she saw the girl flush as the caller spoke to her, and a slow smile spread over her plump face. She was looking so much better, Isabel thought fleetingly; a few days' warmth and rest, with decent food, had worked wonders. Who was this male friend now telephoning?

'Yes – yes. That'll be great,' Isabel heard. 'See you,' and Emily handed the telephone back to Isabel, who replaced it on its base.

'That's a friend,' said Emily, repeating the caller's description of himself. 'He's asked me to have supper.' She didn't say where; he hadn't told her. Probably he meant in the van.

Was she asking permission? No – and why should she? She was twenty-three years old and she understood her own position.

'That's nice for you,' Isabel said brightly. 'He knew where to find you, then?'

She must be assuming it was someone from the site, Emily supposed.

'Yes,' she said.

Isabel did not feel she could ask any more questions, though how had this friend learned where Emily was? She could have got in touch with him on Friday, when she was here alone. Where did he live?

'Better not be late back,' she suggested. 'Douglas won't be happy if we have to let you in after we've gone to bed. And nor will I,' she added, wanting to improve Emily's opinion of Douglas.

'No. OK. I'll be no later than eleven,' Emily said. 'I'll probably be much earlier.'

Isabel did not offer her a key. Last thing at night, Douglas would, as usual, set the security system, recently installed, to ward off thieves. Emily had not been shown how to turn it off; since she arrived, Isabel had not set it in the daytime, giving her a spare key to come and go at will. As Douglas was not happy about this, she had reclaimed the key over the weekend. Emily would need it again while she was working. Perhaps Douglas would forget about it; after all, their cleaner also had a key, and as she could not yet manage the security system, it had to be turned off when she was due. It wasn't very satisfactory and before they went on holiday, she would have to learn to use it or its purpose would be defeated.

Emily rushed upstairs, presumably to get ready for her date, not that she had much choice of clothing. She came down again after only a few minutes and called out, 'I'm off, then.' Isabel heard the front door close behind her.

That evening, after supper, which as usual on a Sunday was soup, cold ham and salad, eaten in the kitchen, there was a programme Isabel wanted to watch on television. She kept the volume down, and Douglas, still with Gladstone, turned away from the set. To have gone into his study would have been unfriendly, but both would have been happier if he had done so, the one not distracted by the flickering screen and its accompanying sounds, the other catching all the dialogue devoid of guilt.

When Emily left the house, the man she knew as Graham was waiting in the road in his van, as he had promised on the telephone. He took her to a pub some miles from Fordswick, where, by a roaring fire, they had a bottle of red wine with their meal. Godfrey needed to soften her up, make sure she would be biddable, a willing accomplice to his plan when the time came to put it into effect. She might have to help him with the details.

Afterwards, parked in a lay-by, he set out, as he had done before with Alice, to seduce her, and this girl knew what she was doing. There was even an erotic appeal about her soft warm flesh as, once he had got past the various layers of her clothing, he was subsumed in it. And Emily, lonely and lost, clasped against him in the cramped bunk, felt warmed and wanted, something rare for her. This was a fleeting solace for them both; she knew it, and was comforted.

Like a stern father, Douglas was waiting for Emily's return. He had despatched Isabel to bed, saying he would wait up for the wanderer, who, Isabel decided, would be lucky to escape a lecture. She heard the doorbell's shrill ring with relief. At least Emily had returned, and on time; Isabel had been harbouring a secret fear that her anonymous friend, who was probably a fellow demonstrator, would bear her off to join some other protest. Ready to rush to the rescue, she lay waiting for the sounds of verbal battle to reach her ears. If they had had a daughter, what a tyrant Douglas would have been, demanding chapter and verse about her every movement. Still, with Emily already in trouble with the law, he was justified in expecting her to conform.

Hardly had the doorbell rung than she heard Emily's heavy footsteps on the stairs. There had been the merest murmur of voices first; Douglas could not have delivered much of whatever lecture he was likely to have in mind. Now he would be shooting the bolts and setting the alarm. Isabel mentally followed him as he did his rounds, then came upstairs. It was too early to pretend to be asleep.

'All right?' she asked, not wanting, if it was not, to know. But what could be wrong? Emily could not be drunk; she had moved too fast for that.

'He drove her back, anyway,' said Douglas. 'But he didn't walk her to the door.'

'No goodnight kiss, then?' said Isabel, aiming to keep the atmosphere light, if it had not already dropped to zero.

'Not at the door, no,' said Douglas, pulling off his Arran sweater. In the fleeting seconds as Emily hurried past him in the hall, bringing with her a blast of bitter winter air, he had sensed an alteration in her – some aura – a muted buzz – he couldn't define it, but, unbidden, the alarming thought of sex had flown into his head. She'd been doing it, he knew for certain. Where? In the fellow's car?

'Well, why not?' Isabel was innocently saying. 'A little kiss between old friends is only natural.'

But Douglas's mind was already running along lines concerning precautions. Condoms, he thought, and if they were not used, what dire consequences might not follow, from fell diseases to, at worst, in nine months' time an infant, for which Isabel would consider herself responsible?

Emily had paused downstairs only long enough to give him a sharp glance as she thanked him for waiting up for her. They heard her now, going to the bathroom.

'I hope that's all that passed between them,' he said grimly, knowing it was not.

Did it matter if more happened, wondered Isabel; many people took such matters lightly these days, and for all they knew, this man might be a past, or even current, lover of Emily's. If so, he might, eventually, remove her.

Each with completely different mental scripts, the Vernons exchanged a light kiss themselves, turned their backs towards each other, and in less than a minute, Douglas was asleep. Isabel, her mind uneasy, lay awake for quite a while.

10

Next morning Douglas, always early on the station platform, saw Alice arrive. He nodded to her as she passed, going to a spot where the first carriages would stop. This meant a quicker getaway in London.

'Emily will be along on time,' Douglas, pacing after her, informed her, though he could not be completely sure that this was true. After that first morning they had not breakfasted together, and for all he knew, she might have changed her mind. Isabel, to beat the worst of the rush hour into Northtown, would have set off for Gifts Galore before Emily was due to leave the house.

'I'm sure she will,' said Alice. 'Rowena's looking forward to seeing her again.' She did not tell this Mr Grumpy that she was going to lose no time in finding an au pair girl. Emily might be a great success; Alice thought she would be, but she would not stay. She was used to a peripatetic outdoor life and would resume it in some way when her legal problems were resolved. This was only a temporary solution.

'If she's not a success – if you're at all concerned – don't hesitate to let us know,' he said. 'Under the circumstances, who can tell? But Isabel has confidence in her.'

And you don't, thought Alice. He was so stiff and seemed so austere, standing there in his charcoal overcoat. Did he never smile?

'Thank you,' she said. 'I'm sure it won't be necessary.'

Douglas nodded again and then, as the train came into view, to Alice's relief, walked back to his usual position. She had not really thought he would risk sitting near her in the train, for that could involve attempts at conversation, though at this hour, most travellers retreated silently into their books or papers. Few were yet ready for the day, which would not start properly until they arrived in London; the journey was a limbo time which some commuters used for leisure reading or for study, while others finished their slumbers. Theirs was not one of the enterprising groups who had developed an educational project, instructing one another, as in some areas.

At Marylebone, Douglas saw Alice ahead of him, hurrying away from the train and turning towards the underground. He wondered where she worked and what she did: some sort of clerking job, he supposed. Was it really worth her while to travel up to town each day? She was still in sight, on the escalator, walking down it, the big black furry hat descending below him. Realising that their timetables overlapped at the start of the day, even to the extent of catching the same tube train, he felt annoyed. He might have to speak to her again, now that they had acknowledged one another.

Walking up to Ford House, Emily felt cheerful. She had slept well. Apart from the night in the police cell, she had been sleeping soundly, though often she had vivid dreams, some of them terrifying, reminding her of past horrors, things she wanted to forget now that she had turned her life around.

Last night, Graham had said he would be in the recreation ground and why didn't she walk back that way with Rowena after collecting her from nursery school? He might be; he might not. Time would tell. Their evening had been good; he'd wanted her to enjoy her meal – which she did – not stinting on the wine. He'd shown no curiosity about her and she'd told him nothing about herself. They had talked about Ford House; he'd been interested in the family and she'd described the big dark kitchen, and the other rooms she'd seen. This morning she felt no regrets for how the evening had ended. She had had a few casual encounters on the site, nothing serious; getting too close, letting someone matter to you, could end in sorrow and rejection. It would be disappointing if he didn't turn up, but life was like that. People came and went. She couldn't look ahead, long-term: not yet. Maybe never.

She reached Ford House, entering by the back door, to find Mrs Watkinson clearing away the breakfast things and it was Rowena who let her in, looking pleased to see her. Her eyes, behind her spectacles, shone.

'Mrs Watkinson, let me do that,' Emily protested. She hung her bulky jacket on a hook near the back door and took the pile of crockery from Mrs Watkinson. Though she was so large and moved awkwardly, she was neat with her hands, as Isabel had discovered in the shop, and Mrs Watkinson stood back to let her get on. There was a dishwasher and Emily needed to be shown the best way to stack it. It was a different make from Isabel's, and though recently accustomed to rinsing her tin mug in dubious water, she had already become familiar with this domestic aid.

'When you were young, I suppose you had a maid to wash up,' said Emily cheerfully, and Mrs Watkinson, though somewhat stunned by this directness, agreed that in her parents' house this was so.

'Some had maids, and some were maids,' said Emily. 'You could always get work, couldn't you, if you went into domestic service?'

'Oh yes,' said Mrs Watkinson, adding, 'There was no shortage of posts for those who would do it, and they were fed and housed, but the employers lost their privacy.'

'I hadn't thought of that,' said Emily. 'Like people now who have big houses and staff living in – the Queen, say.'

'Yes.' She was certainly forthright, this girl, thought Mrs Watkinson, grimly amused. It would not be dull while she was in the house.

'There's time to get these in the machine before I take Rowena to school,' Emily declared. 'Why don't you go and sit down, Mrs Watkinson? I'll do the other household jobs when I get back. Rowena can tell me what she needs for school, and help me find her clothes and so on, and I remember the way. You showed me. Half-past nine, isn't it, she has to be there?'

Godfrey had planned to be outside Ford House to watch Emily take his child to school, but he overslept. After leaving her the night before, he had parked the van in the recreation ground car park again; it was convenient there, with the lavatories and water supply at hand. In the morning, the curious face of Joe Pugh, their custodian, was once more pressed against the misted windscreen, trying to see who was inside. He could not make out anything through the glass. He should report the van to the clerk to the parish council, who employed him, Joe supposed, but he did not want to cause trouble just for the sake of it. The van's occupant had to spend the night somewhere, after all, and as long as he did not take up permanent residence, his presence was not illegal. He'd walk past later; maybe the driver would be stirring then, and Joe could ask him what his plans were. Joe could remember a time when the presence of any stranger in the village would have been remarked on and his business swiftly ascertained, but things were different now; outsiders came to the two pubs, and were welcome customers. The Stick and Monkey was no longer very popular with the few remaining original Fordswick families, of which Joe's was one. After his early ritual, Joe went off to his other job, as lollipop man, shepherding the children across the road outside the village school.

Walking home after the children were safely inside the school, Joe's route went past the nursery school, where the children were arriving. He knew most of them and enjoyed watching their progress; all too soon they were proper pupils at the primary school. He saw the little girl from Ford House, arriving not in the car with her grandmother, but walking with a stout young woman who wore a red woollen cap. She held Rowena's hand and the pair seemed content together; Joe was a connoisseur and could pick out the stressed mothers at a glance. He was glad Mrs Watkinson had found someone to relieve her of this daily duty, though he knew she and Rowena were fond of each other, and the old lady had found a new interest in the child. Much more love and care was lavished on her than had ever been the lot of Alice; Joe, who had worked in the garden at Ford House until back trouble forced him to give up, had always felt sorry for her, a meek, down-trodden girl. If she'd had a bit of spirit, she'd have got out years ago, before she fell for the baby. It was that fellow who'd lodged there, of course; the poor girl's only chance of a bit of fun, and look what had happened as a consequence. The parents could have employed a housekeeper instead of turning Alice into a drudge. She'd had no life, working in Northtown every day and coming home to do the cooking and the ironing. No wonder she'd fallen for the first man to pay her a bit of attention. Still, it had turned out all right; she had the little girl, and her parents' attitude had softened.

Joe went home, and when his wife came back from her morning shift on the till at a supermarket outside Northtown, he told her about the large young woman he had seen with Rowena. Doris Pugh was glad to hear the Watkinsons had found some help, but she saw no need for Alice to go trailing up to London every day. In Doris's opinion, she should stay at home and look after her own child, at least until the little girl was old enough to be at school full-time. It wasn't as though the Watkinsons were short of money. Joe thought this was harsh; the poor woman would never find a husband if she didn't get about a bit, and that, surely, would be the best thing that could happen to her and the kiddie. Joe still believed in men taking care of women. Some kind, lonely widower, he thought, would be ideal. Doris took a harsher view and was realistic about any husband taking on a stepchild, saying that often it wasn't such a good idea. They knew that from experience; their own son's first marriage had collapsed and when his children came to visit, they seemed resentful of his second wife's son and daughter. Although the marriage appeared to work, there were a lot of problems.

'Some chap's been parking by the rec, in a camper van,' Joe told her. 'He was there a couple of nights last week, and he came back last night. If he means to stay, I'll have to mention it, I suppose. Though he isn't hurting anyone.'

'Well, he can't stay indefinitely, can he?' Doris asked. 'Otherwise we'd have all sorts there – caravans and tents.'

'I'll hope to catch him and mention it,' said Joe. 'He sleeps in a bit, mornings. Nothing else to do, I suppose.'

Joe was soft-hearted, Doris thought. Live and let live was his motto, but she held that rules were meant to be obeyed.

When he walked up to the school that afternoon to supervise the children's departure, he took a turn past the recreation ground, and saw the van had gone. Well, that was one potential problem that had been solved; just as well he hadn't brought it to anyone's attention.

Godfrey, however, had not gone far. He had driven to the village where he had taken Emily the previous evening, and had bought a paper and some food; he did not want to attract attention in Fordswick, so he would not spend more time there than he could help before his plan matured. When he returned, he parked in a looping road which was part of a development of modern houses well way from Ford House. He locked his van and walked briskly off towards the recreation ground. It was a bright, sunny day, warmer than the day he met Emily; there was no reason for her not to bring the kid – Rowena – to play on the equipment. Emily had said the grandmother never took her home from nursery school that way; she always drove.

He waited with a sense of anticipation, and soon he saw a group of women and children entering the recreation ground at the distant gate; Emily was distinct among them because of her red hat, and her bulk, though two others were quite large. All wore thick jackets with either leggings or trousers. Godfrey did not stroll towards them. This was not the moment to claim acquaintance with Emily, but she saw him and waved, carrying on, however, towards the playground area. She held the hand of a small child dressed in a bright blue padded suit zipped from neck to crutch. The other children's clothes were in drab colours, though one or two wore bright hats. Godfrey peered at this small individual. She was his daughter. He felt a brief stirring of what anyone else would have recognised as primitive emotion, but he would have described as simple curiosity. This was his daughter, fruit of his loins. He could not see her very well; her woollen cap – red, like Emily's – was pulled down over her ears, but he could see the spectacles.

She wore glasses! His kid had imperfect vision! Godfrey had not considered the possibility of any flaws. He had imagined a perfect child with flaxen hair and large blue eyes, though as he and Alice had brown hair – his was greying now – and both had brown eyes, this was impossible. He needed to see her more closely, to inspect her features.

They were invisible today, so shrouded was she in her winter clothing. And he hadn't got his van nearby; he couldn't give her and Emily a lift home.

It wouldn't be wise to be seen and recognised by those other mothers, in case a straightforward confrontation at Ford House brought no results. Godfrey wasn't sure how he would extract money from the Watkinsons, but he'd do it. After all, she was his, and he had rights. Fathers had rights. He might find out what they were, not that he'd want to lumber himself with the kid for long. He wouldn't be able to cope with her in the camper; that was certain. He'd need a base.

He'd rent a room in Northtown. He'd not need it long. It would be an investment. He could take the kid there, if things worked out that way. He still had some money, and with an address, he'd be able to sign on.

He was sure the Watkinsons would pay him to keep away, as they'd done before, and if they didn't, then he'd set about claiming what was half his: the child. They'd soon pay up then.

Alice might deny he was the father, but there were tests now which could prove it, one way or the other. It would be good to scare those Watkinsons, get his own back for bundling him off so suddenly.

He waylaid Emily that evening, waiting for her in the van near Elm Lodge. She'd said her day would end at three-thirty, but it was getting on for five, and nearly dark, when she came walking down the road.

'You took your time,' he told her, opening the van door and leaning out towards her.

'What are you doing here?' she asked. 'We hadn't arranged to meet.'

'No, but I wanted to hear about your day, and I've found a place to live,' he said.

'What – in Fordswick?'

'No, in Northtown. Just for a bit, while I make plans,' he said. 'Like to come and see it?'

'Isabel will be expecting me,' said Emily. 'She'll be back soon.'

'Leave her a note,' he suggested.

'All right. I won't be long,' she said.

As she walked up the drive to the house, he locked the van and followed her, arriving at the front door just as she, illumined by the security light which had come on at her approach, was unlocking it. Emily felt his bulk behind her and turned around.

'Thought I'd come and help you,' he said, and Emily, giggling, felt a small thrill of daring, similar to when she was on a rope walkway above the ground. Douglas wouldn't want him in the house, she was certain. Well, he wouldn't be there for long.

She didn't go upstairs. He'd follow her, she knew, and then

what would happen? As it was, while she tore a sheet of paper from the pad by the telephone and wrote a note, which she left prominently displayed on the kitchen table, he took a quick tour around the ground floor, looking into the drawing-room, Douglas's study, and the dining-room. He resisted the urge to pocket a small silver snuff box displayed on a shelf.

'Nosey, aren't you?' she said.

'Yes,' he agreed, smiling. 'I didn't get a look round when I came before.'

Godfrey had never had any trouble finding women, short term; his problems were with lasting relationships. He had three failed marriages behind him, one contracted when he was in the army and had soon realised that he missed his freedom. The second did not survive a spell in prison, and the third, under an assumed name in Canada, was probably bigamous as he had no knowledge of a second divorce. He had left Canada to escape arrest; now he had a chance to acquire funds with very little effort.

Emily could ease him into Ford House. Through her, he could reach the child.

'Let's go,' she said, fearful that Isabel would arrive home and catch her with him in the house.

As it was, Isabel had mixed feelings when she found the note. She had been pleased that Emily had a friend who seemed to be fond enough of her to seek her out, despite her pending court case, and Douglas would prefer to be spared her company, but wasn't her behaviour rather casual? Couldn't she have introduced this friend, or was that expecting too much? Isabel was responsible for her, after all; she was an accused person on remand.

Presumably her first day at Ford House had passed off uneventfully. Absently, Isabel pushed the note into her apron pocket before she laid the dinner table and prepared the chops and vegetables; Emily's two chops would not be required tonight. While she was doing this, ready to start cooking when Douglas reached home, she had a sudden fear lest Emily had absconded, and went up to check the bedroom, but her guest's few spare garments were still there.

She was mulling all this over in her mind when Douglas returned. It was too dark for him to prowl round the garden looking at his recent structures and musing over more. He went immediately to look at his fish, which were swimming calmly in their tank, and checked the temperature, scrutinising the aquatic plants for fear they might be ailing, but all seemed well. After that, he went in search of Isabel, who, when she heard his key in the door, had put the vegetables on, and lit the grill.

He pecked her cheek.

'How was your day?' she asked him. No one could say that neither of them tried.

Douglas told her as much as he felt it prudent for her to know about the failings of a new junior clerk and the possible retirement of someone more senior. He never discussed policies except in the most general way.

'Where's Emily?' he asked at last.

'Out for the evening,' Isabel replied.

'Is that wise?' he asked.

'She's not subject to a curfew, Douglas,' Isabel answered. 'We can't stop her seeing her friends. We can only try to do that if she comes back very late, or drunk, or brings them in and disturbs us.'

'I suppose not.'

'It's good that she has people who seem to care about her,' said Isabel.

'We should know who they are,' said Douglas. 'She owes us that.'

In a sense, Isabel agreed; but on the other hand, Emily was entitled to some degree of privacy, despite the reason for her presence in the house.

'I'll go and change,' said Douglas. When he came home, he always showered and exchanged his city suit for dark trousers and a polo shirt worn with a corduroy jacket. It was only recently that he had ceased to wear a tie for dinner. Some husbands were very scruffy; Isabel felt she should be glad that hers was not. Even so, his standards were exacting.

Over dinner, he told her about his plan to elevate part of the garden and create a waterfall above the pond which he had made last year. Isabel listened with part of her attention, while she wondered where Emily was and what she was up to, and about the brothers.

'Douglas,' she said at last, interrupting his rhetorical remarks about the merits of various pumping systems. 'How do you think we can set about finding Emily's brothers?'

'Has she some?' he asked, annoyed by the interruption to his flow of thought. 'Oh, yes – of course, she has. You told me,' he remembered. 'Doesn't she know where they are?'

'She says they're abroad. They've had some row,' said Isabel.

'She must know where they live,' said Douglas irritably. 'Surely they must have turned up for their mother's funeral, at the very least?'

'I'd imagine so,' Isabel agreed.

'It would be advisable for them to take her off our hands,' he said.

'If there'd been any chance of that, I'd have expected her to get in touch with them, not me, after her arrest,' said Isabel.

'Ask her about them again,' Douglas advised. 'Find out the last address she had for them. That would be where to start enquiring for them.' Then he added, as he neatly dissected his chop, 'I suppose she'll be late again tonight.'

But she wasn't. Emily came in at ten o'clock while they were watching the television news.

'I'm back,' she said, putting her head round the drawing-room door. 'I'm going to bed now. Goodnight,' and she was gone before Isabel could ask if she had had a pleasant evening.

There was no doubt, however, that she had. She was radiant, and Isabel's heart sank. She hoped Douglas hadn't noticed.

Emily had not expected Godfrey's accommodation to be anything special, and it turned out to be merely a small room on the top floor of a lodging-house near the railway line in Northtown. On the way there, they stopped to buy pizzas and a bottle of red wine. He'd showered and changed his clothes before he collected her, but she made no comment on his smart shirt and clean jeans; she wasn't exactly fashion-conscious. He liked a woman to look smart, but Emily's appearance was incidental as he did not intend to be seen with her much in public.

With very little prompting, she told him a lot about life at Ford House and he learned that on Thursday morning, while Rowena was at nursery school, the old Watkinsons were going into Northtown to the dentist. Because Emily was there to care for Rowena, they had now arranged an optician's appointment in the afternoon. They would be out all day.

'So you see, I am of use,' she said, beaming.

'You are,' he told her, moving closer. It saved making conversation, and he had gleaned some very useful information.

11

Godfrey had not yet seen Alice. He knew which train she caught; Emily had told him, speaking admiringly about the job she had at an art gallery in London, yet wondering how she could bear to be parted from Rowena. He had been forced to listen to a number of stories about Rowena's wit and cleverness.

'You're obsessed with the kid,' he'd said, and Emily had said that there could not be too much love in the world, telling him that she loved nature, too – trees, flowers, the environment. Just in time, she remembered not to mention the trouble this allegiance had brought her.

'Does the kid know anything about her father?' he enquired.

'Her name's Rowena,' Emily said, reprovingly. 'You know that. No, I don't think so. Mrs Watkinson said to turn the conversation if she asked, but she hasn't, so far. She's bound to be curious when she's older. Maybe they'll tell her he's dead. It would save a lot of explanation.'

Godfrey did not care for this idea at all. He wasn't dead.

'Did they tell you about him?'

'No, except to say he disappeared before Rowena was born.'

'He's got rights, though,' said Godfrey.

'What rights?'

'Rights to the kid – Rowena. He's her father.'

'They weren't married. He doesn't support her. He's got no rights,' said Emily.

'He's her father. He has a right to her. To access,' Godfrey persisted.

Suddenly Emily became impassioned.

'He's got no rights. He didn't bother about Alice, did he? Going off and leaving her pregnant.'

'Maybe he didn't know she was,' Godfrey said. After all, it was the truth.

'That makes no difference. Alice has had all the worry and responsibility, and her parents have kept them – paid for them.'

'He might have paid, if he'd known,' said Godfrey, who would not have done so then and did not mean to now. 'What if he finds out?'

'He won't,' said Emily, confidently.

'You can't be sure.'

'He hasn't been heard of for more than four years. Why should he suddenly turn up?'

Godfrey left it, then. He'd sailed quite near the mark. She knew nothing about him, but she might start putting two and two together if he kept on.

He didn't visit Fordswick on Tuesday. Emily was disappointed, but only slightly. She knew where he was living, and if she wanted to, she could look him up, but she had had another busy day and hadn't really thought about him much. She was eager to tell Isabel about her work, and so far had not had a chance.

*　　*　　*

'It'd be quite nice to stay at Ford House till Alice gets back,' she told Isabel. 'She'd like to hear about Rowena's little sayings, I'm sure.'

'Won't Mrs Watkinson fill her in?' asked Isabel. 'She's fond of Rowena, isn't she?'

'Yes – very. Seems fonder of her than of Alice, if you ask me,' said Emily. 'She never talks about her and she's always on about Rowena. Mind you, I haven't seen them together – her and Alice. Alice isn't there when I am, you see.'

'Well – no. That's the point, isn't it?' said Isabel. 'You're there to bridge the gap.' And the arrangement was only temporary. Though Alice was aware of the true state of things, she might not have told her parents in case they did not like the idea of someone remanded on a criminal charge working in their house.

'Rowena will soon be at school full-time,' said Emily. 'Proper school. That will change things. Make it easier, except for the holidays of course, but they should be able to find a student then, to help out.'

So she wasn't planning on staying. Isabel felt relieved.

'Yes – I suppose they might do that,' said Isabel. 'With Mr Watkinson not well, it must be very difficult for Mrs Watkinson. How is he? The old man?' She didn't know him, except by sight; though they were generous to local causes, the couple had played no active part in village life since she and Douglas moved there.

'Not good. He can walk a little, and speak all right. One hand isn't much use,' said Emily. The man known to her as Graham had wanted to know all this on Monday night; people were kind, taking an interest. 'I might be late on Thursday,' she added. 'Mr and Mrs Watkinson are going to the dentist and to have their eyes tested. Usually they can't go out for long because of having to be back for Rowena, so they're getting it all done while they know she's in safe hands.' Mine, she reflected, proudly.

'Oh – that seems sensible. They must be glad to have you, Emily.'

Isabel had already wondered whether this short term of employment, if carried out successfully, might help Emily when her case was heard. Perhaps Alice could be persuaded to write a commendation. She'd keep it in mind. The hearing was next week: not long to go.

'I wonder who Rowena's father was,' said Emily.

Isabel had heard rumours that he was a handyman who had been working at Ford House, and, more sensationally, that Alice had been raped in Northtown where she went to pubs looking for pick-ups – she had been seen by several villagers.

'I don't know,' she answered truthfully.

'Funny to go around not knowing you've got a little daughter,' said Emily.

Isabel thought that men who donated sperm to fertility clinics did exactly that.

'It must happen quite a lot,' was all she said.

'I don't think a father should have the same rights as a mother,' said Emily. 'Not when they split up, I mean.'

'It depends a bit on the father, doesn't it?' said Isabel. 'How good he is. How responsible. All the circumstances.' There had been notorious cases where the law had granted access to fathers patently unfit to have it, and others where the father should have been awarded custody, yet had not won it. 'What about your father? Did you see much of him after he and Ginnie parted?'

'Not really,' said Emily, and did not enlarge.

'What about Charles and Anthony? They spent time with him, didn't they?' She seemed to recall Ginnie, while she still wrote, mentioning their visits to him. 'You say you've quarrelled, but wouldn't you like to get in touch with them now? We must be able to find out where they are. One of them might help you. They are your brothers, after all.'

'I don't want them to know I've been in trouble,' said Emily. She had gone very red.

'Well – what about afterwards? When it's settled.'

'No,' said Emily flatly. 'I told you.'

'Where were they when you last heard from them? What about when your mother died?' said Isabel. 'They must have been at her funeral, surely?' But that was several years ago.

'I don't know,' said Emily desperately. 'I was ill myself. I wasn't there.' Once again she set her mouth in a firm line, then said, 'I'll go and lay the table now,' and left the room.

Isabel found this conversation disturbing. This was the first she'd heard about Emily being ill, but perhaps it explained her opting out of university – it was obvious that she had never graduated – and her current life style. What could have happened? Had she had a breakdown? If so, there was all the more reason, surely, for the brothers to rally round.

Emily was some time in the dining-room, and when she returned, she said gruffly, 'I'm sorry if I was snappy. I just don't like to be reminded of that time.'

'No – I can understand that,' said Isabel. 'It's just that I think your brothers have a right to know that you're in trouble, so that they can have a chance to help you.'

'And don't I have a right to keep them out of it?' she said.

'I suppose you do,' said Isabel wearily. 'Just as you had a right to express your views about the new road but not to trespass or be violent. There are too many crusades about rights these days and not enough about obligations.'

'Obligations?'

'Yes. I have a duty to you because you're my goddaughter. Douglas has a duty to me because I'm his wife and that means he should back me up when I'm helping you, which he is doing, though, let's be honest, reluctantly. He's very conventional, you know. And it could be argued that my duty to him should take precedence over my duty to you. You failed your duty to keep the peace, but you have a duty to keep our house rules and now you've undertaken a duty to Rowena and her mother. And her grandparents.'

'I've said I won't let you down, or the Watkinsons,' said Emily, and her eyes filled with tears. 'I know Douglas doesn't want me here and I'll leave as soon as I can.'

'Oh, Emily, I'm sorry. I didn't mean to be cross,' said Isabel. She put her arm round the girl's sturdy shoulder and hugged her. 'I only want to help you, but it would be useful if I knew why you've lost touch with your brothers and what brought you to that demonstration. You don't seem to be a violent or a lawless type of person.'

'I can't tell you any more,' Emily replied. 'Only what you know – about losing my flat.'

And I lost my baby, she thought: my child. If Douglas knew about that, he'd go ballistic. Ironically, the notion made her laugh, disconcerting Isabel.

'What's so funny?' she asked.

'Just the idea that Douglas wouldn't approve of me at all, if he knew more about me,' said Emily, with disarming honesty.

'He'll be glad you're not going to be out late tonight,' said Isabel. 'You're not, are you? You're not meeting your friend?'

'No.'

'Have you known him long?'

'No,' Emily replied.

'If you want to ask him round, feel free to do so,' she said. Douglas wouldn't be pleased, but if they met the man, they might feel reassured. What would he be like? Long-haired, with elaborate tattoos and many earrings? Those features would not disqualify him from her approval, for though Douglas might be incapable of looking beyond them, she was not. But perhaps the friend had come on a fleeting visit and had now left the area.

'Thank you,' Emily was saying. What if Isabel knew he'd already been inside the house?

Meanwhile, Douglas, in his lunch hour, had crossed from the ministry to the street where Alice's art gallery was situated. It wasn't far to walk; in fine weather, he often took a turn in the park. He liked fresh air and sometimes thought he should have been a forester or a horticulturist, but such careers were not as safe or as predictable as his had been. He had entered it in his youth, encouraged by his father, who asked him if he wanted security or adventure, and he had chosen accordingly. Douglas's father, who had had a good career in insurance, had always regretted leaving the army after the war, and he had encouraged his son to pursue whatever vocation he wanted, secretly hoping he might choose something challenging which the father could vicariously enjoy. As it was, Douglas's latest exploits in the field of garden development or house improvement were hard for him to enthuse over. Poor Isabel would only just be settled with her newly appointed kitchen or her freshly plumbed bathroom when Douglas would be scheming to make a room in the loft or undertake some other piece of construction which would mean prolonged domestic chaos. He would even begin one task before the last was complete. It was some consolation that he seemed now to be operating more in the garden than in the house. That must be a relief to her. Douglas was, however, competent at all he undertook; that had to be acknowledged; every piece of work was executed thoroughly.

Douglas could not have explained why he had undertaken this expedition. He had seen Alice again only that morning on the station platform, in her same black hat and coat, and, as on the day before, they had exchanged formal greetings. Emily had told him and Isabel where Alice worked, but Douglas had no interest in modern art, which was the gallery's speciality, nor was he concerned with people or personalities. The private lives of the staff with whom he worked, particularly the women, were of no consequence. Those senior to him were simply faces and voices, in his mind completely sexless; those below him were inferior, to be spoken to accordingly though with perfect civility, in the expectation that each would carry out her duties conscientiously and with competence. He was always fair, and even when annoyed was courteous; these attributes compensated for his detachment – which, of itself, carried some advantages. Friendless, but uninvolved, he made his way through life.

At first he did not see Alice in the gallery. It was probably her lunch hour, too. Often, he had sandwiches in the office, and occasionally he went to a small restaurant not far away. He rarely ate with colleagues unless there was something to be discussed which they had chosen not to consider in the office – the proper place, in Douglas's view. He walked slowly round the display of pictures on the walls, liking some and wondering why others were worth vast sums of money, and was studying blurred patterns in various colours which represented, according to its label, summer in Tuscany, when he heard her speak.

'It's lovely, isn't it?' she said. 'One of my favourites.'

Douglas turned sharply, peering at her above his glasses. Without her hat – naturally she would not wear it in the gallery – she looked less drab, her hair lightened by a rinse and her eyes – large and brown – like bottomless pools. The fanciful thought amazed him. Douglas did not go in for extravagance.

'The colours – warm Italian shades—' she went on eagerly, her own colour high as, animated, she extolled the picture's merits.

Douglas had already discovered that the colour combinations and the shapes were pleasing to the eye, if not immediately reminding him of Italy.

'You work here,' he stated, and, lying, added, 'I didn't know.'

'Yes. I love it,' Alice said, warmly. 'I expect you're just browsing, aren't you? I won't disturb you, but let me know if I can help at all.'

'Er – yes,' he said. 'Oh— ' he did not know what to call her. Miss Watkinson, which was her name, seemed very formal. 'How is Emily getting on? You found things all right last night? Is she proving satisfactory?'

'Yes, very,' said Alice. 'Rowena likes her, and she has been very helpful to my mother.' Basely, she did not tell him that she was in contact with an au pair agency.

'Good,' said Douglas, and nodded. 'Well, good day,' he continued, and walked out.

Alice had been startled when she saw him, and had wondered whether to approach him, but here, on neutral ground, she felt secure and confident. Why not? If it had been Isabel, not him, she would certainly have spoken.

Douglas, going home, knew unaccustomed feelings of discomfort as he wondered if Alice would tell Emily that they had met.

At dinner, surprisingly, he asked Emily how her day had gone and what time she had come home, thus learning that her path had not overlapped with Alice's. This, it seemed, was part of the arrangement, something he had not understood. His relief was tinged with worry, for why had he not openly mentioned going to the gallery and seeing Alice? Why should he feel guilty?

Because Isabel would have been astounded at his doing something so entirely out of character, unless he had simply popped in, when passing, to shelter from the rain.

It had not rained, however: not a drop had fallen, either in London or in Fordswick. It had been a bright, clear, frosty winter's day.

12

After Douglas Vernon had left the gallery, Alice thought no more about him.

She was undergoing an interior struggle about whether to stay in her job. Travelling so far each day had always been a questionable step, although her father had encouraged her to take it, and her daily escape was a liberation. Once out of Fordswick and the area, she became a different person, gaining increasing competence in her sphere, well treated by her colleagues, and beginning to enjoy contact with clients. If she hadn't been hidden away from the public in her earlier job, she might have acquired confidence then, and been less vulnerable to Godfrey's unscrupulous approach when she was desperately haunting pubs seeking a social life. Or searching for a man. Was that why she'd done the rounds? What a way to look for one. She should have joined a club or society where she might have made congenial friends through some shared interest. Even without a degree or other training, she could have found a job away from home at a time when her parents were still fit and active. She'd had no will of her own, yet her parents, though demanding, were kind. They were also over-protective, and now they had needs which could not be ignored. Alice was, however, determined to make Rowena the antithesis of herself, teach her to stand on her own feet. Though she regretted almost everything about her relationship with Godfrey, she did not wish undone Rowena's birth, an event which, once it was inevitable, she had dreaded. Nothing had prepared her for the overwhelming rush of love she had felt for the baby as soon as she was put into her arms. It was primeval, visceral; and not universal, for in her ward in Northtown Hospital there had been a mother – married, with an affectionate husband – who had felt nothing for her infant. She had wept and told Alice how dreadful she felt about it. She was suffering from post-natal depression, and would doubtless recover, but Alice had met her some months later and found she was still indifferent to the child. If the baby was the result of rape, or if you hated the father, you might feel like that, Alice conceded, but her own bitterness towards Godfrey did not stop her from loving his child.

She did not know that her father had paid him to go away, but she no longer cherished any affection for him, nor did she expect him to reappear. She had banished him from her mind.

Even with her parents' support for her decision, perhaps she should have found a job nearer home. The old habit of filial duty died hard, and only Emily's timely arrival – and that was due to her mother – had saved her from having to ask for unpaid compassionate leave. Whatever the outcome of Emily's trial, she would not stay for long. Even if she did not hanker for her roving life, Rowena would soon be at school all day, and Emily might not care to spend her time looking after an elderly, sometimes cantankerous couple. Compared with many single parents, Alice was lucky; she was not at risk of being homeless, nor of penury. Some would say she should accept the confines of her life and throw herself into local activities. She could study for an Open University degree, for instance, or do some other course which would qualify her for a career with prospects. Then, when Rowena was older and perhaps she no longer had to consider her parents, she could pursue one. Here her mind shut down. She did not wish her parents dead.

She had a new reason for wanting to stay in her job. She had met a man who worked in a bookshop near the gallery; they both lunched occasionally in the same small self-service café and once, when it was very busy, had shared a table.

A week later they had coincided at the counter, and had quite naturally found seats together again. Both lunched late, and had agreed that they would try to meet there on Wednesday, which was the day after Douglas's visit to the gallery.

Each knew where the other worked, and had exchanged only first names but no further details. He was Paul. This was enough for Alice, for the moment.

Travelling home on Tuesday, she was looking forward to tomorrow; nothing was lost if either could not be there, for another chance would come, or, if it didn't, that was that. Alice did not want to give up this fragile social contact unless it – or Paul – first abandoned her.

He had a wife, of course, and a family; a man like him, aged about forty, thin and rather bald, could not be alone. It was a bit like that film, she thought, *Brief Encounter*, which she had seen on television several times, except that the couple in it were both married and were in the grip of real love, or passion, never fully realised. It was so sad. She didn't let her imagination carry her beyond her and Paul's next meeting, for though she was not married, she had ties, and he must have them, too. At any time, their fragile friendship could be terminated.

Details of two possible au pair girls would be in the post to her tonight, and she should receive them in the morning at the gallery. Even though her parents would never open her mail, they asked her about the rare letters she received because they were so few, and in the past she had had to invent excuses for Mary being such a poor correspondent. Now it was simpler, because she could pretend that they saw one another in London. Since meeting Paul, she had taken to mentioning their lunches, replacing him with Mary as her companion. Mary had a demanding boyfriend, Alice had declared, one who took up a great deal of her time. This drew a snort from Alice's father, and a frown from her mother, making Alice smile secretly. Her parents thought boyfriends a mistake; how they had ever got together themselves baffled their daughter.

Nothing happened to prevent her meeting Paul on Wednesday, but he had had a cold which, he said, he hoped she would not catch.

'They're everywhere,' said Alice. 'My father's got one.'

'Your father?' This was the first personal detail Alice had revealed.

'I live with my parents,' Alice said. 'They're rather old. I think my arrival was a shock to them.'

'Natural, surely?' he remarked. 'And pleasant. To be expected. Egg and cress? Cottage cheese and grapes?' At her elbow, he peered with her at the display of open sandwiches; he had noticed that these were two of her preferences.

She chose egg and cress today, and he picked ham; sometimes he opted for cheese. They both had cappuccinos.

She did not respond to his comment. She knew that her mother had worked in her father's company. Presumably they had fallen in love; that was what you did, wasn't it, before marriage? In those days, anyway. Nowadays people didn't seem to bother too much about marriage, or even love, judging by the papers; it was all sex.

Eating their sandwiches, facing one another across the table, she wondered what it would be like if Paul were to kiss her, and as this thought entered her head, she heard him asking if she would go to a concert or a film one evening after work.

'What? Oh – I don't know! Oh – yes – why not?' she gasped, questions about how to arrange it racing through her head. Emily would be willing to stay late one evening, surely? She would tell her parents she was meeting Mary. Colour flooded her face as she contemplated what to her would be an extraordinary experience, but which most people would find unexceptional.

'When?' he asked. 'This week? Friday? If you haven't got my cold by then.'

'And if you're better,' she replied.

'I will be,' he promised.

They arranged to meet for lunch on Friday, when they could decide whether to go ahead with their plans for the evening. If one of them failed to turn up at the café, the other would know the cold or some problem had arisen.

Alice, in the train that night, felt a lightness of heart she had not known for years. Paul did not know where she lived and that their plan would mean her catching a late train home. It didn't matter; she would do it. Or should she book a hotel room and tell her parents she was spending the night with Mary?

No. She couldn't do that. They must know where to get in touch with her, in case of an emergency. As it was, she would be untraceable for several hours, for she would not be able to tell them what concert or cinema she was going to. A mobile telephone, she thought: if this went on – if she continued to see Paul – she must get one. There was such a lot to think about now, and tomorrow she must answer the au pair agency, requesting further details about Wanda, a girl from the Czech Republic who sounded suitable, and Cecile, who was already in the country, but unhappy in her present post.

When she reached home, a letter was awaiting her. The address was typed, and it was postmarked Swindon. She ignored it while she read Rowena her bedtime story and heard about her day. Rowena had played on the swings and Emily had taught her how to make patterns and little boats out of paper. After she was tucked up in bed, her mother asked her if she was going to open the letter.

'It's probably a circular. Some advertisement,' she said.

But it was from a solicitor's office in Swindon, stating that their client, Mr Godfrey Sutton, wished to have access to his daughter and if it was not freely granted, he would be applying to the court.

'He can't do this,' she said. 'Oh my God! After all this time!'

There was no point in trying to dissemble. She handed the letter to her mother, who, frowning, read it quickly, then reached for a chair and sat down.

'We'll say nothing to your father,' she said. 'Not unless we have to.' Both women had turned pale, and Alice's heart was pounding away in her chest like a sledgehammer. She felt sick and giddy.

'We must find out where you stand,' Muriel Watkinson continued. 'We must ring Thomas Jones in the morning.' The Watkinsons rarely required legal advice, but after Rowena was born they had all made new wills, drawn up by Thomas Jones, a partner in a firm of solicitors in Northtown.

'How has he found out about her?' Alice said. She, too, had sat down, and now her pulse was steadying and she was breathing more easily.

'Maybe he made some enquiries,' said her mother. It wouldn't be difficult, if he grew curious about Alice. Or perhaps he had had a chance meeting with some previous acquaintance from the village.

'But he just disappeared, without a word,' said Alice. 'He didn't know I was pregnant.'

No, thought Muriel, and if he had, he would have driven a harder bargain before agreeing to go.

'You were better off without him,' she said. 'You both were – you and Rowena. He was no good.'

'But having a child might have made a difference. He might have settled down,' she said, as a wistful, fleeting fantasy flashed through her mind.

'Don't you believe it,' said her mother.

'I never thought he'd come back to me,' Alice was saying.

'Don't delude yourself,' said Muriel harshly. 'He's not coming back for you. I don't see him on the doorstep with a bunch of red roses. He must have made some enquiries – employed a detective, perhaps. He's not after Rowena. He's got other ideas. He's after money.'

'You don't know that,' said Alice. 'Perhaps I should see him. Talk it through.'

'Don't act hastily,' said Muriel. 'He can't do it, Alice. He can't take your child away.'

But perhaps he could. There were all sorts of new laws about fathers' rights, and even where they had contributed nothing to the cost of raising a child, or shown any interest in its well-being, or were in other ways unsuitable people to have charge of one, they had been allowed to interfere in their lives and cart children off to unsavoury quarters and sometimes even win custody.

'He's only asking for access,' said Alice. 'Maybe she has a right to meet him. To get to know him.'

'What? At four years old? When all she knows is that he went away before she was born?'

If Rowena were to ask about her father, Muriel had wanted her to be told that he was dead. In her opinion, it would be the simplest way to deal with the situation, but Alice, student of books on child welfare, had said she must be told the approximate truth. She would be curious one day. Even so, satisfying her would not be made too easy; no father's name appeared on Rowena's birth certficate, and apart from the normal child allowance available to every mother, Alice had received no state aid, nor was the Child Support Agency involved in their lives.

'I can't go to work tomorrow,' said Alice. 'I'll have to deal with this. Go over to Swindon and see this man. And talk to Thomas Jones.'

'No. You carry on as usual,' said Muriel. 'It's no good upsetting your father and you will, if you break routine, and nothing is going to happen straight away. Time must be allowed for you to reply to that letter, and no solicitor moves fast, as I daresay you've lived long enough to find out. I'll telephone Mr Jones.'

There she was, still putting her down and taking charge. This was why Alice had sought escape.

'I suppose you're right,' she said. She put the letter away in a drawer in the hall chest. 'It's there if you need it,' she added.

'I'll telephone Thomas Jones tomorrow while your father

is with the optician,' said her mother. 'He needn't know anything about it unless Mr Jones wants me to go to see him. Emily is staying later tomorrow anyway, and I could go to his office while we're in Northtown, but I doubt if it will be necessary. This can be dealt with on the telephone and by the solicitors.'

There was no more to be said. Alice went meekly up to bed, where she spent a sleepless night. Her mother was right: Godfrey was not interested in her or he would have come to the house, made direct contact. But had he been having her watched? How had he found out about Rowena?

She found, on reflection, that she had no desire at all to see him. She felt no yearning to be caught in his arms, to repeat the act which had created Rowena: not with him. To pretend otherwise was to indulge an unrealistic romantic illusion. She had never felt warmed and safe with Godfrey: excited, yes, at first, and eager for experience, but later she had felt used and cheap. It had been a relief when he went away, although she had wept and imagined herself broken-hearted. It was the blow to her pride, the rejection, that had been so wounding, and then, when Rowena was born, her whole life had been transformed and acquired purpose. That was the truth.

She slept at last, fitfully, and in the morning she caught her usual train.

13

When Emily arrived at Ford House on Thursday morning, Muriel Watkinson warned her of the possibility that they might be delayed in Northtown.

'Another matter has arisen,' she said. 'A small problem.'

She did not enlarge, and Emily decided that it was probably something medical and intimate which she did not want to discuss.

'Not to worry,' she said cheerfully. 'I'm happy to stay open-ended,' and she beamed at Mrs Watkinson.

The girl was certainly cheerful, and Robert liked her. Already, after only a few days, she was becoming indispensable, and if she stayed, Muriel's hip operation could be planned. When that was over, she would be able to keep control of things again. Muriel Watkinson had only once lost charge of her life, and even then, when the fact was recognised and accepted, she had soon regained command. The watershed event had been the unplanned birth of Alice which had resulted in her marriage to Robert, who at the time was still married to his first wife. Abortion, though possible if you knew where to go and could pay, was illegal then; there was a divorce and Robert married Muriel. Alice did not know about her father's earlier, childless marriage; there had been no need to tell her.

Robert had known that Muriel had not intentionally trapped him by becoming pregnant. That had been an accident, and when Alice was born the affection that Muriel felt for the baby was tempered with resentment because she had been compelled to give up her career, for Robert decreed that she could not continue her employment in his firm. Hitherto, they had enjoyed their long association, concealing it with fair success. Muriel had a flat in the centre of Birmingham while he and his wife lived in a pleasant suburb. His first wife still lived there, well compensated by the settlement he had made on her, and with a scarcely altered life style, playing bridge and giving lunch parties for other women who had workaholic or absent husbands, or were on their own. There were more of these today, widows and divorcées, than in earlier years. The legal aspect had been handled discreetly by a lawyer with wide experience of such things. Muriel seldom thought about it now, but some frustration lingered. She was not domestic, nor inherently maternal, and had not chosen the new role forced upon her, though Robert was delighted by his belated fatherhood, which soon became despotic. Muriel occupied her spare time with charity work and after Robert sold his business, took on the secretarial work involved with his new position. In those years, the Watkinsons, particularly Muriel, had been active in the village; now, however, their patronage was merely financial. With Rowena's birth, Muriel discovered an untapped well of emotion; she doted on the child, and this sudden, unexpected threat to her granddaughter's security aroused rage such as she had rarely felt. Muriel would never let that man lay claim to her.

Mr Thomas, when she telephoned him from The Crown

Hotel in Northtown where she and Robert had lunch – Robert was now in the optician's, fairly close at hand – was reassuring but evasive. Unfortunately, though access to Rowena might be prevented, there were precedents indicating that Godfrey could succeed, unless Alice denied that he was the father and then there would be the ritual of proving it, which Godfrey might insist on.

'I suppose there's no doubt about it?' he asked. 'His being the father, I mean?'

'None at all,' said Muriel.

'I'll write a temporising letter to the solicitor who communicated with you,' Mr Thomas said. 'As they never married and he has not supported the child, Alice has a strong case, but this man could make things quite difficult. She might have to take out an injunction. There could be some unpleasantness.'

This was legalese for a great deal of trouble, Muriel decided.

'We might pay him off. It worked before,' she said, adding that Alice did not know this, and he should bear it in mind if he dealt with her direct.

Mr Thomas made a note of it, and of the solicitor's address, which she had written down.

'Shall I send you a copy of the letter?' She had meant to bring it with her as she could have had it copied at the stationer's along the road. Alice could get it done tomorrow.

'It might be as well,' said Mr Jones.

How unfortunate, he thought, hanging up. Of course the man was after something, and probably it was money, but as he had pointed out to Mrs Watkinson, if they paid him off again, he would return to ask for more.

Muriel, leaning on her stick as she hastened back to rescue Robert from the optician, felt that matters were in hand;

nothing more could be done at present. If paying off that man a second time were the only way to get rid of him, Robert would have to know. His stroke had not incapacitated him long enough to make it necessary for her to have his power of attorney and he kept tabs on everything they spent. Besides, as Mr Thomas had said, Godfrey might return to haunt Alice in the future, even if he waited until after they were dead, and he could upset Rowena very badly. It could not be permitted.

After she had taken Rowena to nursery school, Emily had hurried back to Ford House. She would give it a great clean-up, polish surfaces that had been neglected in the preceding weeks, make sure dinner was prepared. There was plenty of mince in the fridge, so she'd cook some for herself and Rowena to have with baked potatoes, and make a shepherd's pie which they need only put in the Aga for the old pair's supper. They were a funny couple, so stiff and proud, never saying much. Alice would be about thirty-two or three, maybe more; even so, she'd arrived late in their lives, for Mr Watkinson must be over eighty, and his wife was not much younger.

Polishing a heavy old oak chest in the hall, Emily found that one drawer was not fully closed. A sheet of paper was caught in the top of it. Freeing it, she saw it was a folded letter. Lacking the scruples others might take for granted, she took it out and read it, then sat down in total shock. Little Rowena's father was going to stake a claim to her. How terrible! And they wouldn't be able to stop him. She had seen it happen. Men arrived from nowhere, making demands. Some were affectionate and kind. But there were the other sort, and Rowena's father had walked out on Alice years ago.

Emily cleaned on in fury, resolved to help Alice if he turned up while she was here.

She had not long to wait, but she did not know that Rowena's father, Godfrey Sutton, and the man she knew as Graham, were the same person.

He arrived while they were having lunch in the kitchen, the warmest room in the house. Emily, though used to living out of doors, noticed the many draughty corners. He walked right in through the unlocked kitchen door and found them sitting at the table, Rowena on a tall chair which raised her so that she was at adult height, not with her chin level with her plate. They were laughing. Emily was telling Rowena a story about how she had lived in a tree and gone up and down by a rope ladder.

Eating stopped. Rowena stared at this tall, moustached stranger, and Emily, after her first surprise, said, 'Well, you've got a nerve, walking in like this.'

'Aren't you going to give me any lunch?' he said, but he was staring at Rowena.

'Oh, I suppose we can spare some,' Emily said airily, getting up to fetch a plate and cutlery.

Her back was turned, so she did not see the scowl spread over his face as he glowered down at Rowena who was sitting with a spoon in her hand, halfway to her mouth. She looked away from him, and carried on, carefully inserting it between her small pink lips and chewing with determination.

Godfrey, who cherished no great sentimental fantasy, and had already seen the spectacles, nevertheless expected to see a child he could admire. Instead, he observed a little girl with a pale, thin face and steel-rimmed glasses; her gaze was bent on her plate and not on him. Brown straight hair was drawn severely back from her face into a bunch behind her head. To his eye, she was an ugly child.

Emily, unaware of his scrutiny, said, 'This is Graham, Rowena. He's a friend of mine,' and so Rowena, at four drilled in the perils of stranger/danger, saw no risks attached to him. 'Say hullo,' Emily instructed.

But Rowena wouldn't. It was rude to speak with your mouth full, so she went on eating, still not looking at the visitor. Each had failed to be impressed by the appearance of the other.

Surly little brute, thought Godfrey, bitterly disappointed. He sat down well away from her and accepted a generous helping of mince from Emily. Luckily there would still be plenty for the evening's pie, she was thinking; she'd thickened it with carrot puree to mop up the fat and make it go further, as her mother used to do.

'So where have you been?' Emily asked him.

'Oh, here and there,' he said. 'I had business to see to.'

She was pleased that he had sought her out. Though he'd got the room in Northtown, she didn't flatter herself that it was because of her. After all, he hadn't come to Fordswick on her account; until they met by chance that day, he hadn't known of her existence.

'Oh yes?' she said. 'What's that, then?' Why had he come to Fordswick? He'd never told her why he'd stopped there in the first place.

Godfrey was eating his mince and vegetables. It was nursery food, but then this was a nursery meal, with Emily the nanny; the irony was that the child was his own. Eating, he stared at her across the table, and Rowena, raising her head and munching with her baby teeth, stared back at him through her spectacles. Her gaze was steady, appraising, and unsettling.

'This and that,' he said, curtly.

'Sorry I asked,' said Emily. Affronted, her tone, too, was curt.

'Do you talk?' he asked Rowena, leaning towards her across the table, his knife and fork held upright in either hand in a manner Rowena had been taught was not polite.

'Of course she does, and she can write her name and read a bit,' Emily said proudly. 'But she's eating now. She'll talk later.'

'Hmph.' Godfrey resumed his own meal, which, though dull, was free.

'When'll they be back? The old folk?' he asked.

So he'd remembered they were going out. He'd known she'd be alone with Rowena. Emily wasn't sure how to take this but it explained why he had walked in, as bold as brass, and she decided he must want to see her.

'Not for some time,' she said. 'Four, at the earliest. They're going to the dentist and the optician. They'll be having lunch somewhere in Northtown. Parking's easy for them. They've got a disabled badge because of Mr W. Grandad's not too fit, is he, pet?' she said to Rowena. 'Got a poorly leg.'

Rowena remained silent. She had finished her mince and laid her spoon and fork neatly on her plate. She was a tidy child, Godfrey noticed. Wasn't she old enough to use a knife? They'd mollycoddle her, as they'd done with Alice.

'It's banana custard next,' Emily said brightly. 'We won't wait for Graham as he started after us. Then you can watch television.' She turned to Godfrey. 'The children's programmes start soon. Rowena likes to watch, don't you, lovey?'

Godfrey was nauseated by her sickly endearments. The child was not appealing; why treat her as if she were?

Rowena still made no comment. She accepted a bowl filled with warm custard in which slices of banana were submerged and began to eat. There was nothing wrong with her appetite, her watching father thought, but she was a skinny, unattractive little thing.

In silence, he consumed his own first course, and declined the pudding. Emily was glad; it meant she could finish what was left. No wonder she was overweight, thought Godfrey, looking at her with distaste.

'Any drink in the place?' he asked.

'There's water. Or fruit juice,' said Emily. She and Rowena had been drinking orange juice.

'I mean drink,' said Godfrey. 'Beer. Whisky.'

'Oh, I don't know. I shouldn't think so, and anyway—' Emily had been going to say that she couldn't give him Mr Watkinson's liquor when he got up, stalked from the room, and came back several minutes later with a whisky bottle. It had been in the dining-room, with other bottles, just as he had remembered.

Emily was not at all pleased to see him pour a large measure into a tumbler taken from a cupboard in the kitchen.

'Pardon me,' she said, with heavy sarcasm. 'How did you know where to find it?'

'Most people with houses this size keep drink in the dining-room,' he answered, and, as she glowered at him, added, 'It wasn't difficult to find the dining-room.' He must take care, however; she was none too bright, but she might get suspicious if he seemed to know his way around the house.

Emily was bustling Rowena off to the drawing-room, where she put the television on and settled the child down on the sofa. Godfrey saw that she was thin and small; she wore a sort of overall, dark blue bib and brace corduroy trousers, with a scarlet sweater underneath. She did not look at him as she went off with Emily, who soon returned.

She watched anxiously as Godfrey lowered a good tot of whisky, sighed, and poured himself some more. The Watkinsons might notice, and suspect her of drinking it. She decided to top the bottle up with a little water, for safety. She didn't know if they had drinks at night. Isabel and Douglas had wine, and she'd seen gin and whisky in the house.

'Rowena's shy,' she said, disappointed that her charge had not responded to him. It was strange, as usually she was friendly; she had taken to Emily straight away. 'Such a bad thing's happened,' she added. 'Her father's suddenly turned up and wants to see her.'

Godfrey swallowed a gulp of whisky. How had she discovered this? Did the Watkinsons tell her all their secrets?

'Has he?' he asked. 'How do you know?'

'He wrote to them. Well, a solicitor did. I happened to see the letter. It wasn't put away properly.'

'Well, he's got a right, hasn't he?' said Godfrey. Thank goodness he hadn't told her the name he had used when he was living here.

'I don't think so. He walked out and left Alice. He hasn't paid for anything. Why turn up now, causing trouble?' She hesitated, then said, 'A father turning up after a long time like that can upset a child. Make her feel insecure. Frighten her.' And worse, she thought. 'If she was grown up, or even in her teens, able to understand to some extent, it might be different. But to upset a little kid when she's safe and loved – it isn't right.'

'She's as much his kid as the mother's,' Godfrey said.

'If he was a good and loving father, yes. But he isn't. He's somehow found out about her and wants to get some of the action. I hope the Watkinsons can put an end to it,' she said.

'They haven't talked to you about it?'

'No. I told you. I saw the letter,' she replied.

Godfrey got up and walked to the door.

'Where are you going?' she asked.

'To see the kid,' he said. 'See if she'll talk to me. Make friends,' he added guilefully.

'She'll be watching her programme,' said Emily.

'I know. I'll watch it with her.'

He left the room, and Emily began to clear the lunch things. He was in a strange mood, and he'd drunk a lot of whisky. She stopped what she was doing, poured some water from the tap into the whisky bottle and put it in the sideboard in the dining-room. There were more bottles there; she hoped this was where he had found it. Then she followed him into the sitting-room.

He was standing, legs apart, looking down at Rowena who had curled herself up into a corner of the sofa and was sucking her finger, gazing at the television, resolutely avoiding his gaze.

'Don't you want to meet your daddy?' Emily heard him ask, as she entered the room.

'Graham! Leave her alone. Leave it,' she cried. 'Come away.'

Rowena, intent on her programme, wasn't listening, but she was frightened. Emily saw Godfrey/Graham turn off the set and face the little girl, looming over her.

'Listen to me,' he shouted at her. 'Rowena, don't you want to know your daddy?'

As Rowena burst into frightened tears, Emily seized her in her arms and shouted at him.

'Graham – leave her alone. Get out. Go away. You shouldn't be here.' She hugged Rowena to her, sitting on the sofa, smoothed her hair and said said, 'There, there, pet. He's going. He didn't mean to frighten you.'

But I did, thought Godfrey, turning on his heel and leaving. And I'll frighten both of you more than that, before I'm through. That was just for starters.

Emily heard the front door bang behind him. He had gone. What had come over him? He'd no business to talk to Rowena like that, mentioning her father. She calmed Rowena down and found a video of *Thomas the Tank Engine*, which they both settled down to watch, and eventually Rowena fell asleep. She often napped in the afternoon. Emily left her on the sofa and went into the kitchen to finish clearing up. Before doing so, she made sure all the outside doors were locked, not that she really thought he'd return. What had got into him? It was the drink, she decided.

Godfrey, departing, was furiously angry. Now he'd have to change his simple plan, for he couldn't count on Emily's cooperation.

Emily worried for a while about Graham/Godfrey's attitude and thought it was a pity they had parted after angry words, but he might have upset Rowena quite badly. With any luck, after her sleep, she'd forget about it; Emily would think of something she'd enjoy doing, like making fudge, perhaps. She had planned to take her to the playground; she liked the carousel and the slide. It was most unlikely that Graham would be there, loitering about; she might never see him again and that would be a relief, in a way, as he'd turned so nasty. She'd enjoyed their brief relationship, but brief it was always going to be, for next week she must appear in court and who knew what would happen after that? She might end up in prison, a fate she could not bear to think about.

When Rowena woke, they went into the garden and played ball for a while. Rowena's coordination was not good and she found catching difficult, but as Emily persevered with her, she began to improve. Then they went indoors and made the fudge, which was setting when the Watkinsons came home.

They were tired. Mr Watkinson went straight to bed, and Muriel said she would take him some whisky when she'd got him settled.

'I'll get it, shall I?' offered Emily. 'Where is it?'

'Thank you, Emily,' said Muriel. 'It's in the sideboard. We like a little water with it.'

That was lucky, thought Emily, and she had put it back in the proper place. She took Rowena with her to collect the glasses, and poured out two generous tots.

'The man had some, didn't he?' said Rowena.

'Yes, he did. I don't think we'll tell grandma and grandpa about him coming, though,' said Emily.

'All right,' said Rowena, docile.

'He won't come again,' said Emily. She'd have to trust the child not to blab, but she was a quiet, uncommunicative little soul; if she did mention a caller, it was to be hoped that her story would not hang together and might not be understood.

'You could do with some, too,' she told Mrs Watkinson, handing her the second glass. 'I'll stay and put Rowena to bed.'

'Oh, thank you, Emily,' said Muriel. 'That would be kind.'

If Rowena did mention Graham, and she was challenged, Emily would say that yes, someone had called, but she had not mentioned it because the Watkinsons were so tired after their long day in Northtown. She could say that as he was a friend, she hadn't thought they'd mind. Some nannies and au pair girls entertained quite freely when their employers were off the scene, she knew. She'd met a few of them.

14

Isabel was home before Emily returned.

The Watkinsons had asked Emily to stay late today, she remembered, but how late? Was she still at Ford House, or had she met her mysterious friend again? In case she had left a message, Isabel took a look round, but could see no note, and there was nothing on the answerphone. No doubt she'd be back soon, and meanwhile Isabel would start to prepare the evening meal. Putting on her apron, a linen one printed with herb designs, she felt a crackle in the pocket and drew out a crumpled piece of paper. It was the note Emily had left on Monday. There was no point in keeping it; why had she not thrown it away at the time? Isabel was about to put it in the bin when some impulse made her look at it again. Then, still holding it, she went to her desk to find the letter Emily had written four years previously, breaking the news of her mother's death.

She took it from its envelope, unfolded it, laid it down and put Monday's note beside it and the envelope. Something had struck her when she read it, and must have been the subconscious reason why she had not thrown the note away. She stared at them, then took both to a better light and scrutinised them closely.

There was no doubt about it. The letter dated four years ago, and Monday's note, in ballpoint pen on a piece of paper taken from the block by the telephone, were not in the same handwriting. The note was in a rounded, clear script; the letter was in spiky, rather upright cursive.

What could this mean?

Isabel put the note, and the original letter, into a large envelope. Had Emily got someone else to write on her behalf from Spain? But why? Wouldn't she have mentioned it if she had hurt her hand or was in some way unable to write herself? Isabel had had other letters from her in the past, thank-you notes for presents, until some years ago they ceased and she stopped sending gifts, but there had been enough of them for her to recognise the style of this. Wouldn't she have noticed a change then, if there had been one? This difference was distinctive.

An incredible, unacceptable suspicion had to be confronted. Was this girl, who certainly did not remind her at all of the child Emily, an imposter? And if she was, why was she posing as someone else, and who was she? And where was the real Emily?

Isabel's head began to reel. She sat down on the sofa and tried to reason clearly. If Emily was a fake, how had she known about Isabel and where to find her, and that as they had not met for many years she might get away with the deception? Had she decided, when arrested, that it was a chance worth taking? At worst, Isabel would have declared her to be a fraud and gone away; the girl would have been at risk of being accused of adopting a false identity, but was that an offence? Couldn't you call yourself by any name?

Emily hadn't been keen to see Toby and had spent very little time with him, disappearing into her bedroom until after he had left the house. Then Isabel had swept her off to the cinema and she'd been ignorant about Jane Austen. What could be behind this impersonation, if it was one? Or had Emily had some major illness or accident which had caused her to put on weight and develop a quite different style of handwriting? That was possible: a head injury, brain damage, could have been responsible for a metamorphosis.

There were no scars on that shaven skull.

Then there was the matter of the brothers. Emily had sheered away from talking about them, had professed not to know where they were, and had not wanted them located, which had seemed puzzling, to say the least.

The real Emily would speak Spanish, unless a brain injury had expunged such knowledge from her memory. How could Isabel catch her out on that? What trap could she set? How could she plausibly ask her to translate some Spanish phrase? There were no books in Spanish in the house.

She could devise a ruse. It would be simple – she could get a Spanish book from the library or a bookshop. Emily either would or would not be able to translate a passage. That was the thing to do: postpone an explanation until then, and meanwhile play along. Douglas must not get a hint that anything was wrong. She wouldn't mention her suspicions until she was sure she had made no mistake. Whoever the girl was, she was good-hearted, and in trouble. And harmless. Or was she?

How could she be certain that the girl posed no threat? Isabel tried to think it through. There was no doubt that she had been among the protestors at the site and had been aggressive. What was her past history? Isabel remembered how quick she had been in apprehending the shoplifters the day she went to Gifts Galore. It wasn't long until her day in court; perhaps it could all be left till then. She could tackle Emily on the way down to face the magistrates, or just ignore it: let it happen.

No. That wouldn't do. If this girl was not her goddaughter, she owed her no duty. What she had was an obligation to discover what had happened to Ginnie's real daughter.

She was briefly tempted to offload responsibility and tell Douglas, after all. He would know whom to contact – 'the proper channels' – to unearth the whereabouts of Emily's two brothers, and, ultimately, the truth.

She couldn't. Not immediately, anyway. He was already hostile towards Emily and he'd be so angry. He'd demand verification, and browbeat the girl, and if he thought she was a liar, he'd certainly call in the local police. Isabel resolved to observe Emily closely and be alert for inconsistencies. Above all, she must not reveal her distrust or the girl might run away, perhaps disappear with the man who'd come to see her. Did he know who she really was? Was it some plot? Were they thieves?

It couldn't be like that. Getting arrested wasn't part of any burglar's plan, and Isabel's involvement could not have been assured; she might have refused to respond to Emily's appeal after her arrest. Whoever she was, and however she had discovered it, she must have known that Isabel had not seen Emily since she was a child.

Isabel made an effort to calm down, and returned to the kitchen. She'd bought some fish in the market and set about making fish pie. Douglas liked it, and Emily ate anything that was put in front of her. She was a delight to cook for, except that she should be on a strict slimming diet. Isabel mixed the potato to go on the top – she cheated by using dried potato chunks, but she added sour cream which lent flavour to the result. Douglas had never discovered this time-saving stratagem. She had just assembled everything and put the dish in a low oven when Emily returned.

'Sorry I'm so late,' she said, breezing into the kitchen. 'Oh, it's lovely and warm in here, and something smells good.' She beamed at Isabel who, despite her misgivings, was pleased to see her. She liked the girl. 'Those poor old things were exhausted,' Emily continued. 'They've had an awful day. You won't believe this, but Rowena's father wants to see her. Can you credit it, after all this time?' She reached into one of her large pockets and produced a polythene bag. 'Alice told me about it. I stayed until she came back as they were so tired after their day in Northtown. There!' She put the bag down on the table. 'Home-made fudge,' she said. 'Me and Rowena made it.'

Me and Rowena. Would the true Emily have uttered such a solecism? But you heard it all the time now; it was even used by David Archer on the radio soap, and he had had a good education, hadn't he?

'Oh – Emily, thank you,' said Isabel, rather faintly. 'How delicious. You must have had fun making it.'

'Yes, we did,' said Emily. 'They're not going to give in to him,' she added. 'To the father.'

'What if he just turns up?' said Isabel.

'I suppose he might,' said Emily. 'He's sent a letter. Well, a solicitor sent it for him.'

'How worrying,' said Isabel. 'Maybe he has rights?' she added.

'Wrongs, more like,' said Emily robustly. 'They do it, though. Leave girls pregnant and go off and then come back wanting more.'

Isabel decided not to ask more of what.

'The child should be considered,' she replied. 'Most fathers should be involved.' But there were some who should never be allowed anywhere near a child. However, presumably Alice had, at some point, liked Rowena's father. What had happened?

Isabel had thought herself in love with Douglas, and had liked him. Did she now? He had become so cold and so aloof. The mere fact that she wanted to keep her worries about Emily from him was indicative of the lack of trust between them.

If Toby were to come down again, he could say something to Emily, refer to some past episode, a childish exploit they had shared, which would prove, one way or the other, whether Isabel's fears were unfounded. Perhaps he knew some Spanish and could test her.

She wanted to be mistaken. She would not challenge Emily herself by mentioning picnics shared so long ago, or swimming trips. Such things could be genuinely forgotten.

'Thank you for the fudge,' she said again, and, forgetting Alice and Rowena, hugged her, thinking, Judas.

In the night, sleepless, Isabel told herself that there must be an explanation for the inconsistencies in Emily's history. She would turn out to be, after all, who she said she was; no imposter would have risked meeting someone who had once been close to her and would be likely to realise that she was not genuine. Besides, the police had her details; they would have detected bogus papers, and wouldn't they have taken fingerprints? But with none to check against – and Emily's was established as a first offence – how could a substitution be detected?

Round and round in Isabel's aching head went all these contradictory theories until she concluded that Emily must have had some serious illness or been in an accident which had changed her personality, caused her to put on weight, and altered her handwriting. Such things were known. Convincing herself, Isabel at last fell into a troubled sleep. She was still asleep when Douglas got up; since their move, with the boys adult and now seldom at home, she had stopped feeling it was her duty to be down for breakfast at the same early hour as he.

Emily, too, avoided him. After that first morning, she had stayed upstairs until he left, and she slept later now. At the site, the noise of the security men, the clearance workers, and the tree-fellers had aroused the protestors, but after a time you learned to burrow your head into your sleeping bag and ignore all except the loudest racket. If you stayed put, you were an obstacle to those anxious to remove you. Now, she slept soundly, not afraid of being physically disturbed. For the last few days she had woken feeling calm and peaceful; briefly, she was in tranquil waters, unthreatened until she had to go to court. No one, at the moment, wished her any harm.

But someone wished harm to that poor little girl. Emily could not accept that a father suddenly appearing after a four-year absence, demanding what he saw as his rights, was thinking of the child.

Continuing their discussion from the night before, she said as much to Isabel at breakfast, which they had together, Emily still enjoying cornflakes every morning.

Isabel, whilst agreeing to some extent with what she said, found her point of view extreme and said she was ignoring the father's feelings in all this.

'Surely he has a right to get to know the child, to build up a relationship, if they've been estranged?' she said.

'If he's really nice, he'll be content to take it gently,' said Emily. 'Rowena's father isn't thinking about her. He just wants to get at Alice.'

This could be true.

'There was that king in the Bible,' Emily went on, brandishing her spoon above the bowl of cereal. 'Two mothers were quarrelling over a baby. Each said it was hers. The king, to settle it, said the baby should be cut in half and a piece given to each mother. The real mother cried and gave up her claim because she wouldn't harm her child.'

'King Solomon,' said Isabel. 'Where did you hear that story, Emily?' She could distinctly remember Ginnie's atheism and her spurning of the Sunday school to which Matthew and Toby went each week. Isabel, though doubt ridden, wanted her children to be exposed to the Christian religion and adhere, as much as possible, to its rules, which on the whole were excellent.

'Oh, Mum read it to me,' she said.

'Did she?' said Isabel, and her tone indicated her disbelief.

'Or my grandmother. Yes, maybe it was her,' said Emily glibly. She spooned the last of the cornflakes into her mouth and got up quickly, turning away from Isabel. 'More coffee?' she asked, picking up the old enamel jug in which Isabel always made hers.

'Oh – yes, please,' said Isabel. 'Thanks.'

Emily made a business of pouring it and Isabel let the moment go, but her heart was pounding fast. Ginnie would never have told her Bible stories; her paternal grandparents were in Botswana and Ginnie's parents lived in Scotland. Ginnie and the children had, however, spent a year or two with them after the marriage break-up; the grandmother might have sought to counteract her daughter's views.

'Was that when you visited her in Wales?' she said lightly. 'Your grandmother?'

'That's right,' said Emily. 'I liked seeing her. She's dead now,' she added.

Gotcha, thought Isabel, and a wave of sorrow swept over her. Was the Scottish grandmother dead? And the grandfather? 'That's why you didn't get in touch with her, when you were arrested?' she added, making sure.

'Yes,' said Emily, digging another hole, and falling into it.

'Did she go to Ginnie's funeral?' asked Isabel. 'Was she well enough?'

'Who?'

'Your grandmother. She must have been very sad.'

'She couldn't. She was dead herself,' said Emily. 'You're asking a lot of questions,' she added. 'Don't you know all this?'

'How could I? You told me so little when you wrote about Ginnie, and you didn't answer when I wrote back. Perhaps you never got my letter.'

'No,' said Emily. 'I didn't.'

And that, thought Isabel, is probably the first truthful thing you've said throughout this conversation. She felt rather sick. Should she challenge her now, straight off, before things got even more complicated?

But Emily was getting up, clearing away her breakfast things, putting them in the dishwasher.

'I must go,' she said. 'I don't want them to think I'm not coming. Poor old things, they were very tired last night, and Alice looked so worried.'

'I'm not surprised,' said Isabel. 'I hope they can deal with this business of the father. If they turn him away, Rowena may hold it against them later on.'

'If she finds out,' said Emily.

'She will. Most people get found out in the end,' said Isabel. 'Unless they're very clever and extremely lucky.'

Unlike you, my dear, she thought; you're neither, and I'm going to track down your grandparents when you've gone to work. Failing them, I'll find your brothers. If she tried hard enough, perhaps she would remember where they went to school or university; surely she had known some details about them in their adolescent years? A school or college might know where they were now, if the administration could be persuaded to yield the information.

When Emily had gone and could not witness her activities, Isabel found what she was looking for in an old address book. Ginnie's name appeared, with an address in Scotland, near Stirling, c/o William Campbell. How very lucky that she hadn't thrown the out-of-date book away when sorting things before the move to Fordswick. No telephone number appeared beside the address, so, before she had time to change her mind, she rang directory enquiries. The efficient voice informed her that there was no entry for that name and address.

If the Campbells were still alive they could be ex-directory, or they might have left the district. She could write to them, and mark the envelope *Please forward*.

It was time to leave for Gifts Galore. Isabel picked up a pad of writing paper and an envelope, shoved them, with the address book, into her bag, and left the house. She wrote the letter as soon as she had opened the shop and was ready for business. She said that she was Emily's godmother and had lost touch, asking Mrs Campbell how to contact Emily and her brothers. It was very important, she wrote.

Assuming Mrs Campbell was still alive, she might not receive Isabel's until Monday or much later, and if she replied at all, it might be by letter, not the telephone. But Isabel felt sure that she was dead. That part of Emily's story was very likely to be true.

Nevertheless, she popped out to catch the morning post with her urgent missive.

*   *   *

Up at Ford House, things were, on the surface, normal. Alice had gone to work, and the old Watkinsons were creakingly beginning their day. Muriel had slept badly and still looked very tired. No wonder. The poor old thing must be worried sick, thought Emily, who had to remind herself that she was not supposed to know about the solicitor's letter. She kept bright and brisk herself, getting Rowena organised and setting off with her to school. She had almost forgotten about Graham's visit of the day before and his abrupt departure, but Rowena hadn't. When Emily collected her from school, she said, 'I hope that man won't come again today,' and Emily, shocked, assured her that he wouldn't.

'You didn't mention him to grandma, or to Mummy, did you?' she asked anxiously, and Rowena shook her head. 'He is a friend of mine, you see,' Emily explained. 'But they mightn't like me giving him lunch, without asking them.'

Rowena seemed to understand.

He was sitting in his van, not far from the nursery school, when Emily and Rowena walked past a few minutes later, but he did not speak to them. Emily ignored him, and hoped Rowena, who was running ahead with some friends, hadn't noticed him.

Emily knew he'd seen them, however. That was why he was sitting there: to watch them going by.

Why bother?

When she walked back, after taking Rowena in and helping her remove her outdoor clothing, he had gone.

15

All the way up in the train that morning, Alice worried about the threat Godfrey's return imposed, and wondered if she could go ahead with her plan to spend the evening with Paul. She had given advance warning to Emily and her parents that she and Mary were going to a film, and Emily was staying to put Rowena to bed, but things had changed now. Last night she and her mother had discussed the new situation, and Alice thought she should put Mary off. Her mother urged her to stick to the arrangement, pointing out that though they had met for lunch, it was the first time she and Mary had spent an evening together since Alice began working at the gallery.

'Nothing will happen until Godfrey hears from Mr Jones,' Muriel Watkinson had said. 'Even if he caught the post to the Swindon solicitor this afternoon, Godfrey won't know about it until Monday, and it's more likely that Mr Jones won't write until tomorrow. Then there's the weekend.' Mr Jones might telephone the other solicitor, but she thought it wasn't probable.

Mr Jones had murmured something about making Rowena a ward of court, but that decision could be postponed; unless her father could smuggle her out, such a course would stop him removing her from the country, but it might cause other problems later on. Muriel was sure that Godfrey wanted money, not the child, and Mr Jones, at this stage, had kept to himself his awareness of the risk that the one might be used to obtain the other.

Things changed so fast. Until she opened that letter, Alice had been happy and exhilarated, with this new friendship – she did not think of its potential as being more than that – and the novelty of the evening with Paul ahead. Now, she felt as if her and Rowena's very existence was threatened. The prospect of Godfrey – a total stranger to the child – taking Rowena off to some flat or house, with perhaps a wife and other children there, and a whole alien environment, was terrifying. Despite the restrictions of her own childhood, Alice understood that in their repressed, inarticulate way, her parents loved her. She had always felt physically, if not emotionally secure, and to have had that stability jeopardised when she was a child would have been horrific. If her parents had parted, and she had been passed to and fro like a parcel, presumably she would have adjusted, as many modern children in similar circumstances seemed to do; but if she had not known her father and had suddenly had to meet a strange man and spend time with him, she would have been frightened beyond measure. Surely the courts would not permit such an intervention? Even to think of it filled her with terror.

She had barely noticed Douglas on the platform, answering only when he repeated his now customary stiff greeting. He, watching her in the train from his seat several rows away, saw that she was not concentrating on her book. Very little of her face was visible below her large fake-fur hat, but she seemed distracted. Isabel, had she known that Douglas was observing this, would have been amazed; he never seemed to notice if she was upset or unwell. As the journey continued, Alice was unaware of anything other than her huge new dread. She had never expected Godfrey to enter her life again, not after the first faintly hopeful weeks after he left. Men did reappear, though, and women took them back. Battered wives resumed the treadmill of violence, but he had not been violent; merely insensitive; and she was not a wife. He couldn't have any legal rights to Rowena.

Standing up when the train slowed for the terminus, she moved forward and found herself near Douglas, who looked down at her and said, 'Are you feeling all right, Alice? You look rather pale.' And indeed, what he could see of her face was ashen, with dark shadows under her eyes. Unfamiliar chivalrous feelings swept over him. Did she need help of some sort?

She did, and for a moment was tempted to tell him why. He was solid and safe, a successful middle-aged man who would know how to deal with Godfrey.

But Mr Jones was a similar man, and a professional; it was his job to handle people like Godfrey and he would do it. The moment passed.

Not, however, for Douglas. He stayed near her as they descended the escalator, and stood beside her on the platform waiting for the tube train to arrive. The sign said it would be arriving in two minutes, and he filled the interval by asking her which train she normally caught in the evening. She told him, and said that tonight she was probably going to be late as she was meeting a friend.

'How pleasant,' he said, stiffly.

'We might go to a film,' she said. Her voice was high and nervous.

She was overwrought, he thought. What could be upsetting her? She had seemed so composed when she came to see Emily, and also yesterday, in the gallery.

'Emily continues to be satisfactory, I hope,' he said.

'Oh yes. She's staying late again tonight, to put Rowena to bed. It's good of her to do two nights in a row.'

'I'm sure she doesn't mind,' said Douglas. 'She seems very fond of the child.' Rowena's praises had been sung throughout dinner, and her accomplishments described.

'It's mutual,' said Alice. 'Rowena likes her too.'

'Good,' said Douglas, and then the roar of the wind heralding the advancing train ended their conversation. They both had to stand for most of the trip, and exchanged no more remarks, but Douglas kept thinking about her as he completed his journey. It was unusual for him to have anything in his head except matters of work during the day, but at lunch-time he decided to go to the gallery once more. Alice would be hatless there, and if he took a good look at her, he could confirm or dismiss his deduction that she was unwell or anxious.

She was leaving the gallery as he arrived. Wearing her all-enveloping black coat and hat, she walked quickly up the street, and, astounded at himself, Douglas found that he was following her. What was he doing, stalking the woman like a man obsessed? Was this how those weird fixations, mentioned in the press, began? Part of him was intrigued by her; her past – illicit, in his opinion – fascinated him, and he found her pale, waif-like appearance curiously magnetic. The other part of him deplored her conduct, regretted her show of independence, and thought she should be staying at home to care for her child, for with her wealthy parents' backing, she could have done so without hardship. This censorious part of him also condemned Isabel's venture into shopkeeping; since she started Gifts Galore, she had become unpredictable – joining the golf club, for example, and acquiring friends he'd never met. When she said she was only going on a theatre trip or to the cinema with other women, which, very occasionally, she did – he cared for neither form of entertainment – how did he know it was true? She might be seeing someone.

Who? How could she have met some other man?

Easily, was the answer, either in the shop or on the golf course. He had suggested that the subscription was an extravagance, when she could play so seldom since she spent so much time on shop business, but she said it was her money and she thought it well worthwhile. She played even at weekends, when she should be looking after him, he having spent the morning toiling in the garden, erecting more pergolas, for instance, and excavating the attractive pond before winter sent him inside. He had a plan to fit new cupboards in the spare bedroom, now occupied by Emily. Isabel was opposed to his scheme, maintaining that those already there were adequate, and if he moved them to another wall, which was his proposition, the room would need redecorating.

That was part of the project. Doing it up would occupy more time. Such work was relaxing for one who spent his days stressfully dealing with intricacies of government. Isabel was not convinced he was exposed to excess stress in the office, except possibly in the area of personal relationships. He often grumbled about the obstinacy of various colleagues, or their lack of attention to detail, which was vital in affairs of state.

This business of importing Emily into their household had been deeply unsettling, and was a fresh example of Isabel's new intransigence, but it was because of Emily that he had perforce become acquainted with Alice, and was now walking down a West End street behind her. She entered a small café, and Douglas went in too. He saw her walk straight to a corner table where a middle-aged, balding man stood up and greeted her, leaning forward to kiss her lightly on the lips. Douglas, astounded, turned and hastened out, not daring to risk her seeing him while he was spying on her.

He was outraged. All sympathy over her pallor vanished. Was this why she chose to work in London? To meet her lover? Douglas forgot his occasional lunches with colleagues when some important matter of policy had to be discussed off the record. Without a trial, he condemned her.

Alice, toying with her sandwich, wondered whether to tell Paul that she could not meet him later, but could not bring herself to do so as he asked her what she would like to do – which film she might want to see, or would she rather he tried for concert seats?

She chose a film. *Shine* was showing, and neither of them had seen it. Alice had not been to a cinema for years, except to take Rowena to *Babe*, a film about a pig who functioned as a sheep-dog. Her parents considered Rowena still too young for such a jaunt, but it had been a big success and Alice was determined to take her to suitable future films. Paul told her about a book he was reading – it was easy for him, working in a bookshop, to read any new book that came along, and he often saw proof copies in advance of publication. Alice tried to be interested, but her thoughts kept turning to Godfrey and his letter. Like Douglas, Paul noticed her pale face and her shadowed eyes. He wondered whether to suggest postponing their date, but if she had some problem that was bothering her, going to the cinema might take her mind off it, and do her good. When he knew her better, he could ask her what was on her mind.

He kissed her again when they parted, each saying that they would see the other later. Paul returned to his bookshop, and Alice to the gallery.

*   *   *

Isabel was on her own today in Gifts Galore. A supplier arrived with an order, which she took in, checked and unpacked, and she had a steady flow of customers as the morning wore on, but business would not really pick up until nearer Easter. On her way home, she'd pick up something exotic from the delicatessen for the evening meal, just to see if Douglas noticed. Emily had said she would stay at Ford House until after supper and have hers there; she would be late home because Alice was going to have a night out in London, so she would give the old couple their meal and clear it up.

Isabel was glad that Emily was showing such a thoughtful side to her nature, but she was a kind and generous girl. Isabel had grown fond of her and, whoever she really was, liked having her around.

Later, she remembered how that had been in her mind earlier in the day.

Emily set off to nursery school with Rowena at their usual time. It was still extremely cold; there had been no rain since she came to Fordswick and the ground was like iron. Well wrapped up, they walked along the road. Going through the recreation ground was a nicer route, but it took longer, and Emily kept that for the return journey, when perhaps the day would have warmed up a bit. They walked along, hand in hand, the large young woman in her baggy jacket and red woollen cap, and the small girl in her blue snowsuit, also with a red hat.

Godfrey saw them leave. Then he drove his van through the gates of Ford House and stopped at the front door where he pressed the bell hard, and, almost at once pressed it again.

He knew from what Emily had said that the Watkinsons had aged and grown fragile since he last saw them five years ago, but even he was shocked when, after a considerable delay, the door was opened and what he thought of as an old crone stood before him.

Muriel Watkinson was fully dressed, in black trousers and a long purple cardigan over a black roll-neck sweater. She was leaning on a stick and seemed to have lost several inches in height; her hair, which he remembered as iron grey and thick, was now white and wispy. She looked up at him, frowning, seeing a strange, burly man standing on the doorstep, and slowly she realised, with horror, who he was. He had put on weight, his hair was grey, and he now wore a moustache. She tried to shut the door, but he pushed it open, almost knocking her over as he did so, thrusting past her into the house. He closed the door behind him and as he advanced towards her, she was forced to retreat, but she waved her stick at him, and stopped at the foot of the staircase.

'How dare you burst in like this,' she said.

'You know who I am,' he said. 'I want my daughter,' and he stood looming menacingly above her. Muriel thought he was going to hit her.

'Alice received your solicitor's letter. An answer is on its way to you. You have no rights in this,' she said, gripping her stick, thankful that the child wasn't in the house at this moment.

'You'll find that isn't so,' said Godfrey. 'But I'm prepared to come to a reasonable agreement. Fifty thousand pounds will see me on my way.'

'I won't discuss the matter,' Muriel replied. 'You will hear from our solicitor. Please leave,' and she made a move towards the door.

'The old man may think differently,' said Godfrey. 'He did before. Now there's the kid. That alters things.'

'It does,' agreed Muriel. She hoped he could not see that she was shaking. 'The child is safe here, and looked after. If you lay claim to her, Alice will demand child support from you and that will be a price you won't want to pay.'

'I won't pay a penny. You're going to,' he declared. 'The old man will see the sense of it. Where is he?' and he turned away from her abruptly, heading towards the room which he remembered had been Mr Watkinson's study.

Muriel raised her stick and brought it down sharply against the side of his face. His head jerked away in a reflex response.

'Don't you dare disturb him. He's not well,' she said, raising it again as Godfrey reeled back, his hand to his smarting face.

'You old bitch,' he said, and he took a step towards her, but she held the stick upraised, ready to strike him again.

He caught hold of it, wrenched it from her grasp and flung it across the hall, where it clattered across the floor, coming to rest against the wall.

'What are you going to do now, you stupid old cow?' he sneered, and he stood close to her, one fist clenched, as if to strike her.

She waited for the blow, incapable of further belligerent action, but not of speech.

'What a worthless man you are,' she said. 'You come here threatening an old woman and a mother and her child.' She would not speak Rowena's name. Why should he learn it? 'You're a good-for-nothing bully.'

He hit her then, striking her with his fist against her face, and she stumbled sideways, tripped, then fell, uttering one faint cry.

Godfrey stood over her.

'Fifty thousand pounds,' he said. 'I'll telephone to arrange collection. I'll want the cash on Monday.' They could get it by then: phone calls to their bank and stockbroker would produce it.

'You'll go on wanting,' Muriel replied, still on the ground.

'Then don't say I haven't warned you,' Godfrey answered, and he banged out of the house.

When Emily returned from leaving Rowena at nursery school, she came in through the unlocked back door and collected the vacuum cleaner, intending to go upstairs to make the beds and sweep the bedrooms. In the hall, she found Mrs Watkinson lying on the floor, making little mewing sounds.

Emily was on her knees beside her in seconds.

'Oh, Mrs Watkinson! Whatever happened? Did you fall?' she gasped. 'Oh dear! Can you speak? Where does it hurt?'

'I'm all right, Emily. Just help me up,' said Mrs Watkinson. 'I slipped. There's no need to be alarmed.'

She had tried to get to her feet but, without help, had found it impossible. The only way would be to roll over and kneel, then stand, but she had not got the strength, and she had fallen out of reach of anything solid to hold on to for leverage. After she had been there for some time, she had remembered that Emily would be returning soon and would find her.

'You may have broken something,' said Emily. 'I'd better call an ambulance.'

'There's no need for that,' said Mrs Watkinson testily. Whilst prone, she had made herself breathe deeply and steadily to slow her pounding pulse, and had moved her limbs, one at a time. All were working. 'I may be bruised, but that's all.' People called ambulances for the least thing these days: cut fingers, indigestion. They were intended for serious emergencies. 'Now, let me hold your arm and see if you can help me up. Bring my stick over first.'

Emily discovered that although Mrs Watkinson was small and frail, she was heavy, but slowly, with Emily's assistance, she managed to stand and, propped on her stick, to limp into the drawing-room.

'I think some brandy,' she told Emily. 'From the dining-room. Just to pull me round.'

When Emily had poured some into a glass and Mrs Watkinson had gulped a mouthful down, she revived. After a pause, she sipped some more. Then she managed a weak smile at Emily.

'That's better,' she said. 'I felt a bit shaken. That's all.'

'Better stay there for a bit,' said Emily. 'Are you sure you haven't broken anything?'

'Quite sure,' said Muriel, who wasn't, but thought she would not have been able to move at all if she had. 'Perhaps you would see how Mr Watkinson is getting on,' she said. 'He may need some help. He's had his breakfast. Oh, and don't mention my little tumble to him.'

'I won't.' Not yet, thought Emily. 'Leave it to me,' she said, and she went into Robert Watkinson's room, where he was fretting, impatient to get dressed, complaining because his wife had not attended to him as promptly as was usual. He was quite a tyrant, Emily considered, but maybe he couldn't help it; it must be frustrating to be so restricted in his movements. The old girl ruled the roost now, and she didn't want him to learn about her fall, though if she was badly injured he'd have to be told. Did he know about the threat from Rowena's father, or had that been kept from him? She must remember that she had found out only by chance.

Mrs Watkinson was looking better when Emily returned to her, having installed the old man in a chair by the window, where he could look across the garden to the trees. Emily had taken to putting crumbs out to tempt birds to the concrete balustrade bordering the terrace on to which he looked, hoping he might take an interest in them.

'You stay there while I finish clearing up in the kitchen,' Emily instructed. Interrupted by the accident, she had not yet gone upstairs to make the beds and vacuum round. She bustled on. Robert Watkinson saw her come round the side of the house and cast breadcrumbs on the terrace wall. Soon the birds would come, thrushes and the robin, maybe some tits. He enjoyed seeing them. He must tell her so; she was a good-hearted girl despite her odd appearance. Robert believed in encouragement, realising too late that he had denied it to his own daughter.

Where was Muriel? Normally, once her morning chores were done, she read the paper to him, a routine which, since Emily's arrival, now took place earlier. She had been with them for only a few days, yet she had made a big difference to their lives. He watched the birds squabbling over the crumbs, huge starlings fluttering down to scare away the smaller birds. It was ever thus, the weak intimidated by the large and powerful. Now he knew what it was to be a lesser mortal and he did not like it.

Muriel came at last, with *The Times*, and sat down to read it to him. Soon Emily arrived with cups of coffee for them both. She left them peacefully together. They seemed quite fond of one another. Touching, really.

Just before it was time to fetch Rowena, the telephone rang. This was a rare event; Emily did not recollect it happening before while she was there. She answered it, and went to tell Mrs Watkinson that she was wanted by a Mr Jones.

Muriel was already on her way out of the room towards the hall, where the instrument was on a table. Why didn't they have a cordless one, like Isabel, wondered Emily as she took the old woman's elbow and helped her to the chair beside it. She'd suggest it to Alice – but of course, she would have gone back to Isabel's by the time Alice returned from her evening out. She must remember to mention it on Monday, or she might pop up over the weekend to see if they were all right.

Muriel was listening intently, then nodding.

'I see,' she said. 'So there's nothing to fear, then. I'll tell her. Thank you.'

'Good news?' asked Emily, who had waited in the offing, ready to help Muriel move back to the drawing-room.

'I suppose so,' Muriel replied. She looked at Emily's round, concerned face, and the urge to confide became overwhelming, for what if Godfrey returned and really knocked her out? 'Mr Watkinson doesn't know about this, Emily. He isn't strong enough to stand it, but I'm going to tell you. Just in case I have another, more serious fall. Rowena's father has expressed a wish to see her. We hadn't heard a word from him since he left – we were not aware he even knew about her birth – but he must have discovered. Alice had a letter from his lawyer on Wednesday.'

'Oh, goodness! That's awful!' Emily made a good job of pretending this was news to her.

'Yes, it is. I got in touch with our solicitor yesterday – Mr Jones. That was him on the telephone just now.'

'Oh,' said Emily again. 'And he says it can't happen?'

'Not exactly,' said Muriel. 'He said the lawyer it was supposed to be from doesn't exist. He checked, before replying.'

'What does that mean?'

'Oh – that Godfrey – that's the father – wrote the letter

himself, with a fake address. He could have done it at a print shop, it seems.'

Emily didn't know much about print shops, but she took this on trust.

'Well, that means he's just trying it on,' she said. 'Doesn't it?'

'Probably,' said Muriel. 'He'll be wanting money, not Rowena.' But how could they be sure? Could so vicious a man have paternal feelings?

'And if you pay, he'll go away?' Emily was saying.

'We're supposed to think that,' Muriel answered.

'He'll be back for more,' said Emily.

'I agree.'

'But what can you do?'

'I'm not sure. Mr Jones is going to write to the false address and see what happens. If his letter is returned by the post office, it might be useful as evidence of uttering threats, extortion – something like that,' she said. 'But in fact he didn't utter threats. Not in the letter. It simply said that he wanted to see his daughter.'

'So what happens now?'

Muriel was strongly tempted to tell her about Godfrey's visit and that he had caused her fall. But the girl would want the police called in. Perhaps she should have told Mr Jones what had happened this morning. She could ring him back later, when she had had time to think and was feeling stronger.

'He might come round,' she said. 'He might try and see her without our cooperation.'

'He'll have me to reckon with, if he does,' Emily declared.

16

Few of the children at the nursery school could put on their warm outdoor clothing unaided, and the small cloakroom was crowded. Emily always went in to help Rowena clamber into her padded snowsuit.

Rowena wanted to go home through the recreation ground, but Emily said they must hurry back. She mustn't mention Mrs Watkinson's fall; the old woman wanted that kept from her husband, and Rowena might blurt it out, if she knew. She hastened along, holding the little girl's hand, walking quickly down the road towards the junction where they would turn off for Ford House. They had gone only a short distance, other mothers and children near them, when Godfrey's camper van drew up beside them.

He jumped out, opened the rear door and said, 'Get in. It's cold enough to freeze an elephant. I'll run you back.' Then he plucked Rowena up and put her into the back of the vehicle.

Emily had not expected to see him again. They'd parted after angry words, but here he was, wanting to make amends, bearing no grudge. A lift would get them home all the faster. She clambered in beside Rowena and fussed over her, fastening the seat belt round her while Godfrey slid the van into gear and drove off. At the junction he turned left, taking the road that led out of the village, not the turn for Ford House.

'This isn't the way,' said Emily. 'Graham, Ford House is in the other direction.'

He did not answer, his foot hard on the accelerator, the van's engine roaring as he drove towards the main road that led to Northtown.

'Where are you taking us? We have to go back to Ford House,' said Emily, not yet frightened, only puzzled.

'Thought we'd give the kid a treat. Get some pizzas, take her back to my place. I've got a video – something about dogs. Kids like that,' said Godfrey. He reached out and picked up a video so that Emily could see its title: *101 Dalmatians*.

He needed Emily. If he'd snatched the kid and left her standing, even Emily would have caught on that something was up and would have have raised the alarm, and he couldn't manage the kid on his own, not when he had to make phone calls and write letters, force the Watkinsons to pay up. Not unless he drugged her, which might be necessary later. Emily would cooperate once she knew there was cash in it for her, and she'd keep the kid quiet.

Rowena had sensed the tension and that Emily was upset; besides, she knew this wasn't the way home and she didn't like this man.

'We can't do that. We must get back. Turn round, Graham. The Watkinsons will worry,' Emily said.

'We'll phone them. You can say you met a friend and you'll be back this afternoon,' he said.

Put like that, it sounded reasonable, but in the circumstances, it wasn't.

'We've got to go back,' Emily told him, urgently. 'Please turn round, Graham.'

Should he tell her who he really was? Godfrey was tempted, but it was too soon. He'd wait until he'd got them in his room. She'd see the sense of it then. To hell with it, he was the kid's father, after all. When Emily knew that, she'd be on his side. After all, she fancied him, and no one else was going to want her, with her shaven head and lumpy body – no one fanciable in return, that is.

Rowena began to snivel. This friend of Emily's was horrid.

'I want to go home,' she whined.

Emily wanted to reassure Rowena, but Graham was showing no sign of slowing down or turning. He was driving fast along the Northtown road.

'Graham, please take us back,' she repeated. 'Rowena's hungry, and her grandparents are expecting us.'

Godfrey hadn't reckoned with the kid needing feeding. Not for hours. His line about the pizzas had been just a placatory sop. He'd planned to take them to his room and leave them there together; there was no video recorder in it, since it was just a cheap room, but they could have the television from his van, if that would keep them quiet. The video box was one he'd lifted, empty, from a supermarket shelf. Emily could pacify the kid while he made a phone call. The money'd soon be up front; people like the Watkinsons only had to call the bank and they'd get an advance on some security or other – the house, or their investments. It would all be over by this evening and he'd be on his way.

Rowena's wails grew louder, and Emily said, 'She wants to go home, and so do I. We could go on a picnic another day. Children don't always like surprises, and the Watkinsons will be angry. I may lose my job.'

'You won't need it after today,' he said airily. 'You'll be rich.'

'What do you mean?' But a dreadful fear was beginning to sweep over her. Mrs Watkinson had warned her to keep close to Rowena, and she had had a mysterious tumble in the house while Emily was out. Then she remembered Graham's remarks about a father's right to see his child, and how he had stared at the little girl.

She would not utter it. She would not put it into words.

'They'll pay to get her back,' he declared, and, horrified, she knew that she was right. His name wasn't Graham; he was Godfrey Sutton, Rowena's father, and he'd come to Fordswick to get the child. Meeting Emily, he had set her up to help him. Even worse, he had no feelings for Rowena; none at all.

Emily, as a small child, had been taken by her father, late at night, from her mother's house where they had lived tranquilly after her parents separated. Life had been much better since they parted, with no more rows. She did not miss her father; he used to hit her mother when they disagreed, then would turn to Emily, calling her his little girl, his pet, but he hit her too, sometimes. Even at that age, she knew that he did it to upset her mother. When he seized her, she had been pushed into the back of a car and driven a long way, to a house where she had been locked in a room for what had seemed like months but was in fact days. A woman was there, someone thin and dark and angry who, while her father was at work, beat her on her body, where because of her clothes the bruises wouldn't show. Then the police had found her and she went back to her mother. After that, there had been a further interval of peace until her mother remarried and acquired two step-children, and the courts had insisted she spent time with her father. When she was thirteen, after a fierce row with the dark woman whom her father had married, she ran away. In various ways, she had been running ever since.

She could run again, but this time, she must take Rowena and get back to Fordswick.

'I see,' she said slowly. 'You've got a plan.' He had lied to her from the beginning.

'That's right,' he said. He knew she'd play along when she understood. She was like a dog who would attach itself to anyone befriending it. In the driving mirror, his eyes met hers, and Emily forced herself to smile.

'Rowena's hungry,' she insisted. The child's whines had settled into a weary grizzle. 'Couldn't we stop now and get the pizzas? Or some fish and chips? Then she'll probably go to sleep. She usually does, after lunch.'

'Well – if we see a takeaway place,' said Graham/Godfrey. It would be a good move if it kept them quiet.

The extent of his treachery was sinking in. He'd used her, encouraging her to apply for the job at Ford House, asking her about the Watkinsons. A deep anger filled Emily, but she had learned to deal with rage and harness it, and she was a survivor. She gazed ahead to see whether she could recognise where they were. She had been to Northtown so few times and only once, that first day, in daylight. They were entering the outskirts of the city now, approaching the district where Gifts Galore lay to the north of the city. On her exploratory trip, armed with the five pounds Isabel had given her, she had walked round this area and had bought the flowers for Isabel, who was not her godmother at all but a total stranger. She had never expected her bluff to work, that Isabel would not disown her instantly, recognising she was nothing like the real Emily, whose identity she had adopted after they met in a hospital ward more than a year ago.

Godfrey was slowing down because there was a line of cars and buses held up by traffic lights, and gazing out, Rowena a little quieter now, sucking her thumb, Emily recognised the florist. Delia, it was called. Though she couldn't see it, Gifts Galore was further on, and, she remembered, there was a chip shop not far away. That first morning, as well as buying flowers and her red hat, she had spent some of Isabel's five pounds on chips. Here was her chance.

'There's a chip shop,' she exclaimed, and pointed. 'Rowena and I'll pop out and get some.' She had no money on her, but they needed none; they'd run into Gifts Galore where they'd be safe.

'You leave her here with me,' said Godfrey.

Rowena had not followed this conversation. What happened next gave her a shock, for her dear Emily pinched her hard and instantly she yelled. Under cover of the noise, Emily unfastened her own and Rowena's seat belts.

'For Christ's sake!' Godfrey pulled the van up, the near wheels on the pavement. He'd have to humour them. Horns blew and cars swerved to get past them. 'I'll go,' he said. 'Make her keep quiet.' They'd be causing an obstruction but he shouldn't be more than a few minutes.

He got out of the van and crossed to the chip shop, taking the keys, but Emily couldn't have driven it except possibly across a field where there were no obstructions. The moment he had gone, she pulled open the sliding door and got out, dragging Rowena with her, then set off down the pavement towards Gifts Galore.

Godfrey, in the chip shop, had met a queue. He could not risk waiting to be served; a traffic warden or the police might come along. The kid would have to do without. Hurrying back to the van, at first he did not see that it was empty. Then, realising they had gone, he stared round wildly and saw the pair scurrying along the pavement beyond the traffic lights.

It was no good running after them. He jumped into the van and drove off in pursuit, passing them and parking further on, leaving the engine running as he leapt out to head them off. They had just reached Gifts Galore, though, seeing him, Emily would have chosen any shop. She pushed Rowena through the doorway, but before she could follow the child, Godfrey grabbed her by the arm and twisted it behind her, cuffing her on the head, frogmarching her back to the van as, shouting, she struggled to break free.

People saw and heard it. Though it was over in seconds, there were witnesses, but they froze where they stood, and by the time a woman realised this was an abduction, Godfrey had hauled Emily into the van, hit her across the nose, and banged her head hard against the side of the window to stun her while he drove off.

Isabel, behind the counter, adding up accounts while two customers were browsing round the shelves, was aware of a commotion at the door and a small, screaming child seemed to hurtle across the threshold. The nearest customer, quickly recovering from her instant stupefaction, stooped down to comfort her.

Later, everyone agreed that it had happened so fast. Isabel never saw Emily, but one customer said someone in a red wool hat had been at the doorway. Quietening Rowena's hysterical sobs took priority over further action and at first Isabel did not recognise the little girl, but she kept gasping something, and at last, held in Isabel's arms, the word 'Isabel' was recognised. As they ran, Emily had gasped, 'We'll go to Isabel. Remember, with the biscuits.'

Rowena didn't, for some time, but at last she did, and, later, muttered 'Emily', and 'Nasty man'. By the time the police arrived, summoned because a few of those on the pavement outside the shop had seen Emily being hauled away, the van, with Emily a prisoner inside, was long gone.

Most of the people on the pavement had walked on, regardless, but two conscientious women came into the shop behind Rowena and asked Isabel to dial 999. Rowena was still making a lot of noise, her screams now modified to great gulping sobs.

One of the women had seen the red-hatted individual and the child hurrying along the road. Then suddenly the child had gone and a man was forcing the adult figure – at that distance, the witness was not sure of its sex – into a white camper van which was drawn up with its nearside wheels on the pavement. It was so swift; the second witness, who had not seen Rowena pushed into the shop, but who had also seen the red-hatted person forced into the van, said that she had seemed to turn and face her assailant in the doorway of Gifts Galore, as if to prevent his entering.

The police took more than ten minutes to arrive. It seemed an age, but in that time Isabel persuaded Rowena to calm down and, incredulously, thought she recognised her when her snowsuit hood had been pushed back, but she had to be sure. Remembering how she had taught her sons, at an early age, their names and address, she asked the still sobbing child hers, and heard her say 'Rowena' quite distinctly. The little girl continued to utter shuddering sobs at intervals, but one of the helpful women had been into Isabel's kitchenette behind the shop and poured some warm water, laced with sugar, into a mug, which Rowena was persuaded to sip. That helped to settle her. At this point the customers began to fade away from the shop, leaving only two, one of whom had witnessed Emily's abduction.

'I know who she is and where she lives,' Isabel, chilled with shock, told them. 'I'll shut the shop.'

The woman who had been in the shop when Rowena burst in now said that she must go, but the other one, who had fetched Rowena's drink, turned the sign on the door.

'Done,' she said. 'I'll stay till the police come. There's no one left but me who saw that person in the red hat being taken off.'

'It was Emily,' said Isabel.

'Emily,' Rowena muttered, and gave a huge sigh. 'Fish and chips,' she added.

'Heavens – the poor child's hungry,' said the unknown woman. 'Have you got any biscuits?'

Isabel had, and the good Samaritan went to find them – plain digestives in a screwtop jar. Rowena accepted one and began to nibble.

'I must ring up her grandmother to say she's safe,' Isabel was saying. 'Goodness knows what's happened. Emily looks after her,' she added. 'In Fordswick. However did they get here?'

The police arrived as she finished speaking, and the telephone call to Fordswick was delayed while explanations began.

'You should be out chasing that van, rescuing that girl – Emily, is she?' said the witness to Emily's abduction. 'They'll be miles away by now. Rowena's safe enough.'

She was a brisk middle-aged woman, sturdy and competent. Isabel later discovered that her husband was a research scientist, and she taught languages part-time at Northtown High School.

Whilst to Isabel the identities of those involved, apart from the driver of the van, were clear, and the fact that Emily might have saved Rowena from being abducted with her, the police needed chapter and verse, stage by stage. They did summon more help on their radios, and the van's description was passed on, with a call put out to stop it. Then they asked the witness to describe both Emily and the man.

It seemed to take for ever, and meanwhile Emily was at the mercy of a kidnapper.

Rowena could not be questioned without a responsible adult being present. Isabel said she would fill that role, but she was not a parent or guardian, nor was she part of the social services. Valuable time was lost while the correct procedures about all this were discussed, during which the teacher noticed Rowena wriggling around on Isabel's lap.

'Shall I take her to the toilet or will you?' said the woman, giving Isabel a meaning look.

'I will. We'll just be a minute,' Isabel said, pushing Rowena gently off her lap and leading her through to the rear of the shop.

While there, she washed Rowena's face in cold water and told her everything was all right and she would soon be home with her granny. When they returned, Rowena was eating another biscuit and Isabel said calmly, 'Emily fetched Rowena from school as usual – nursery school, that is, in Fordswick – and this man in the van picked them up to give them a lift home. Rowena seems to have met him before – I'm not sure where – and she didn't like him. She thinks he's called Graham.'

'So Emily knew him.' The police latched on to that, but they had learned very little, so far, about Emily, because they would not listen.

Their reinforcements did, however. A woman inspector had arrived while Isabel and Rowena were in the washroom, and Isabel's new friend, whose name was Valerie, was soon satisfied that serious efforts were in hand to trace the van. Isabel explained that Emily was her goddaughter, who was staying with her at present and working temporarily as a mother's help at Ford House, where Rowena lived with her mother and grandparents. The inspector nodded, taking it all in, and agreeing that by this time the grandparents would be very worried.

'Emily usually took Rowena to the recreation ground on the way back from her nursery school,' said Isabel. 'They may assume she's done that today, but they'd have lunch around one, I'm sure.' It was now half-past; Isabel was quite surprised that it wasn't mid-afternoon; all this seemed to have been going on for hours.

'Why don't I ring up Mrs Watkinson and tell her a watered-down version of what's happened and that I'm bringing Rowena back?' she proposed.

The inspector agreed. 'We'll drive you back,' she said.

'You don't trust me,' said Isabel, incredulous.

'It's not that – but after all this, don't you think she'd be better sitting with you in our car, not strapped into the back of yours in an adult belt on her own?' said the inspector.

Isabel saw the point of this, and the atmosphere lightened.

'May I just ring my partner up and see if she can come in to mind the shop this afternoon?' she said. 'Otherwise, it'll have to stay closed.'

'If she can't, I will – if you'll trust me,' said Valerie. 'I was going to go home to polish the silver. We're having people to dinner tomorrow. The silver can wait, or stay tarnished.'

Joanna was not answering her telephone, so a message was recorded and Valerie was left in charge, her name and address having been noted by the inspector as well as by Isabel. She knew how to work the till as she had previously helped a friend in a shop, and would make a note of sales so that the records could be made up later. Every article was marked with its price. The inspector said they would bring Isabel back once Rowena had been safely returned.

'We'll need statements from you both,' she said.

'Maybe you'll have found Emily by then,' said Isabel. She had written the Watkinsons' telephone number in her diary in case she needed to contact Emily while she was at the shop, and now she dialled it.

The ensuing conversation was quite short.

'Mrs Watkinson, it's Isabel Vernon,' she said. 'You must be wondering why Rowena is late back from school. She's with me.' There was a pause, as she listened while Muriel spoke. Then Isabel continued. 'I'll bring her back as soon as I can. Emily has had a slight accident. Don't worry. We'll be about half an hour. Rowena's hungry and I'm giving her something to eat.' She replaced the telephone and then said, 'Let's pick up some sandwiches or chips to eat on the way. That is, if you don't mind, since it's your car we're using,' she added to Inspector Kent.

Isabel had successfully implied that she was speaking from Elm Lodge, and Muriel, keeping their troubles private, had not betrayed her immediate panic lest Godfrey had waylaid the pair and kidnapped Rowena.

17

Emily knew about the strength of men. She had experienced
its force before Godfrey pushed her into the camper van. As
he seized hold of her, the blow to her head prevented her from
resisting when he twisted her arm behind her and thrust her
inside, banging her head against the window frame so that she
was stunned. Emily had been in fights before, but he had the
initiative and as soon as they were moving, he reached across
and punched her nose, then thumped her head against the
bodywork again. She was yelling and crying, and kicking out
with her feet, but he had one arm across her body, forcing her
against the seat, and she was too badly incapacitated by the
pain he had inflicted to use her own full force in her defence.

He swung the van out of the traffic into a side road where he
stopped and grabbed her shoulders, banging her head forward
against the dash. Blood was pouring from her nose and her
defiant cries had become feeble wails as he banged her head
again, and she lost consciousness.

The silly bitch! She'd ruined it for both of them! Now
what could he do? He should have left her in the street:
cut his losses and run off, but now he was stuck with her,
a witness to his intentions and a victim of his violence.

He'd dump her somewhere miles away and make sure she couldn't talk.

Engaging gear, with Emily slumped against the side of van, he drove on, out of Northtown, into the country to the east, away from this city which he had been familiar with five years ago but which had altered in the intervening period, with revised traffic systems in the centre, and new roads and buildings round the perimeter. He was desperate now. What had begun as a demand for his rights, which he was prepared to sell, had become abduction and extortion. The kid, a pathetic little sniveller like her mother, wouldn't be capable of describing what had happened, and even if old Mrs Watkinson put two and two together and did the sum, she could prove nothing. Emily couldn't be allowed to tell the tale.

Emily was silent, out cold beside him as he turned into a minor road, driving between fields and through several small villages, all of which were quiet. It had begun to rain, a light, fine drizzle. The miles rolled by, Godfrey avoiding major roads where he thought the police could be looking for him. Eventually he came to a wooded area where he saw a track leading off the road, and he drove down it. There, following his usual pattern of improvisation, he stopped the van, pulled Emily from it, and dragged her into a thicket of now mostly leafless bushes. He pulled her hat off and stuffed it in his pocket. Its bright colour was a giveaway. Then he looked at her. Her face was white and she was breathing heavily. She was out for the count, and if he left her here, the cold would get her. On their journey, he'd thought of dumping her in the road and driving over her, but it wouldn't be easy, and it would be murder. Godfrey was not a murderer.

Instead, he left her there to die. Or to recover. After all, she was strong. If she did, he'd be well away before she could describe what had happened. But no one would see her lying in the undergrowth, and a night of recent temperatures should be enough to stop her talking. She deserved no sympathy, upsetting his plans in that stupid way. After all, he hadn't meant to hurt the kid, just to use her as a hostage. There might eventually be a hunt for Emily, but this woodland was more than sixty miles from Northtown. By the time she was found, she would probably be dead, but he would not have killed her and he would have disappeared. Used to living in his van, he'd left nothing of any consequence in his rented room. He need not go back there to run the risk that his vehicle might be recognised by some busybody who had seen him snatch Emily.

Godfrey gave her a few final kicks in the ribs before he left her. Silly cow. She'd spoiled everything. They could both have made a packet, not that he'd have given her much of it, but now he was back where he started from.

Who was she, anyway? Just some girl, not worth worrying about.

By the time Isabel telephoned her, Mrs Watkinson had already rung the police. She had not yet told her husband about Godfrey's visit, but that, and his threats, and Emily and Rowena's failure to return from nursery school, were enough to cause her great alarm. Much earlier, she had called the school itself to ask if Emily had collected Rowena, and learned that they had left normally. Then she rang the mother of one of Rowena's friends to find out if they had walked back together and if she knew of any reason for their being so late. The mother had not seen Emily and Rowena on the way home; her own child had lost a shoe and she left the school premises some time after they did.

The police spoke reassuringly to Mrs Watkinson and said that an officer would be round directly, but the likelihood was that the pair had simply been delayed.

Probably they had. Mrs Watkinson tried to believe that they were in the playground, having lost all sense of time, as she prepared to take her husband his lunch. Since she had been coming to Ford House, Emily had been doing this, but today Mrs Watkinson wheeled it in on the tea trolley as she felt too shaky to carry a tray. Robert Watkinson asked where Rowena was. She often ran in to see him when she came back from school, telling him about her morning's work and showing him her drawing or whatever she had done that day. He looked forward to her bright smile and chatter. None of that had been important when Alice was the child returning from her school, an irony he had begun to notice.

'They're late,' Muriel admitted. 'I expect they're in the playground. Rowena loves the slide. Emily may have forgotten the time.'

'Does she own a watch?' asked Robert. 'She doesn't look as if she's got sixpence to bless herself with.'

'Yes.' Muriel had noticed her wearing one that looked expensive.

'An odd sort of goddaughter for Isabel Vernon to have,' Robert remarked.

'She's a nice girl,' Muriel said. 'She's just not interested in her appearance.'

'She certainly isn't,' said Robert. 'I wonder what she and Douglas Vernon find to talk about.' Robert and he had met when the Vernons first came to the village and Douglas had sampled the church. He still went occasionally.

'Come to that, what do you suppose he and Isabel discuss?' said Muriel. 'Of course, they've got their sons.'

'I hope her shop succeeds,' said Robert.

'So do I. Eat your lunch, dear,' said Muriel, taking the cover off his sausage and mash, the sausage sliced up and easy for him to manage.

As she left the room, using her stick, which she had hooked over her arm while she wheeled the trolley, the telephone rang.

It was Isabel Vernon.

When Muriel saw a police car turn in at the gates of Ford House, she supposed it was in answer to her call reporting Rowena and Emily missing. Robert, meanwhile, had grown querulous when he discovered, as Muriel removed his lunch things, that they were still not home. After Isabel's telephone call, she had explained that Emily had had a slight accident and Isabel Vernon was bringing them back.

'I'm sure it's nothing much. Perhaps she twisted her ankle,' she said. 'Sensible to go to the Vernons.' Except that Elm Lodge was not on their way home from school but perhaps Robert wouldn't think of that.

He did, however, and said so.

'Maybe Isabel met them in the village,' said Muriel. 'Anyway, they're safe.'

'What else would they be?' grunted Robert. Muriel, once so equable and efficient, was getting short-tempered and anxious in old age; he wished she would take things more calmly.

'It's a pity they didn't ring sooner,' said Muriel. He mustn't find out about Godfrey. It would send his blood pressure soaring, and then he might have another stroke. As the police car drew up outside, she hoped he had nodded off and had not seen it. He would think her ridiculous for calling them in when the pair were less than an hour late.

But it was much more than that now. It was getting on for three o'clock and the light would soon begin to fade. Muriel moved away from the window where she had been watching for Isabel, and reached the door before the bell rang.

A uniformed woman police officer stood on the step and said she was Inspector Kent. Behind her, Isabel Vernon was helping Rowena out of the car. Another police officer – a man – was assisting. There was no sign of Emily.

Rowena was clinging to Isabel's hand, but when she saw her grandmother, she let go and ran forwards, to be embraced. Muriel, stooping, managed not to lose her balance as the child burst into tears.

'There, there, dear. It's all right,' said Muriel, holding her. 'Come along in.'

She looked across the child's head at the adults. It seemed clear that everyone was going to enter the house.

'Rowena's had a bit of a fright,' Isabel said. 'We'll explain.'

Poor Mrs Watkinson: she looked exhausted as she led them all into the drawing-room. Isabel had told the inspector about Mr Watkinson's poor health and that Emily had been helping with Rowena and the housework. Now, she stooped down and took Rowena's hand, crouching so that their faces were at the same level.

'We must tell your grandmother what happened,' she said. 'Don't cry, Rowena. Perhaps you and I could go into the kitchen and make some tea, while Inspector Kent talks to granny. You can show me where everything is.'

'Yes. That's good idea,' said Muriel, and to the adults, 'Please try not to disturb my husband. He's in his study, probably dozing. Go along, Rowena. You show Mrs Vernon the way.'

Rowena understood Isabel was connected to Emily – sort

of a mother, Emily had said. She trotted off, dragging Isabel along, while the two officers went with Muriel into the gloomy drawing-room where the fire had burned down. PC Darwin soon attended to it, murmuring that it was nice to see a real fire. Only that morning, Emily had brought in coal and a pile of logs, one of the duties she had undertaken without being asked.

For a few minutes Muriel and the police were at cross purposes, while it was established that though she had reported child and helper missing, they were here because of Rowena's irruption into Gifts Galore, and that Emily had been abducted.

'It may have been pure coincidence that it was Mrs Vernon's shop and not one of the others,' Inspector Kent said. 'Except that Emily had been there with Mrs Vernon, and Rowena has said something about stopping for fish and chips. There's a chip shop not far away and witnesses saw Emily and Rowena hurrying up the pavement together.'

'But what were they doing in Northtown?' Mrs Watkinson asked, bewildered.

'We know only what we have been able to learn from Rowena,' said Inspector Kent. 'She says someone she calls "that man" and also "the nasty man" stopped in the road near the school and said he would give them a lift home, and they got into what she says is a van. He drove off very fast, and wouldn't go the right way.'

'It was Godfrey,' said Muriel at once. 'It must have been Godfrey. He came here this morning, in a white van. One of the kind you sleep in.'

'Godfrey?'

Muriel looked at Inspector Kent's concerned face. She was a woman of about forty, with alert grey eyes and a large, generous mouth; it was a pleasant face, thought Muriel vaguely. She would have to be told.

'Rowena's father. She doesn't know that's who he is. No one does, except us. My husband and I, and our daughter, of course. Alice. Rowena's mother.'

'And where is Alice? Mrs Vernon says she has a job in London.'

'Yes. In an art gallery.'

'She's there now?'

'Yes.'

'Does she know Rowena and Emily were missing?'

'No,' said Muriel. 'I was wondering how soon I must telephone.'

'Well, as Rowena is safe, I think it can wait for a little while longer,' said the Inspector. 'Colin, would you go and see if you can help Mrs Vernon with the tea? Maybe you could bring ours and have yours with her and Rowena. What about Mr Watkinson? Should we have a look at him?'

Muriel shook her head.

'He'll call if he wants anything,' she said. 'He has his tea at half past four. We've got an alarm fixed up so that I can hear him from this room.'

'Right,' said Inspector Kent.

Colin Darwin went off to find the kitchen, and Inspector Kent then told Muriel the story they had pieced together from what Rowena and the two women witnesses had said. During their conversation, Colin Darwin returned with a tray, poured them each some tea, and left. Like a good butler, he told Isabel in the kitchen, where he proceeded to show Rowena some card tricks.

'Most people just melted away,' said the inspector. 'No one took down the number of the van.'

'Nor did I,' said Muriel. She had to tell the inspector why she couldn't do it. She was lying on the floor when he drove off.

As she related what had happened, Inspector Kent made notes, checking that she had got everything straight, including the details about the letter from the non-existent solicitor. Muriel got up and left the room, limping on her stick, to fetch it. She'd never sent Mr Jones the copy; there hadn't been a chance to get it done.

'Is someone looking for Emily?' she asked, eventually, and Inspector Kent said that a general call had gone out for the man and his van, and now they had a name for the driver, though Rowena had kept calling him Graham.

'She got muddled, I expect,' said the inspector. 'They both begin with G, after all.'

'And people saw Emily being dragged into the van. She didn't go willingly?' Muriel wanted to know. 'She could have been his accomplice.'

'I don't think so, Mrs Watkinson,' said Inspector Kent. 'She's Mrs Vernon's goddaughter, vouched for by her. How could she have known this man?'

Muriel had to agree that it was unlikely.

In the kitchen, moving from card tricks into building a card house, Colin managed to ask Rowena when she had seen the man in the van before today.

'Can you remember?' he asked gently.

'Here,' said Rowena, setting a card against another forming the wall of the large bungalow being assembled on the table.

'Here?'

'Mm.' Tongue protruding, concentrating, Rowena placed another card.

'In the house?' Isabel asked this question.

'He had lunch. He ate rudely,' Rowena stated. 'Emily got cross.'

'She knew him, then?'

'S'pose.'

'Did she ask him to lunch?' asked Colin, fearful of pressing her too hard but anxious to discover what she knew.

'He asked. It was rude. He just came and said to Emily, "Where's my lunch?" Or something,' said Rowena.

'So he ate lunch with you and Emily.'

'Mm. Then he got cross and so did Emily and he went away,' said Rowena.

Colin did not ask her any more questions. They went on constructing the house, adding a storey, making it palatial. Then Rowena gave a mammoth yawn.

'There might be something on television,' said Isabel. 'Shall we go and see?' When there were suitable programmes, what a useful child minder it was. She hoped Rowena wasn't too young for what might be shown now.

'Maybe Grandma's got a video,' said Colin, father of two, guessing.

'He had one. That man. In his van. It was the Damnations,' said Rowena.

Colin knew exactly what she meant.

'Did he, indeed?' he said.

He had not heard Muriel Watkinson's revelations about Godfrey Sutton; later, when he and Inspector Kent compared notes, it seemed certain that a kidnap had been intended and that Emily had foiled it.

Meanwhile, there was no sign of her.

Robert Watkinson wanted his tea and a visit to the lavatory just as Muriel and Inspector Kent had reached the end of their discussion.

'Emily was so good with him,' sighed Muriel. 'She's only been working here for a week, yet I've already come to rely on her.'

'I'll help him,' said Isabel, coming in with Rowena. 'Rowena's tired. Perhaps she could watch telly or read a story with her granny. She'd like that. Wouldn't you, Rowena?'

Rowena was sucking her finger again. She nodded.

'He'll wonder why you're here,' Muriel warned Isabel. Robert would not have expected Isabel to linger, after returning Rowena.

'I'll tell him,' said Inspector Kent 'Someone must. I'll keep it to the minimum.'

Muriel subsided on the sofa, while Colin looked in a box containing several video tapes and offered Rowena a choice. She picked her favourite, Postman Pat.

'You can't go wrong with him,' said Colin cheerfully, and, making sure they were both comfortable, sitting on the sofa with Mrs Watkinson's leg resting on a stool, the fire well made up and safe, he left them to it, going to radio headquarters to see if there was any news of Emily.

There was none.

18

Alice knew nothing about the day's events.

She would have to be told without further delay. There were witnesses to Emily's abduction and, with the hunt on to find her, the media might hear of it, though the names of those concerned would not be officially released. Alice, however, need not be alarmed, for Rowena was safe, and the father was hardly likely to try to snatch her again. He was on the run, with his captive.

After Mr Watkinson had been given a version of events which left out all reference to Godfrey Sutton, since that was his wife's wish, and had been persuaded that Rowena and her grandmother were best left watching television, Isabel and Colin Darwin made sure the remote control for the old man's set was by his side and left him to hop channels. The Watkinsons were well equipped with television sets; Alice had one in her bedroom, Colin had discovered, going on a quick surreptitious reconnaissance of the house; knowledge of its layout might be useful.

Anticipating that, with such frail employers, an emergency was possible, Isabel had asked Emily if she knew how to get hold of Rowena's mother while she was at work. As a result, the gallery telephone number was pinned up on the fridge.

'The proper course would be for a local officer to go to her place of work and tell her,' said Inspector Kent. Seeing Isabel's expression, she added, 'It would be handled tactfully.'

'Isn't that using a hammer to crack a nut? Couldn't we just telephone her? I realise she's got to know – she can't just come back on the train as usual and find out,' said Isabel. Then she remembered. 'Oh – she was going to meet a friend tonight. Mary. They were going to the cinema. Emily was to stay late and put Rowena to bed.'

'Tough. She's going to have to stand Mary up,' said Inspector Kent.

'I'll ring her,' Isabel decided. Short of using force, they couldn't prevent her. 'You can talk to her then, if that's what you want. It will be less of a shock if I tell her. If she hears it's the police she may think something dreadful's happened.'

But it had. Emily, the mysterious girl who was not, after all, her goddaughter, had been abducted in the street and had disappeared, and it was only thanks to her that Rowena had escaped kidnap.

'Right,' said Inspector Kent. 'That's a good way of doing it, and after that we'd better get you back to your shop.'

Isabel had forgotten all about Valerie, her temporary relief. Outwardly calm and functioning, inside she was frantic with anxiety about Emily. However, Inspector Kent was right; after speaking to Alice, she must get back to Gifts Galore.

Alice was assured that Rowena was unharmed, but she said she would come home at once, catching the first possible train. She asked about her parents, and was told that all was calm. At this stage, there was no need for her to know that Godfrey had assaulted her mother earlier, but when she returned, she would have to be told. Mrs Watkinson had said she did not need to see a doctor, and perhaps, medically, it was unnecessary, but one was called. The CID were dealing with this case now: they would find evidence that there was a bruise on her face, and there might be others on her body. These injuries, if witnessed, recorded, and preferably photographed, would support the prosecution case when Godfrey Sutton was arrested.

'I should stay here till Alice gets back,' Isabel had said.

'Colin will stay until the CID get here. He's made friends with Rowena.'

'The CID?'

'Yes. Detectives,' said Inspector Kent. 'It's departmental.'

Isabel knew about departments. Douglas was affected by them daily.

'Oh – right,' she said. 'Well, I'll go back, but I'll shut the shop. When Emily's found, I must be available. I'll try my partner's number once again.'

'Ring from here,' suggested Inspector Kent. 'The Watkinsons aren't going to mind a few calls at their expense.'

Isabel did so, and Joanna answered. The bare facts were soon related, and Joanna said she would go straight to the shop to relieve Valerie and meet Isabel there. Cutting the line, Isabel meditated for a moment. Then she did something almost without precedent. She telephoned Douglas in his office, and told him most of what had happened.

'Emily's still missing,' she declared.

*   *   *

That wretched girl, was Douglas's first reaction, as he replaced the receiver. She'd been nothing but trouble since she arrived and now she had landed herself in personal danger.

'It'll be that damned man she's been going out with,' he had said. 'Mark my words, he's at the bottom of all this. Why else would he want to take her out unless he had her lined up as an accomplice?'

'We don't know that, Douglas,' she responded. He might be right, however. It was a dreadful thought.

'Hm. Well, it's all very regrettable,' he answered.

'Douglas, Emily is in great danger. That man has abducted her. God knows where she is or what will happen to her.'

'Well, we can't do anything. It's in the hands of the police, you say. Now it's up to them,' he had replied.

But when their conversation ended, he remembered Alice. Isabel had said that she was on her way home. She had looked so wan this morning and now she had to deal with those decrepit parents, one of whom had been assaulted, though, it seemed, not injured, and a daughter who had briefly been a kidnap victim. He forgot the treacherous kiss that he had witnessed; now she was in distress, and who better to come forward as a saviour than himself?

He had every excuse for leaving the office early. He told his section head that his wife's goddaughter, temporarily on a visit, had been abducted and was missing. He felt it was his duty to get home as soon as possible, and the section head agreed. Hurrying to Alice's side, it did not occur to Douglas that though the reason he had given for leaving early was a valid one, Isabel might be in need of some support. Why else had she rung him up? He never asked himself that question.

Soon he, too, was heading for the station, hoping to catch the same train as Alice.

He was just in time. The train was about to pull away from the platform as he reached it. He jumped aboard as the doors were about to close, and walked along it, seeking her. He found her in the third carriage, sitting by the window, staring out unseeingly. Douglas took the empty facing seat – neither was accustomed to finding plenty of room on their homeward journey – and stretched out a hand, laying it on her black-covered knee.

'Alice, my dear,' he said. 'I've heard the news. I came at once to see what I can do to help. Poor little mite. At least she's quite unharmed, I'm told.'

Alice had felt the light touch on her knee. Slowly, she turned her head to face him. It took her a few seconds to come back to earth and recognise him.

'Emily's not,' she said. 'He's got her.'

'Well – yes,' Douglas admitted. 'But she's not a little girl,' he pointed out. 'She's well built and strong.'

'You don't know Godfrey,' was Alice's reply.

'Godfrey?'

'The man who's got her. He's Rowena's father,' Alice said.

'Oh – is that so? Oh dear!' This part of the story had not been relayed to Douglas.

'Emily saved her,' said Alice. 'Didn't you know that?'

Perhaps Isabel had mentioned it.

'I believe she did,' he acknowledged.

'Oh – I hope she's all right,' Alice said. She turned to face him, her eyes brimming with tears. Douglas had an urge, which he suppressed as insane, to remove her enormous hat, stroke her hair, and murmur soothing words. 'Rowena and my parents think the world of her,' she added. And behind Emily's back,

Alice had been planning to replace her with a foreign au pair who might not be such a success.

'Yes – well, I'm glad,' Douglas said.

'How much do you know about what happened?' Alice asked him, and he had to reply, very little; the two had been abducted from Fordswick on their way back from Rowena's nursery school, and somehow Emily had managed to rescue Rowena but not herself.

'They stopped in Northtown, for fish and chips, or something. They only know what Rowena has been able to tell them,' Alice said. 'And there were some witnesses who saw him force Emily into his van.'

'They'll trace the van,' Douglas said, soothingly. 'The police will be looking for it everywhere.'

'If they find it, it may be too late,' said Alice.

'He won't hurt her,' said Douglas. 'She's a tough girl. She's been living rough for weeks. She can take care of herself.' It might be wise not to mention the assault on Mrs Watkinson; Alice might not have been told about that yet. Was the man who attacked her really the child's father?

'Better than most, I'm sure,' Alice was agreeing. 'But he won't want her around to give evidence against him.'

'Oh – she'll be all right,' Douglas repeated. 'He'll probably drop her off somewhere and try to save himself.'

'I hope you're right,' Alice said.

He did not question her too closely, telling himself that it would be wise not to let her dwell on what could have happened to Rowena, but he knew so little about the affray – for that was what it had been: no doubt about it – and felt at a disadvantage.

'Perhaps he just wanted to get acquainted with Rowena. Spend some time with her. Get to know her. If he is, as you say, her father,' he suggested, trying to strike a positive note.

'He is,' she assured him. 'Unfortunately.'

'Yes – well, that's as may be,' said Douglas. 'And please don't misunderstand me. I don't approve of his methods. There are legal ways of going about these things.'

'You can't believe you'd approve of him seeing her, by some arrangement,' she said.

Douglas thought that a father was entitled to a share in his child, if he acknowledged her as his and took some responsibility for her. He was about to express this view in a tactful manner when a youth pushing a refreshment trolley came into the carriage.

'Ah – tea,' said Douglas. 'That would be welcome. Don't you agree?'

Alice did. She allowed him to buy her a polystyrene cup full of a fluid purporting to be tea. After drinking his, he took out his mobile phone, which he almost never used, and rang Elm Lodge to get an up-to-date account of events from Isabel, but there was no reply. Where could she be? Surely she hadn't gone back to the shop? She was becoming far too unaccountable, what with that and golf at weekends and on summer evenings. It was all most unsatisfactory.

Facing him, her eyes closed, was a different sort of woman; one who had fallen from grace, it was true, but who was more sinned against than sinning. He eyed Alice approvingly, unaware that she had closed her eyes to protect herself from his conversation.

Only then did she remember Paul, and their arrangement to meet. She couldn't get hold of him now to say she would not be coming. She could not ask Douglas if she might borrow his mobile phone as she did not know his bookshop telephone number; they had never communicated except in the café. Well, he'd soon realise, when she didn't turn up. There was nothing she could do about it now. Rowena's ordeal and Emily's present predicament were of far more importance. After a while, she opened her eyes, and felt mild comfort in seeing Douglas, reliably solid, sitting there. He met her gaze, and saw her smile faintly.

'That's better,' he said, reassuringly. 'The police will be doing their best to find Emily, and your daughter is safe. That's the main thing.'

It was. He was right. As long as Godfrey could be stopped from ever entering their lives again.

Emily was very cold.

She hurt. Her legs hurt, and her side, and her head, but that was nothing new. Why had she been hit this time? What had she done? But she didn't have to have done something wrong. Just being alive was her offence, and peace came only when the woman went away, though then she was locked up. Was she shut in a cupboard again? Or was she in the kitchen, flung against the wall after being beaten?

Lying in the dark, so cold and full of aches, she felt chilled right through but there was silence all around her. No one else was there. She drew up her legs, wincing, because every part of her seemed bruised, and felt brambles catch against her clothing. Then she remembered that she had got away – had fled that life and had been living in the woods. She wasn't up a tree now, nor in a tent, but she was in the open air. Feeling safe, she lost consciousness again.

* * *

In Fordswick, Mrs Watkinson had been examined by the doctor and her bruises had been noted. Against her inclinations, but persuaded because the more evidence produced to convict Godfrey, the longer he would be locked up, she allowed the lesions to be photographed. She did not confess to hitting him with her stick. Her injuries were not serious, but she was shaken and must take things quietly for the next few days. The district nurse would call in to help both her and Mr Watkinson. Isabel had driven Valerie home from Gifts Galore, and then returned herself, but with no news about Emily, she was restless, and she was worried about the Watkinsons. She left a message for Douglas, and went back to Ford House. Although there was a police officer in the house, she could be useful there until Alice returned. As she drove up the road, Isabel saw two uniformed officers emerging from one house and entering the gateway of its neighbour. She had been told that enquiries were proceeding in the village; someone might have seen the van, even seen Emily and Rowena being picked up. The police wouldn't have much luck, she thought, except possibly among the parents of children who were pupils with Rowena at the nursery school.

That factor had been taken into account, she discovered, when Colin Darwin opened the front door at Ford House and let her in. The staff and all the parents were being questioned. Mrs Watkinson had described the wanted man, but there was no photograph, unless Alice had one.

'Among her souvenirs,' said Colin, telling Isabel this.

'Poor thing – she must have had an awful time,' said Isabel.

'People do, unfortunately,' Colin said. 'Rowena seems all right. She's playing snap with my colleague in the kitchen. Her mum should be home soon.'

'She's young enough not to realise how much danger she was in,' said Isabel. 'What if Emily hadn't saved her?'

'Who knows?' said Colin. 'He'd probably have demanded a ransom, and might have given her up if he was paid, but would the Watkinsons have told us what was going on? Might they have tried to handle it on their own?'

Because their own solicitor was already involved, he might have learned what had happened and persuaded them to tell the police. It was unlikely that the child's father would have done her any physical harm, but he might have tried to take her out of the country. Suppose he had taken a shine to her and decided he would hang on to her? Isabel and Darwin debated this, sitting by the fire in the drawing-room. Mrs Watkinson was lying down in her bedroom, and the old man was watching television. It was nearly time for the evening news.

'I'm glad you're here,' Colin told her. 'You know Alice. She'll need a friendly face, when she realises what's nearly happened.'

'I'm glad not to be alone,' said Isabel. 'I'm worried sick about Emily.'

She almost told him her suspicions about Emily's identity, but decided this was not the time. There must be a reason for her impersonation, and perhaps it was a good one. Isabel, in a week, had grown as fond of the gauche, ungainly girl as if she really were Ginnie's daughter.

Doris Pugh had been on early shift at the supermarket. She was at home when the police knocked at her door, but she could tell them nothing about the stranger in the camper van who had given a lift to Rowena and the nanny, as Emily was being rather grandly described. However, she remembered Joe mentioning such a van being parked by the recreation ground for several nights. The enquiring police officer was invited in, and Joe was summoned from his shed where he was working on a stripped-down motor mower. As a sideline, he overhauled them. He also bought old ones at sales when they were going cheap, did them up and sold them on at a profit.

He remembered the van, could testify as to which nights and mornings it had been parked near the toilet block which was his charge, and could provide its make and registration number. He was part of a Neighbourhood Watch scheme in the village, and made a habit of listing the details of any vehicles left overnight in the parking area, and those of any unfamiliar cars that aroused his curiosity. He had not been able to observe the camper van's driver, who had been either absent or invisible behind steamed-up windows and flimsy curtains when Joe had seen the vehicle. He had noticed it parked elsewhere in the village subsequently, and on the previous Friday, a week ago, it, or its twin – he couldn't see the number – had been drawn up some hundred yards beyond the gates of Ford House, pointing away from the village centre, too far for him to recognise the individual sitting inside. This was significant information; it linked the van with a possible interest in Ford House. The interviewing constable noted it all down; much later, it was collated with Mrs Watkinson's statement that Emily had come for her original interview that day. Possibly she had known the driver, and, if so, she and Rowena had not been abducted by a total stranger, but had willingly got into his van.

Now, however, the police could provide an accurate description of the vehicle, which should help locate it.

In Fordswick, other officers learned that a stranger answering the description of the wanted man had eaten at The Stick and

Monkey. He hadn't had much to say but he'd had quite a lot to drink. All this was corroborative; now they knew who they were looking for, had a description of both him and his vehicle, but no sightings since he had forced Emily into his van.

The six o'clock news carried a brief item. A woman had been abducted from a shopping centre in Northtown earlier that afternoon and a man driving a white camper van was being sought in connection with her disappearance. A description of the wanted man followed.

Godfrey, now near Leicester, heard it on the van's radio and wondered why he hadn't let Emily go. After all, without the kid, she was no use, and, without the kid, there was no case against him, just her word. He could have disappeared: no harm done, even if he'd gained nothing, and he could have tried to bleed the Watkinsons another time.

She'd angered him by her defiance. That was why he'd done it. She'd enraged him. She had to learn her lesson.

Well, she wouldn't testify against him now.

Emily, lying in the darkness, heard strange cries and moans. Someone was in dreadful trouble: why did no one help them? Surely a nurse could hear the patient's groaning? And why was the ward so dark and cold? And so quiet? Usually there were footsteps going past, trolleys clanging, and the television. Had someone taken all the blankets from them? Were the moans coming from the girl in the next bed, the one who had lost her baby? She'd been told she could have another, no trouble at all; it had just been bad luck.

'Maybe it wasn't meant to be,' she'd said to Emily. Both of them were grieving. 'Maybe there was something wrong with it.'

Emily had never thought that anything was wrong with hers. It had died because she'd had that awful pain, and she'd had surgery because something was the matter with her insides. It didn't seem too likely that she would ever have another.

The other girl had a visitor: a man she had been going to marry, the father of her lost baby. She told Emily she wasn't going to marry him now. The baby had been a last throw to keep them together and she saw now that it wouldn't do. She told Emily all about herself: her childhood, her parents parting and her mother's later marriage to a Spaniard, then her sudden death. One of her brothers worked in Madrid; the other was in South America. When she recovered, she was going to visit each of them in turn. There had been a godmother whom she hadn't seen since she was tiny, though she used to write regularly and send presents.

As they both recovered, she told Emily a lot about her family, and the godmother, and where they had lived. Emily liked the stories about their safe family life. Even in Spain, it had been secure. After the other girl left, she had pretended it was her life, not the one she had endured until she had run away.

Poor girl, thought Emily, lying there in the dark, cold and aching. If she went on crying like this, and groaning, unattended by the nurses, she would never get to South America.

Emily did not realise that the moans she was hearing were her own.

After a while, they stopped.

19

As soon as its doors were open, Alice was off the train and running along the platform. Douglas, slower, panted after her, and pursued her to her car, calling to her.

'Wait – Alice!' he gasped. 'Wait, please! Shall I drive you home?'

Flustered by his delaying interruption, she turned round in annoyance.

'Thanks. I'm fine,' she said, wrestling with her key in the dark. It was always awkward when she could not see what she was doing, and now Douglas shone a tiny torch, attached to his key ring, on her car door. His own car had a remote control lock which he simply pressed as he approached. 'Thanks,' she said again, getting in and starting the engine, which fired the second time. She revved it, and roared off, scattering gravel from the parking lot. All Douglas could do was follow, catching her up when she had to stop at a junction for some passing traffic. He kept behind her, right to the gates of Ford House, obliged to peel off then. Isabel would bring him up to date with what was happening and he could go round later, offering his services in case of need.

Isabel, though, was not at home. There were no signs of

dinner preparations, but then, in fairness to her, he was earlier than usual. He found her note, and checked the answerphone, but there were no messages. Even looking at his docile, gently swimming fish, checking the temperature in the tank and casting in some food, did not appease him. He wanted plaudits for his mercy mission, though all he had achieved so far was to provide Alice with a cup of railway tea, his comments and some sympathy, which he had felt was not wholly appreciated. Of course, she did not know that he had come home early solely on her account. And now Isabel was up at Ford House, on the scene. After only a few moments' deliberation, Douglas looked up the Watkinsons' telephone number and dialled it.

A male voice answered.

Douglas gave his name. 'I believe my wife is there,' he said. 'Who's that speaking?'

'Police Constable Darwin, from Northtown Central,' Colin answered. 'You're aware of events, I take it? She telephoned you, I believe.'

'Yes, yes,' said Douglas testily. 'I'd like a word with her. I'm at my own house,' he added. 'Rowena's mother has probably mentioned that we travelled back together.'

She hadn't. Alice had entered the house less than half an hour earlier, intent on rushing straight to Rowena, but Isabel had intercepted her, calming her, preventing her from upsetting Rowena and Muriel Watkinson. An emotional display would not help anyone; Rowena had not realised the gravity of the situation or that no one knew where Emily was, though she had asked. Luckily she was young enough to be distracted when no proper answer was forthcoming.

Isabel, and a woman police officer who was also in Ford House, were still filling Alice in with the details of the afternoon's incident when Douglas telephoned.

'Rowena's mother is being told the full story at this moment,' Colin told him. 'Mrs Vernon is explaining her involvement.'

'Her involvement?' He was unaware that she was connected with events, except as far as Emily was concerned.

Colin caught on quickly.

'I don't want to interrupt them at the moment,' he stated. 'I'll ask her to telephone you when she's free.'

When she's free, indeed! Douglas was seething. He was the one who should be consoling Alice, plying her with brandy, generally in control.

'She's been wonderful,' Colin was enthusing. 'So good with Mrs Watkinson and Rowena.'

Oh, has she, thought Douglas. He took a deep breath, trying to control his sense of outrage. 'Please ask her to telephone, as you suggest,' he said in icy tones, and replaced the receiver.

For several minutes he paced the floor, fuming with frustration, while Colin Darwin mentally noted that Douglas Vernon had not enquired whether Emily had been found. Douglas's wrath was interrupted by a ring at the front door. A police officer stood outside; he wanted to know if Douglas had seen a white camper van parked anywhere in the village during the past week, and a man thought to be its driver, described as around forty, with greying hair, a moustache and sideburns, somewhat corpulent, and with dark brown eyes.

Douglas hadn't, but he interposed with questions of his own. Was this enquiry linked to the disappearance of his wife's goddaughter, one Emily Frost, aged twenty-three? She had spent several evenings in the company of an unknown man who had collected her with a vehicle not observed by Douglas, who assumed she had known the man previously.

The police officer, on a procedural enquiry, had not linked this house with the missing woman. He paid some attention to what Douglas was saying, and, admitted to his study, offered a chair, and even shown the fish, wrote down the information he was given.

Slowly, evidence about the stranger in the village was accumulating. Several people had seen a white camper van, either in the car park by the recreation ground or elsewhere. As the evening drew on, those who worked outside Fordswick were returning home, and among them a man was found who, while walking his dog, had seen the van stop outside Elm Lodge late on Sunday night. Someone had got out and it had moved off immediately. The passenger had gone into Elm Lodge. This witness was very certain; he walked that way each evening at about half-past ten, and he might meet other dog walkers, or see passing cars, but a camper van unloading someone at that hour was unprecedented. Some of those questioned knew very little about their neighbours and could not say who lived where, but this man knew the Vernons were the occupiers of Elm Lodge; as he walked past daily, night and morning, he had observed Douglas's achievements in the garden. He had seen the signs of tasks in progress: pergolas being erected; the installation of the pond; the presence of a hired cement-mixer parked neatly beside the fence; the piles of patio stones. In winter, with the hedges bare, the results of Douglas's labours were visible from the road; in summer, climbing plants and vegetation blurred the view.

'He's a busy man, that Mr Vernon,' the witness volunteered. He'd never spoken to him, but he knew him by sight. 'Goes to London every day,' the man said. 'Something in the City, isn't he?'

His evidence was duly noted, and that of several women

whose children were pupils at the nursery school and who had seen Emily and Rowena get into a white camper van that morning. Some had seen a stranger answering the description of the wanted man, and one who was a child minder had noticed Emily sitting on the bench beside him in the recreation ground. After some thought, she remembered when it was: the previous Thursday. She had seen neither of them before, but the next week, Emily was in charge of Rowena.

'Did they look like old friends?' she was asked, and it was difficult to answer as she had not paid them much attention.

'They weren't sitting up close,' she volunteered. 'There was plenty of bench space between them.'

This did not, however, rule out the possibility that they were in collusion, that Emily had been a stool pigeon to decoy the child away; the officer interviewing the woman felt the possibility warranted the information being passed on at once to his headquarters, where it reached Detective Inspector Cox, now investigating the case under the direction of Detective Superintendent Golding. It was possible, some considered, that she was involved. Perhaps she had thought better of her collusion, freed the child, and reaped the consequences.

None of the police officers knew the true circumstances which had brought Emily to Fordswick. No one, yet, had asked Isabel about her.

Eventually Alice had absorbed the story. Isabel stayed on at Ford House while Rowena was put to bed, finding in the fridge Emily's preparations for the evening meal which, she was touched to find, seemed to be fish pie, not unlike the one she had made a few nights earlier. Alice, returning to the kitchen, explained that they had a weekly order from a travelling fish van which visited the village, and she did a major shop on Saturdays. She was much calmer now. Her mother had been persuaded to go to bed, and her father accepted the explanation that it was the shock which had made her rather tired and necessitated the visit from the doctor. Nothing was mentioned about Godfrey's assault.

'He'll discover eventually,' warned Isabel.

'Let's keep it from him while we can,' said Alice wearily.

Was it wise to have so many secrets? Isabel still had a few herself.

'You poor thing. This is dreadful for you,' she said.

'Things did seem too good to be true,' Alice admitted, at last sparing a fleeting thought for Paul, and for the gallery. Both were now past history. 'I'd begun to look for an au pair girl,' she confessed. 'I didn't think Emily would last long, whatever happens in court when her case is heard.'

'Will she be found in time to appear?' wondered Isabel aloud. Would she be found at all?

'I didn't say anything to the police about that,' said Alice. 'And of course my parents don't know about it.'

More secrets.

'I suppose the police will have to be told, if she doesn't come back soon,' said Isabel. 'I needn't do anything about the court yet.'

'She may just walk in. Or telephone from somewhere,' Alice said. 'If she gets away from him, that is.'

'Do you think she will?'

'She'll try, won't she? He'll have to stop eventually, even if it's only for petrol. She'll get a chance, surely?' said Alice. 'He's not going to kill her, is he?'

Isabel looked at her.

'You tell me,' she said. 'You're the one who knows him best, or did. Why did he take her, when Rowena got away? There was no point.'

'Revenge,' said Alice. 'She'd got the better of him, rescuing Rowena. He wouldn't like being the loser. And I still don't know how he found out about Rowena.'

'Where's he been all this time?' she asked.

'I've no idea. I don't suppose Mother enquired,' said Alice, with a wry smile. 'He just vanished, years ago. I didn't realise I was pregnant until later.'

'It must have been awful for you. Quite frightful.'

Alice looked at her in amazement.

'It was, but no one's ever realised that before,' she said.

'Surely your parents did?'

'I doubt it. They were simply shocked,' she answered. 'And angry. Disapproving. I was in disgrace – I still am, though they backed me in the end, and when Rowena arrived, Mother fell for her. She really loves her.'

You think she loves her more than you, thought Isabel. Well, perhaps she does.

'That's wonderful for your mother,' she said. 'It must have renewed her. Given her a fresh interest.'

'Oh yes – and she has been such a help,' said Alice. 'I couldn't have managed without her – without them both.'

But you've only just gone back to work, thought Isabel. What sort of life have you had, these past four years and more? And of course you'd have managed on your own, if you'd had to: you'd have surprised yourself.

'I expect you've got friendly with some of the mums in the village,' she suggested.

'It's difficult,' said Alice. 'Not because I'm not married – it's because I'm different. Living with my parents, in a big house. All that.'

Isabel wondered how often Rowena had friends round to play, or went to other houses. That might increase now that she went to nursery school, but no children had come round during Emily's brief spell of work at Ford House.

Alice had opened a bottle of wine. At least the house wasn't teetotal, Isabel had reflected. They were sitting with their glasses by the fire when Colin Darwin opened the door and showed Douglas in.

'Isabel, aren't you coming home?' he demanded, and then, to Alice, 'Ah! How's the little girl?' His voice, Isabel noticed, altered as he spoke to her.

'She's fine, thank you,' said Alice. 'Would you like some wine?'

He'll refuse, thought Isabel. He's really come to take me home to cook dinner. And she hadn't given it a thought.

But she was wrong. Douglas, simpering – there was no other word for it – was accepting. Isabel could almost see his brain cells calculating the alcohol level, were he to be breathalysed on the way home. One, even two glasses of Alice's rather good wine would be acceptable and would keep him below the limit. She wondered who bought the wine. Did Alice get it on her weekly supermarket trips? Or was it chosen by her father, just as Douglas patronised a wine club and ordered various bottles by the case?

'It was nice of you to speak to me on the train.' Alice knew she had been brusque, even rude, at the station, but now, mellowed by the wine, with her child asleep upstairs, she made amends. 'That tea helped. I knew Rowena was safe but I'd had such an awful shock.'

'Of course you had,' said Douglas kindly.

Isabel had already realised that he had come home early, but now she learned that he had travelled back with Alice. She listened, waiting for fresh revelations.

'If you hadn't been there,' Alice was saying carefully, 'I'd have been in a bad way, on the journey. Waiting to find out if she was really safe. But you were on the train.' She hadn't been so grateful at the time, regarding him with some impatience, but with hindsight she knew that his mere presence, equipped with his mobile telephone which he would have let her use if she had been unable to wait for further news, had been calming, and he had made sure her car would start. If it hadn't, he would not only have driven her home but would probably have made arrangements for the rescue of her car. Reflecting on all this, she beamed at him.

It was time to interrupt this idyll.

'I expect you want your dinner, Douglas,' Isabel said abruptly. 'I'll be off.' She turned to Alice, who, after all, didn't know Douglas as well as she did, and who was a damsel in distress. 'You're all right now. Rowena won't register how serious it could have been. I'll ring you in the morning and I'll pop up if you need any help.' It was her weekend for the shop but Joanna had offered to stand in for her. 'If you write your shopping list, I'll do that, if you want to stay at home,' she promised.

'May I let you know in the morning?' Alice said. 'When I see how things are here?'

'Of course,' said Isabel.

'Thank you so much for everything,' said Alice. 'I do hope there'll soon be news of Emily.'

'So do I,' said Isabel. 'She's the one who needs the thanks.' She got up to go, wondering how long Douglas would linger, eyeing Alice up, for that was what he was engaged in doing: no doubt about it.

She felt no pang of jealousy, merely utter weariness; the hypocrite, so swift to condemn Alice and now casting himself in the role of her cavalier. Fat chance that he would volunteer to do the shopping for Ford House. Driving the short distance home, she wondered if Emily had somehow got herself back to Elm Lodge. What if she were in the house, preparing dinner?

She indulged the fantasy until she let herself into the silent house, but fantasy was what it was. Where was she? Who was she? Before she left Ford House, Colin Darwin had implied that Emily might have been in league with Godfrey in a plot to kidnap Rowena. Isabel had said that it was out of the question. She had already emphasised that Emily had arrived in Fordswick only the week before, but if the police continued to develop that theory, they might look for evidence to confirm it. Weren't they often desperate to make arrests and apportion blame without always seeking out the facts?

Instead of condemning Emily, they should be looking for her.

Douglas returned half an hour after Isabel reached home. He had brought in coal and logs, talked to the old man, and promised to play chess with him.

'Oh, what a good idea!' said Isabel, but she was not deceived. He'd do it to curry favour with Alice.

Dishing up the hastily assembled meal, she contented herself by saying that she hoped he would manage to find time.

'I shall make the time,' said Douglas piously. 'It will be simple while the weather's bad, keeping me from the garden.'

Had he always been so sanctimonious? Isabel studied him across the table: his long, lean face with the thin lips, his gaze now bent towards his plate as he expertly twirled spaghetti round his fork. She could imagine him in a homespun cassock and sandalled feet, evangelising like some latter-day Saint Francis, yet he seldom went to church: not that church attendance was necessarily consistent with sanctity. When did I become so critical, she asked herself: was it as recently as Emily's arrival, seeing him through her eyes? It was disloyal, but perhaps it was high time, she thought, and anyway, how far should loyalty extend?

'I'm sure they'll be grateful,' she said shortly. 'It's going to be difficult for them now, without Emily. Muriel Watkinson is very lame, and the old man needs a lot of attention.'

'That foolish girl,' said Douglas, loading his fork again. 'Getting mixed up with someone so undesirable.'

'Which do you mean?' asked Isabel smoothly. 'Alice or Emily?'

'I meant Emily, of course. But Alice was no wiser, clearly.'

'We haven't met him, so we don't really know what he's like,' said Isabel. 'Except that he's violent. He must have got something, or why did he succeed with Alice?' Emily's was a different case: he must have turned up here, seen that she could be of use to him, and was vulnerable. 'And anyway, we're guessing that he's the man Emily was meeting,' she added. If only she'd been less scrupulous about Emily's right to privacy and had questioned her about her alleged friend. She should have shown more interest, not that it would have made much difference, for how could anyone except Alice and her parents have known who he really was? Though someone in the village might have recognised him from the past.

Douglas was, for once, keen to listen to her, bidding her tell him all she knew about the day's events. She described Rowena's propulsion into Gifts Galore, and how her anguished howls diverted attention from Emily's failure to follow her through the door.

'She shouldn't have accepted a lift from him,' he said.

'Douglas, we know that now, and so does she, poor girl,' said Isabel. 'But assuming he was this friend she mentioned, she had no reason not to. He's the villain, not Emily.'

There was no need to tell Douglas what Rowena had said about the man coming to Ford House, nor about the letter Alice had received demanding access. If he were to carry out his promise to play chess with Mr Watkinson, he might reveal these details, which Muriel had wanted to conceal from her husband.

'It could have been a long-term project,' said Douglas. 'If he knew Emily at the site, and found out about her connection with you, he could have planned to use her, and followed her here. The police think so. That constable mentioned it before I left. He'd heard it from his headquarters.'

'I know,' said Isabel. 'But it's a crazy idea. He could hardly have arranged for her to be arrested.'

'He might have tried to engineer it,' Douglas said.

Silence fell, while Isabel could almost hear the cogs in Douglas's brain interconnecting as he tried to construct a plot whereby Emily was set up to be arrested and would logically arrive at Elm Lodge, giving Godfrey the opening he sought. If he'd had this scheme in mind all along, it would have been far simpler to persuade Emily to leave the site voluntarily before being evicted. They could still have come to Fordswick and she could still have staked her claim to Isabel.

Such a scheme was sheer illusion. What was true was that Emily was an imposter. How had this pretender learned so much about the real Emily, and known Isabel's address? And where was she now? Imprisoned somewhere, terrified? Or dead?

20

Emily had been dreaming that she was in a warm bed, in a warm house, where no one planned to harm her. She had two brothers, Charles and Anthony, who were both older than she was, and were abroad. She had never met them, but that was odd, as they were her brothers. The figure of her mother was dim: first it was a presence, faintly scented, then a slender woman with fair curling hair, wearing summer clothes – a top and cotton skirt in indeterminate colours. She sang hymns and took her to Sunday School, and let Emily help her when she was cooking. That image faded, to be replaced by that of a tall, dark woman, smartly dressed. This was not her mother, yet in a way she was: Emily, struggling, tried to remember her name. Izzy-something, it was, or Bella, but neither was quite right and she could get no further. Then, suddenly, she saw another, sharper figure: someone very thin, with brown hair drawn back from her pale, lined forehead and pushed into an elastic band. Emily was crying, and the woman was coming, not to comfort her but to punish her. This was not her mother. Her mother had gone away and there was no one to protect her. That was why she was living in her father's house, and this woman was his wife, who hated her. At this point, unable to bear the memory of what followed, she lost consciousness again, but not for long, and this time she fought against her growing awareness, because with it came recognition that she was icy cold, soaking wet, and ached all over. If she could lapse back into her earlier dream, comfort would return. She tried to feel the warmth again, the softness of a bed. The well-dressed, dark woman whose name she could not properly remember was part of that; there was a kitchen, fish pie, a shop. And a little girl.

Rowena: that was her name; she remembered it quite clearly, and had an instant's flashback to some struggle and of her own hand pushing the child towards a doorway, but after that, everything was blank.

She had to save the child. The child was in great danger, and somehow in her mind the child became fused with herself in peril as a little girl. Rowena's safety was threatened; she must be rescued. Emily lifted her head, and her almost hairless skull brushed against the tangled branches which had shielded her from the worst of the rain which had fallen during the long night. Now dawn was breaking, and the intense darkness round her paled. As she tried to sit up, an excruciating pain spread across her side and chest, so that she could scarcely breathe. She fell back again, and it was some minutes before she was able to make another effort, this time, despite the agony that movement caused her, managing to roll over and, after a further pause, edge forward on her stomach. It was a wormlike progress as she inched slowly along, and she did not know where she was going, only that Rowena was in terrible danger. Stopping frequently, she progressed a few yards towards the track before, once again, she became unconscious.

It was Saturday morning. Dry now, though a grey, raw day, the wooded area appealed to stalwart walkers. Much later, two of them, booted and wearing hats and weatherproof clothing, came upon her.

No one knew who she was. She was barely breathing when the paramedics arrived. One of the walkers who had found her, Donald Parker, a retired inland revenue official, had covered her with his coat, and his wife wrapped her scarf around Emily's cropped head. She had remained with her while he went off for help, heading along the road to the nearest house, but hoping to flag down a passing motorist. The couple had reached her from the other side of the copse, crossing several fields to get there, and had left their own car at the starting point. As he trudged along the quiet road, ignored by the few cars who drove past, Donald began to wonder if he should have returned to his own vehicle, but that was a good half hour's walk away. He gestured at another car; of course the drivers were not stopping lest he be some violent maniac, he realised. He stood in the road waving his arms at the next one, but had to jump out of the way as it showed no signs of slowing down. The driver shook his fist and yelled at him. Being assaulted himself by an enraged driver would not help the person – male or female, it was difficult to to decide – lying battered in the woodland.

At last a post office van approached. The postman stopped, wound down his window, listened to what Donald had to say and promised to fetch help immediately. Donald hastened back to reassure his wife and to stand near the roadside, ready to guide the ambulance when it arrived, which as he had walked some distance, was soon after he reached the entrance to the track.

Donald had said the casualty had wounds about the face and head and looked as if she – it was probably a she – had been attacked. While he was about it, the postman, a public servant, also called the police, and they arrived in a patrol car while the paramedics were loading Emily into their ambulance. They could not tell how badly she was injured; blood had congealed on her face and clothing, and bruises and contusions were apparent, but hypothermia was the most obvious threat to her life.

When they reached the hospital, there was nothing on her to indicate who she was or where she came from. Emily owned few possessions anyway, and those she had were at Elm Lodge. The wheels of officialdom ground away while she received emergency treatment. A fractured skull was suspected, but the priority was to treat her for exposure. It was mid-afternoon before anyone made the connection between the missing girl abducted from Northtown the previous afternoon, and the unidentified woman who had been saved from freezing to death only because she was overweight, was warmly clad and, unknown to the medical staff, was accustomed to living out of doors.

There was no photograph of Emily to circulate. Isabel had told the police that she had not got one of her as an adult, and that she had no knowledge of where one might be found. It was Alice, when Isabel went up to Ford House on Saturday morning, who suggested that the police might have a mug shot of her.

'Don't they take one, if you're charged with any crime?' she said.

But Isabel thought that was only if you were sent to prison. Emily had spent a single night in a cell at the police station.

'They can't take snaps of everyone they haul in off the streets.

Drunks, and such,' she said. 'Anyway, I don't like the idea of making public the fact that she's been in trouble. It's Godfrey they should be hunting. He knows where she is. He's probably got her tied up in his van.'

'He'll get rid of her,' said Alice. 'He took her in a fit of rage. Then he'll realise she's a handicap to him – her actual presence, as well as her threat as a witness. He'll dump her somewhere, without regard for the consequences.'

And in no condition to talk, they both thought, while Isabel pictured her being thrown on to a railway line or into a canal.

'She's strong,' she said. 'She'd put up a fight.'

'He got her into his van, didn't he? He'd know how to knock her out,' said Alice bluntly.

She sounded tough. Maybe she was not what she seemed, superficially: a timid mouse subservient to her parents, and dependent on them. For the first time, Isabel wondered about the nature of the intimacy between Alice and this man. It had resulted in the birth of Rowena, but by what sort of process? A man capable of this sort of action was hardly likely to be a tender lover. Douglas, for all his shortcomings, would be incapable of violence; he was simply selfish, dull, and unimaginative, like many other people.

'Not knowing anything about poor Emily is awful,' said Isabel.

'I know. Look, I'll get off and do the shopping, if you really don't mind being here,' said Alice.

'Not at all,' said Isabel. 'Douglas is at home, if Emily miraculously turns up. I suppose the police will let us know if there's any news.'

'Don't count on it. They're not always marvellous at communicating,' said Alice. 'I'll take Rowena with me. We'd better carry on as normally as possible. Godfrey won't risk trying to grab her again. He knows he's in serious trouble. That's one thing Emily's achieved – ensured Rowena's safety.'

It was probably true. Isabel saw that Alice was now quite calm, convinced that Rowena was in no danger. She watched them leave; then, before going to see what she could do for the older Watkinsons, she rang Douglas. There was no point in his trailing up here hoping to chat up Alice, which, thinking Isabel was going to do the shopping, he might have in mind.

He had, but he hid his frustration.

'Good – I'm glad she feels up to it,' he said.

'She seems fine,' said Isabel.

Poor Douglas, she thought, putting down the receiver. She didn't think he'd try anything with Alice; he was too cautious, and Alice spelt trouble. Or might he, as a fling in middle age, find that an irresistible challenge and take the risk? And if he did, would Alice welcome an approach from him? One could never tell, but it would end in tears and it would be a pity if she were hurt again. Maybe, when all this was over, they – Isabel and Douglas – should take a holiday somewhere rather nice, and try to regain something they had lost: if they had ever had it.

The manager of the boarding-house where Godfrey had so briefly lodged took scant notice when the youth employed to clean the rooms and make the beds reported that he had not slept there last night.

'So what? Found himself a lady friend, I suppose,' said the manager.

'He's left a few things. Some shorts and socks,' said the youth, Jason, who did not like this work, to which he had been guided by the Job Centre, but he hoped it would lead to better things, such as employment in a large hotel. 'There was a toothbrush, too,' he added. 'He's not taken anything.' Lodgers did: towels and toothglasses, even sometimes sheets, walked away.

'He'll be back,' said the manager. He'd paid a week up front.

'He had a camper van, didn't he?' Jason persisted. 'I wondered why he wanted a room when he'd got that.'

The manager, who had other things on his mind, sighed.

'Ours not to question the whims of guests,' he said. Their Mr Graham – that was the name under which he had registered – had every right to indulge his own. 'Maybe he wanted a bit of warmth.'

'Well, he did have a woman in,' said Jason, smirking slightly. 'Monday, it was.' He remembered, because the man slept in next morning, so that Jason had had to skip his Tuesday cleaning, and when he did get into the room, on Wednesday, there'd been unmistakeable evidence, including wisps of pubic hair, some black, some fairish. It had quite turned him on, thinking what had happened.

'That's no crime,' said the manager. Though Mr Graham had paid for single occupancy.

'No, but about the camper van,' Jason persisted. 'It was on the news. Some woman was snatched up the town, by a bloke in a camper van. I thought it might be him. Did you take the number of his van?'

'No,' said the manager. 'It wasn't parked on these premises.'

However, it had been parked outside, in the road, where Jason had seen it. He hadn't taken full note of the number, but he remembered some of it; it was a C reg. He worried at it, working on without enthusiasm. Because the abduction was local, it was real, not some distant crime that meant nothing, and his mother had been rabbiting on about it after watching the news, wondering what things were coming to in Northtown when this could happen in broad daylight not two miles away from where they lived.

He didn't want to be involved and he didn't want to get in wrong with the manager, but the thought of the fairish pubic hair kept nagging at him. When he had his break for lunch, he went to the nearest public telephone, which was in the next street, and anonymously told the police that when passing by last Wednesday night, he'd seen a white camper van outside the boarding-house.

Rather surprisingly, a patrol car arrived not fifteen minutes later, and Jason, left in charge because the manager had gone down to the betting shop, admitted two uniformed officers into the building. All innocence, he listened to their enquiry and said that yes, he'd seen such a van outside, and he thought it belonged to the lodger in room twelve, Mr Graham, who was out at present and who hadn't been in all night. Jason had been able to describe Mr Graham. He'd seen him on Tuesday morning, when he'd come to do the room and was sent away. The man had come out of his room soon afterwards and had gone to the bathroom on the floor below. He'd worn jeans and had a towel round his shoulders, and, said Jason, had longish greying hair, a moustache and sideburns, and copious grey hair on his chest. Funny that his pubic hair had been so black.

When they asked to see the room, he led them there, but he kept quiet about the bed linen. Anyway, it had gone to the laundry. The room however, had been less than won-derfully cleaned, and Mr Graham's pants and socks were there. The toothbrush, if they were lucky, might yield a fingerprint. It was bagged up, like the socks and shorts, and removed.

If Mr Graham reappeared, his garments could be returned, assuming he had been eliminated from the enquiry, said one of the officers, giving Jason a receipt for the items and telling him they might want to speak to him again.

'Thanks, lad,' said one of them.

'I've done nothing,' Jason answered.

'You've answered our questions and shown us the room,' was the reply, and one of the two policemen gave him a broad wink.

'Makes quite a change to have such a public-spirited lad at large,' he said to his colleague as they went off to make their report.

'Hope he doesn't get it in the neck from the manager,' said the other officer.

The manager wasn't very pleased, but hearing that the police had arrived in response to an anonymous tip-off, agreed that Jason had been right to cooperate. They'd only have come back with a search warrant, otherwise, and besides, obstructing the police in their enquiries was an offence.

Emily was drifting in and out of sleep. She was warmer, and though she hurt – her ribs and legs, and her head – the pain was distant, as though it was being felt by someone else. She opened her eyes and looked round, seeing screens and pale walls, and realising that her arm was connected to some form of medical equipment. A face bent over her, looming large, female and black, smiling.

'You're safe now,' said the nurse. 'Just relax. Can you tell me your name?'

Emily heard her words, and managed to murmur, 'Emily,' and 'Where's my baby?' before she submerged again.

Examining the patient had revealed no signs of recent childbirth but the nurse had caught the name. She made a note of it, and reported it to the police officer who was waiting close at hand, for it was certain that her injuries had been caused by a savage attack involving blows and punches, and her head had been banged hard against something solid. Her face was badly battered, bruised and swollen, and her broken nose had bled freely. She was in a critical condition.

Lying there, time rolled away and she was back in the hospital where she had met the other Emily, the real Emily Frost, who had talked about her life, so that when she, the second Emily, had been discharged, she had taken her name. It was easy. You could call yourself any name and it was legal. She had some proof of her identity: a letter addressed to her at an address in Spain.

The real Emily had found the letter tucked inside a book, *Possession*, by A.S. Byatt, which she had been meaning to read for years and had taken with her to hospital where, at last, she should have time. Mortified when she realised that she had never answered the letter, she had told the usurping Emily that it was from her godmother, about whom she had already spoken. After so long, Isabel would have written her off, she said. Later, when the real Emily was in the bathroom, just before she left the hospital, the aspiring one removed the letter from the book. So she had learned Isabel's address.

She dreamed again. She was in care, in a home where there was scant supervision and some girls went out on the street. Others wished for more intervention from the staff; the few rules here were easily ignored. People bunked off school, Emily among them. Then, in a shop where both were seeing what they could pick up without paying, she met Carol, who encouraged her to abscond from the home and took her to a flat where the two of them stayed with friends of Carol's. It was then that Emily met Billy, and, for a while, things were wonderful, for Billy was sweet and kind and needed to be cared for. He couldn't read or write, and Emily began to teach him. He tried so hard to learn, but he found it very difficult. Emily drew letters on the backs of food packets and with money which they got from begging in the street – Emily had almost given up stealing – bought children's comics. In return, he watched out for her, would let no one bother her or bully her, and stole food for her. Then Billy was picked up by the police and carted off. No one knew where he had gone and it was rumoured that he'd been sent to a detention centre. He'd been arrested for passing another youth some packages a man had given him. They'd been drugs, only Billy hadn't understood; Emily had known nothing about it. After Billy went away, she discovered she was pregnant. She didn't realise, at first, what was happening to her body. The interludes with Billy had been sweet and gentle, nothing like what had happened in the home when several of the boys had overpowered some reluctant girls or talked them into submission. It hadn't seemed the same at all.

Carol had said it would be all right and she'd get money from the state, even her own flat, or she could get rid of it, but then Carol had left to move in with a new boy-friend she'd been seeing recently. Friendless once again – the others in the flat, which was not much better than a squat, had never had much time for her – and frightened, sick, and feeling ill, Emily felt completely lost, but she knew she wanted to have the baby. Unable to think of an alternative, she decided to go home. Surely her father would help her now, even if it was only by finding her somewhere to go?

It was evening when, tired and with a stomachache, she reached the house after hitching several lifts, and to her dismay, her stepmother was alone. When she came to the door, she looked Emily up and down and sneered, 'Well, well! Come back, have you, now you're up the spout.'

She'd seen it instantly. Emily hadn't realised that it showed already.

'I must go to the toilet,' she gasped. She was exhausted, and she had a dreadful pain. In desperation, she pushed past the woman, entering the house and hurrying upstairs to the bathroom, where she found that she had begun to bleed.

When she emerged, the woman stood on the tiny, narrow landing, waiting for her, arms akimbo, scowling.

'You needn't think your father'll want you back,' she said, as Emily, who had washed her face, came slowly towards her, holding her stomach. 'You little whore. You're nothing but filth. You'd best get out before he comes back and shows you what he means.'

'But what am I to do?' Emily's voice was a wail. 'Where am I to go?'

'You should have thought of that before you started shagging around,' said the woman. 'Now, you get out, before your dad sees the state you're in.'

'Where is he?' asked Emily.

'At work,' said her stepmother. He was now a security guard, on night shift at present, and she was expecting a caller in an hour or so, a man she had met while working in a bar. She entertained him weekly; it was a cash arrangement that suited both of them, but she must get rid of this wretched girl before he arrived. 'He won't want to have anything to do with you,' she added. 'I'm surprised you dared to show your face here after how you've behaved.'

So am I, thought Emily, considering how you treated me when I lived here. Time hadn't altered things; she'd never been wanted here and she wasn't going to find any support. She'd been stupid to come.

'Aren't you even going to give me a cup of tea?' she said, wondering if she could possibly ask for some money.

'I am not,' said the woman. 'You are leaving now, and if you don't go willingly, I'll make you.'

She'd raised her arm, and Emily, afraid that she would hit her, as she'd done when Emily was a child, ducked away from her, pushing at her to get past. Taken by surprise, her stepmother stumbled backwards, lost her balance, and fell down the stairs, somersaulting over till she reached the bottom of the short, steep flight, where she lay on the ground, motionless and silent.

Emily gazed at her in horror. Then she walked slowly down the stairs herself and stepped fastidiously over the recumbent body. Calmly, she went into the kitchen, where she made herself a cup of tea, found some bread and cut herself a slice, spreading it with Marmite. Coolly, she washed up the mug she'd used and wiped everything meticulously. Then she went to a jar on the dresser where, years ago, money had been hidden under a bag of sugar. It was still used as a hiding place and in it she found over three hundred pounds. She took it all.

Her stepmother was groaning when she left, but Emily spared her no compassion. It had been an accident, but if she died, she couldn't say who had pushed her down the stairs. Emily had left the house, her long wavy hair hiding her face as she hurried away to the main road. Her stomach still hurt, and she could feel more blood seeping from her body, dampening the toilet paper she had used as padding.

This time, she'd headed north, away from anyone she knew, and a lorry driver had taken her all the way to Leeds where, realising she was ill, he had dropped her near the hospital. He'd left her then, not wanting complications for himself. In the hospital, her baby had been prematurely stillborn and she had needed surgery because of internal damage caused by injuries she had sustained earlier in her life. Doctors had asked her if she had ever been in a road accident, but she would not answer any questions. Her stepmother had kicked and punched her often enough, but that was over now.

After her discharge she had nowhere to go, and was terrified that she would be arrested for murdering her stepmother. She had to lose herself. In the Leeds hospital, she had said her name was Rose Smith – Rose was her mother's name – and as soon as she was able, she had cut her long hair short. A place was found for her in a hostel where she stayed for several weeks, growing daily stronger, soon helping with the cooking and eating everything that was put before her, gaining weight inexorably. When she left, she had her hair shaved off, told the DSS that she had lost all her papers, and easily became Emily Frost. She lived rough, begging, and using the money she had stolen to buy food until she heard about some people who were going on a demonstration to prevent a new road being built.

It was the perfect way to escape. Still imagining herself to be the object of a murder hunt, the new, shorn Emily, now stones heavier, had left her past behind.

21

On Friday night, Paul and Alice had arranged to meet in the foyer of the Meridien Hotel. It was not far for either of them, was near the cinema, and whoever arrived first could wait there comfortably for the other. Paul, unaware of Alice's past pub experience, had suggested it, sensing that if he were delayed, Alice might have felt awkward on her own in a bar.

There was no sign of her. He sat down to wait for her, reading a proof copy of a book he had just acquired. Though it was compelling, he looked up from time to time, anxious not to miss her entrance, but the minutes passed and she did not arrive. After half an hour, he asked if there was a message for him, but as they had never exchanged surnames, she would have been forced to refer to him simply as Paul, from his particular bookshop. However, there was nothing.

At lunch time she'd been planning to stick to their arrangement, but since then she must have regretted her acceptance, yet she hadn't rung the bookshop to cry off. It was a pity that she hadn't let him know. After another half hour, he gave up and left a note addressed to Alice, care of her gallery, which intrigued the concierge. He would go round to see her on Monday, find out what had made her change her mind, but, on second thoughts, perhaps it was best to cut his losses. They might still meet at their lunch place, or perhaps she would eschew it in future.

Paul, a divorced man with two teenaged children who lived with their mother, went back to his bachelor flat in Clapham feeling very much let down. He hadn't thought her frivolous; rather, someone who had been wounded.

When news broadcasts that night mentioned the abduction of a woman from a street in Northtown, he had no idea that this was connected in any way with Alice. He did not know where she lived except that it was with her parents.

Paul worked some Saturdays, and this was one of them. Reading the paper in the tube on the way to the bookshop the next morning, he saw an item about the abduction and merely glanced at it. There was a description of a man wanted in connection with the incident. The kidnapped woman was still missing. The police were looking for a white camper van, containing probably a man and a woman.

What a world, he thought, turning to the leader page. Later that day he decided to walk round to the gallery which, like his shop, was open, though he knew Alice never came in on Saturdays. Her work was mainly concerned with cataloguing and despatching invoices, though she sometimes dealt with customers. He asked a member of the staff if she was ill, saying that they had arranged to meet the previous evening and she had failed to arrive.

'Stood me up,' he said, embarrassed but determined.

'She went home early,' said Alice's colleague. 'She had a call from home – rather awful. Her little girl's nanny was abducted and it seems whoever did it tried to grab the child, too. She's all right, though – Rowena.'

'Oh – Rowena,' said Paul, nodding wisely, anxious not to betray his ignorance of the child's existence. 'Oh dear!'

'The nanny's still missing,' said the man. 'Alice was so pleased to have found her after her previous child minder left, and she was excellent. But you know that, of course.' He looked curiously at Paul, intrigued; Alice had seemed to have no social life at all.

'Yes,' agreed Paul.

'After this, she'll give up and find something nearer home, I guess,' said the man. 'I think it's been a strain, commuting all that way each day, and with the fares, it can't be cost effective. But she liked escaping from that village of hers – what's it called? Fordswick – that's it.'

'Well, thanks,' said Paul. 'I'm glad to know what happened.'

'I expect she was too busy with the police and all that to let you know,' said the man.

'I'm sure you're right,' said Paul.

He still hadn't learned Alice's surname, but now he knew where she lived. At least she hadn't turned him down because she'd changed her mind, but they were still almost strangers, and it seemed that she had serious problems, with Rowena – what a pretty name – and a disappearing nanny. Poor Alice.

Alice and Rowena arrived back from the supermarket in a cheerful mood. Rowena had wanted to know where Emily had gone but Alice had managed to deflect her curiosity, and they had survived the stresses of the crowded aisles and check-out queues. Rowena was good at finding things they needed regularly; she considered herself too big to sit on the trolley but she kept close to her mother, for having your eyes level with most people's lower bodies was like being in a jungle among moving trees.

Isabel saw them return and helped them unload the car. That morning, she had persuaded Muriel that Robert Watkinson must be told the full story. The police would be coming back and forth; when Godfrey was found, she might have to give evidence about his attack on her so that he could be charged with that, as well as his abduction of Emily.

'You can't pretend for ever,' she said. 'If he's sent to prison for a long time, Rowena will be safe.'

But Muriel was still hoping the whole thing might disappear – just go away. She said so.

'It can't. It won't,' said Isabel. 'Goodness knows what's happened to Emily. Suppose she's badly hurt? He must be punished. People can't go around behaving like that and getting away with it.'

'I can't endure the thought that he might come back and threaten Rowena again,' said Muriel.

'Well, he may, if he gets away with it this time.' said Isabel. 'You'd have to make her a ward of court and get injunctions against him ever coming near her, and all sort of things, to protect her.'

Finally, Isabel had persuaded Muriel, and while Alice was out, Robert was told the basic facts.

Rage filled him, as Muriel had known it would, and, fearing another stroke, she urged him to breathe steadily and calm down.

She loves him, Isabel recognised. She really wants to spare him.

'Alice doesn't know I paid him to go away,' Robert explained to her. 'She simply thought he'd abandoned her. He might have married her, otherwise. Silly girl – she'd have fallen for it. She had, hadn't she?' He spoke strongly. Isabel didn't think he looked at all likely to expire. 'If I were fit, I'd find the fellow and thrash him,' he went on. 'How dare he try to kidnap Rowena? Muriel, you should have told me about the letter,' he continued. 'I've lost some of my physical strength but not my wits, any more than you've lost yours through being lame. But where's your sense, woman? If you and Alice had told me, we could have taken some steps to prevent all this. You say that Jones discovered that the letter was bogus, didn't he? But by then it was too late.'

The police had removed the letter; it was evidence, and Godfrey's fingerprints might be on the paper.

Hearing Robert call his wife 'woman' made Isabel squirm with distaste.

'We couldn't know he'd meet Emily and use her as a means of getting into the house,' she said. It was no good loading her guilt at not showing more interest in Emily's so-called friend on to the Watkinsons. 'You're going to have to tell Alice what you did, aren't you?' she said. 'Eventually, I mean. Knowing the truth may cure her of any hang-ups she's got about him – blaming herself, for instance, because he just went off. The fact that he was bought off proves what a creep he was.' She'd nearly used a stronger word, but did not want to add disapproval of her language to their shock.

'We will tell her,' they agreed, and Isabel had said she would occupy Rowena while they did so. She made coffee for them to drink during this revealing interview. Mr Watkinson was much less fragile than she had expected; when she brought the tray in, before Muriel and Alice joined him, there he was, standing at the window leaning on his sticks and looking out.

'Emily was a great one for the birds,' he said. 'She used to feed them and I was enjoying watching them.'

'I'm glad,' said Isabel shortly. She suspected that he had developed the tyranny of some invalids, accustomed to their needs being considered before those of anyone else and reluctant to relinquish this power even when recovered enough to do so. 'Do you have physiotherapy?' she asked abruptly.

'I gave it up,' he said. 'Driving me to the hospital is too much for Muriel.'

Perhaps she was wrong about his self-absorption, but he was undeniably autocratic.

'You could have it here. Privately,' said Isabel. Surely they carried private health insurance? Even if they did not, they could afford to pay.

'I didn't like the woman.' Robert said. 'Too bossy.'

'Try someone else. A man,' she suggested. Of course he wouldn't like being told what to do and made to exercise his limbs by a mere woman. He was a controlling chauvinist, different in variety from Douglas and of an earlier generation, but he was one. Their chess games might be most successful, she decided. She would encourage them. 'I'll ask around,' she offered. 'See if I can hear of one.'

There was a lot that could be done to help this family, who were not held back by poverty. Money did not bring happiness, but it could solve problems.

Leaving the couple and their daughter to discuss the situation, she took Rowena out. It was still cold, a raw, grey day; it might be wise to avoid the playground, in case there was village curiosity about what had happened yesterday – the police were still making enquiries in the area – so they took a ball into the garden and played catch, as Emily had done before. Running around, both warmed up and enjoyed themselves.

Alice joined them, after more than half an hour, and so that she and Isabel could talk without Rowena understanding what they said, persuaded her to demonstrate her skill on the swing. A few pushes set her off, and then she kept the motion going by herself. Alice looked subdued.

'You know they paid Godfrey off before, don't you?' Alice asked her, and, not waiting for an answer, added bitterly, 'No wonder he thought they'd be good for more money.'

'They saved you both,' Isabel said. 'You and Rowena.'

'They hid the truth,' said Alice.

Don't we all, at times, thought Isabel.

'They love Rowena,' she pointed out. But they hadn't let their own daughter grow up properly. 'They wanted to protect you,' she said gently. 'It's natural. Look, we'll talk about it another time – maybe you can come down to supper later on, when all this has been sorted out.'

'I'm not going to be able to go back to London,' said Alice.

'Well, not yet,' Isabel agreed. 'When Rowena's older, perhaps, if you still want to. But there are opportunities in Northtown, you know. Time enough to think about it when your mother's had her hip done, and your father's better.'

'Will you help me?' Alice asked.

'Of course, if I can,' said Isabel. Poor girl, she must be well into her thirties, yet she was more naïve than any teenager. No wonder Godfrey had been able to exploit her. 'I think you must be rather lonely,' she said. Like me, she thought, recognising it, but she had taken action. She had the shop, and golf. 'You might take up golf,' she said.

'Golf?' Alice stared at her, and then she began to laugh, becoming almost hysterical.

'What's so funny? It's a good game, and gets you out of doors,' said Isabel.

'It's going for a walk without meeting traffic,' Alice said.

'What's wrong with that?' said Isabel.

'Nothing, I suppose,' said Alice. 'But I've never been much good at games.'

'The ball doesn't move, in golf. It stays still while you hit it, not like tennis.'

'I could always have a go,' said Alice.

'And you could make a putting green here, on the lawn,' said Isabel. 'Douglas will do it for you,' she promised. 'He loves that sort of thing. Creative gardening. Projects. Pergolas and arbours.'

Rowena's swinging had slowed down. She slid off and came over to them.

'Time to go in,' said Alice, but she was smiling. Paul, and the London fantasy, were already part of another life.

The au pair girl wasn't, however. Cecile had telephoned, and Muriel had said her daughter would ring back.

'Arrange to see her. Get her to come down here,' said Isabel. 'You must have some help. If she's not suitable, there will be others, but she needs to see your set-up. And meet Rowena, of course. Say you'll pay the fare,' she added, for it was obvious that Alice had no experience of this sort of thing.

She left then, intending to telephone the police from home to see if there was any news of Emily. When she did so, she learned that there was nothing to report.

'Why bother?' Douglas said. 'They'll let you know if they find her.'

If, he'd said; not when.

Isabel did not answer. She found bread and cheese for their Saturday lunch, and heated up some soup. They ate the meal in almost total silence, apart from Douglas mentioning that he was thinking of getting a second tank to enable him to stock fish which were incompatible with those he already had. Isabel listened as he spoke of varieties which preferred deep water, and others which liked skimming about on the surface. Just like people, she was thinking.

After the meal he departed to attend to them, and she went upstairs to Emily's room.

The bed was neatly made. In a drawer were her few clothes and the letter which Isabel had written to the real Emily, four years ago, commiserating with her over her mother's death.

Had she found it somewhere? Stolen it? Who was she really? Had she no family of her own?

Isabel wondered if her own letter to Scotland would bring any answers.

Emily's condition had deteriorated when, late on Saturday afternoon, the police made the connection between the battered, hypothermic patient brought in by ambulance that morning and the woman who had been abducted from Northtown the previous day. That evening, PC Colin Darwin came to Elm Lodge.

'We think we've found Emily,' he said.

'Oh!' Isabel felt a lifting of the heart, but then she looked at his expression. 'It's not good,' she stated. She held the door wider, and he came into the hall.

'No. I'm afraid not,' he said and went on to explain. 'We can't be sure it's her,' he said. 'She had no papers on her – nothing to say who she is, but she fits the description. She's unconscious,' he added. 'She's very poorly.'

'I must go there at once,' said Isabel.

'It would be helpful,' Colin said. 'We do need to confirm that it's her. I'll drive you. It's a police matter, and it started on our patch.'

'Oh.' So she need not seek out a hospital in an unfamiliar town on a raw winter's night, alone. 'Thanks,' she said. 'I'll get my coat and tell my husband.'

Douglas, however, had come out of his study, where he had been finishing his book about Gladstone.

'Tell me what?' he asked.

Isabel explained.

'I'll drive you there,' he volunteered at once.

'There's no need,' said Isabel. Of course he'd insist on driving her; she should have known that. Gratitude vying with resentment made her answer curtly. 'The police will take me. You'd better stay here in case Alice has a crisis,' she said, continuing slyly, 'after what's happened, it's quite possible one of her parents might collapse.'

'Ah! That's true,' he admitted. 'Perhaps I should give them a ring and make sure they're all right.'

'It would be neighbourly,' said Isabel.

'No news of that fellow – what's his name?' asked Douglas.

'None at all,' said Darwin. There had been some alleged sightings of Godfrey Sutton, one of which had led to the discovery of what might be some of the man's possessions in a Northtown boarding-house, but as yet there was no firm proof of ownership. Meanwhile, forensic scientists had been examining the ground where Emily had been found; they might have discovered traces from whoever had dumped her there, such as tyre marks, or signs of her being dragged along the track.

Colin told Isabel what he knew as they drove along. Then

they chatted about other things. He played golf, she discovered. She told him she had recently taken it up.

'It gets me out at weekends,' she said. 'I like it. It's a new club and they're nice to women, which isn't always so at golf clubs, I've been told.'

'Your husband doesn't play?'

'No. He's a garden construction enthusiast,' she said. 'I mean, he's not into plants and things. More fancy rockeries and fences. Bowers, and so on.'

'Oh,' said Colin. 'Well, couples can't be in each other's pockets all the time, can they?'

They chatted easily, driving through the night. The journey took them just over an hour, and at the hospital they were quickly shown to the ward where Emily lay in a side room on her own.

She was almost unrecognisable. There were lacerations on her skull, crusted over now, and her swollen face was purple with bruises. Various wires and tubes connected her to complicated machines.

'She's very weak,' said the sister in charge, but Isabel did not need to hear the words. Tears sprang to her eyes.

'Oh, Emily, what has he done to you?' she whispered, going straight to the bed. She put her hand over Emily's plump fist which lay on the sheet. 'Where's her earring?' she asked. But the answer was obvious. A surgical dressing on the ear lobe showed that it had been torn out.

'Perhaps to prevent identification. Perhaps in anger,' said the policewoman who was on duty in the ward. 'They've looked for it where she was found, and they'll be examining that area again tomorrow, when it's daylight.'

'I see,' said Isabel. 'Do you think she can hear us talking?' she asked the sister.

Pityingly, the nurse shook her head.

'No. I'm afraid not,' she said. For now only the machinery to which she was attached was keeping Emily alive.

But Isabel didn't want to believe it. She bent over Emily.

'Emily. I'm here – Isabel,' she said. 'Don't worry. I'll look after you.'

Perhaps the nurse was wrong.

22

It had become a case of murder.

During the night, Emily's heart had stopped and had not responded to resuscitation techniques. The cumulative effects of exposure and her various injuries were probably the causes of her death, but a postmortem would reveal the details.

Isabel had stayed beside her to the end, holding her hand with the bitten nails, and she wept for Emily. Who was she, really? Who else should be mourning? And must she, Isabel, tell the police about her false identity?

There was no need to decide now. She was the only person who knew the truth, and it made no difference to the magnitude of the crime that had been committed. A young woman had been cruelly abducted, beaten up and left to die. Now it was in the hands of the coroner and of the police. Poor Emily would be taken to the mortuary and the secrets of her body would be exposed.

PC Darwin drove Isabel back to Fordswick. He had asked her if she wanted to telephone her husband, but she declined. He'd be asleep, she said, and there was no point in disturbing him.

In the car, at first they did not talk. Isabel was stunned with grief. After a while, she spoke.

'It's funny – she's only been in the house for two weeks – not even that – and I've become so fond of her,' she said.

'Well, she was your goddaughter, wasn't she?' said Colin.

Isabel had already explained that she had no knowledge of the whereabouts of Emily's two brothers, and that to all intents and purposes, she was the next-of-kin.

'We'd lost touch,' she said. 'I hadn't seen her since she was a child.' It would all have to come out. She would be obliged to explain about Emily's arrest and court appearance – and now the court would learn that death would stop her answering to her bail. 'There's more to it than that,' she said. 'I don't think I can face telling you now.'

'Don't try,' said Colin. 'You may feel more like it later. It's Sunday morning. We both need breakfast. We'll stop somewhere.'

They found a Little Chef, and, to her surprise, Isabel was able to put away bacon, eggs, sausage and tomato. Colin ordered baked beans and fried bread, too. They talked about holidays and how he hoped to take his children sailing.

'What does your husband like doing?' Colin asked. 'Apart from garden construction?'

'Tending his tropical fish. Reading biographies about past statesmen,' she said. 'Riding his bike for exercise. A real bike, not a stationary one.'

'As we both play golf, I might see you at that club you've joined,' said Colin.

He smiled at her. He must be at least ten years younger than she was.

'Emily isn't – wasn't – who she said she was,' she heard

herself declare. 'I haven't told anyone. I know, though. I'm certain.'

And over the remains of their hefty breakfast, she gave her reasons.

'You'll have to make a statement,' he said, when she had finished.

'Yes. Obviously. I suppose you'll have to try to find out who she really was.'

'Someone among the protestors may know more about her,' he said. 'They are quite clubby; they hang in together, help each other out. There are all sorts involved from academics downwards.'

'She was no academic,' said Isabel. 'I doubt if she'd passed any GCSE exams. She didn't seem to have heard of Jane Austen.'

'What a dismal failing,' Colin said, laughing.

'Why are you only a constable? Why aren't you an inspector?' Isabel demanded.

'I'm a recent joiner,' Colin answered. 'A mature recruit. I was a teacher. Maybe I will be an inspector one fine day.'

When they reached Fordswick, she made him stop in the road outside Elm Lodge.

'Douglas might hear the car and I don't want to wake him,' she said. 'I can't face it. Perhaps I'll sleep in the spare room.'

'Emily's room? No, don't. Don't touch anything in there. I'm afraid we'll have to send some forensic guys out to see what they can pick up about Emily.' The body would be fingerprinted as routine. 'There might be traces from that man – Godfrey – Graham – whatever he's really called – on things she's left there.'

'There isn't much,' said Isabel. 'She had hardly any possessions.'

'Even so,' Colin said. 'Don't wash any clothes she's left there. Knickers – anything like that.'

Isabel stared, then understood.

'I expect she washed them,' she said sadly.

'Never mind. Maybe she didn't. Even if she did, there may be something else – a hair – anything that links him to her so that when we find him, we can prove the connection.'

'I understand,' said Isabel. 'And I'm glad you said when, not if.'

He walked her to the door, and waited while she opened it, then went quietly away.

Before she went upstairs, Isabel left a note for Douglas on the kitchen table. It stated simply that Emily had died, and that as she had not arrived home until four o'clock in the morning, rather than disturb him, she had gone to bed in Toby's room. She added that the police had said nothing in Emily's room was to be touched, since now she was a murder victim. That would prevent him indulging any sudden fancy to rush in there, embarking on his cupboard scheme or wielding a purifying paint brush. He wasn't going to like it when he found out that Emily had been an imposter. She'd avoid telling him for as long as possible.

She wanted to have a bath, but that would disturb Douglas. Part of her wished he'd heard her come in, just as she, when the boys were growing up, listened half consciously for them. He'd appeared fast enough when she came back with Emily, such a little while ago. This time, he'd known she was with the police and not driving herself. It did not cross her mind that he was worried about her on that cold winter's night, with no idea of where she was; she thought it was all a matter of control. He could not have stopped her from going to identify Emily; last week he might have believed he could prevent her attending the court hearing. But if he had heard her return tonight, would he have sat with her and listened to her talk about the dead girl? That was what she wanted to do. Would he have been kind, or merely dictatorial, thinking he knew what was best for her, which in his view, since nothing could be altered, would be to erase it from her mind?

Hugging a hot water bottle, Isabel got into Toby's bed and pulled the duvet up around her ears. Into her mind's eye swam a memory of Emily, lying on – not in – that high bed, her stout body lightly covered, her bruised and swollen eyelids closed. Had she known what was happening? The hospital staff said that she couldn't have, but while she was lying helpless on the ground, presumably all night, being rained on, wet and cold, hadn't she been very frightened?

No one would ever know.

Isabel tried to remember her competently dealing with the shoplifting schoolchildren in Gifts Galore and happy with her job at Ford House. Whatever had gone before, she had been content at Elm Lodge, and she had never known that Isabel had found her out. That was good.

If this hadn't happened – if Emily were still alive – what would Isabel have said to her? Eventually, she would have had to challenge her. What was the true story? She couldn't have committed any major crime, or it would have been discovered when she was arrested. Would the police discover who she really was? How had she got hold of the real Emily's letter, and such detailed knowledge of her background?

At last, Isabel drowsed off. She was woken when Douglas came into the room, carrying a cup and saucer.

'I've brought you some tea, Isabel,' he said. 'I'm afraid you've had a sad time, my dear.'

He was dressed in his usual weekend garb, corduroy trousers and a Shetland sweater, his shirt collar neatly arranged over its turtle top.

'Oh – oh – what? Yes.' Isabel, slowly surfacing, felt amazement at his adoption of this ministering role.

'What happens now?' he asked. 'I suppose there is all the business of an inquest.' He frowned, in distaste.

'Well – yes, for identification, and so on, but it will be adjourned,' she answered. Colin had explained it to her. The opening might be delayed, since the dead girl's true identity was not known. 'It's a formality. No arrangements can be made until much later. It's murder, you see.'

She sat up, accepting the tea from him, grateful for it. He noticed she was wearing one of Toby's shirts.

'It was on the radio news,' he said.

'Oh! What did it say?'

'Simply that the woman abducted in Northtown on Friday afternoon had been found in a wooded area of Bedfordshire, and that she had died in hospital. She was not being named until her relatives had been informed.'

'I see.'

'I imagine that's normal procedure,' said Douglas. 'There are the brothers, after all. Probably the police will trace them.'

Would they bother, since she was not Emily Frost, their sister?

'They keep her,' she said. 'In the mortuary. Frozen. Chilled, anyway.'

'Yes,' Douglas acknowledged.

'She was soaked right through when they found her,' she said. 'It came on to rain, and she must have been out all night.

Of course, she was well padded – overweight, I mean – and used to sleeping out. Otherwise she might have died more quickly. I don't know if she even knew she'd been rescued.'

'The police want to talk to you,' said Douglas. 'A Detective Inspector Cox rang up. He said you were going to make a statement, and they'll come here to save you going in to Northtown.'

'Oh,' said Isabel. 'When are they coming?'

'In about an hour. I said you might want a bath and so on, first,' he said.

'Oh – thanks. Yes, I would like that,' said Isabel.

'I took it upon myself to telephone Alice as soon as the bulletin was over,' Douglas said. 'I knew that she would be anxious to hear the news and that with a child there, the household would wake up quite early.' When he rang, Alice had already known that Emily was dead.

'I expect she was glad you did that,' said Isabel. 'We – the police and I – discussed how to tell them last night, or rather, this morning, and we decided not to disturb them during the night. Someone was going to go round early today to break it to them.'

'I see.' There was no need to tell Isabel he had been pre-empted by officialdom.

'Well, I'd better get up,' said Isabel. 'Thank you for the tea, Douglas.'

She handed him the cup and saucer, and, somewhat discomposed, he took them from her and went over to the door.

'I'll put the bath on for you,' he told her.

He'd done two kind deeds already today, when normally they were as rare as laughter on the moon. Oh Emily, what have you accomplished, thought Isabel, getting out of bed.

'Thanks,' she said, awkwardly.

'By the way, Toby's coming down today,' said Douglas. 'He telephoned. He said he had something particular to say to you about Emily. He was rather mysterious. I told him what had happened. He hadn't heard about it.' Douglas liked to think that both his sons took heed of world affairs, but ignored, as he did, trivial events.

'Oh, that's wonderful,' said Isabel, but it was the prospect of Toby's coming, not what he had to say about Emily, that delighted her.

Douglas went off to turn on her bath. She'd suddenly looked joyful, almost young, because she would see Toby soon. She never looked like that when she saw him. Leaving the bath running, he went morosely off to feed his fish. Watching them swim round, some rapidly, like the danios and rasboras, in little darting movements, the angelfish and gouramis more sedately, always calmed him. It was a pity people couldn't be segregated into sections appropriate to their natures. He had not been contemplating his piscatorial empire for long before the doorbell announced the arrival of the police.

Douglas admitted Detective Inspector Cox, accompanied by a detective sergeant, both men in plain clothes, and said that Isabel would be down soon. He took them into his study, where neither commented on his aquarium.

'My wife didn't arrive home until it was almost morning,' he said repressively. 'I woke her only because you were coming.'

'I understand,' said Cox.

'It's a pity you couldn't leave her to rest,' said Douglas.

'I'm sorry, Mr Vernon, but we are investigating a murder, and your wife has some important facts to divulge,' said Cox.

Divulge, indeed, thought Douglas. Perhaps she knew that

Emily had a criminal record as long as your arm, which she'd concealed from him.

'I'll make some coffee,' Douglas said. 'Please sit down.'

His study contained a leather-covered wing armchair and a comfortable executive-type chair facing the large desk. There was also a small stool. The two detectives exchanged glances and remained standing, but they moved to look out of the window. The garden was a mass of groves and grottoes separated by elaborate trellis work.

'No gnomes,' murmured Detective Sergeant Fowler. He peered into the fish tank, where, on different levels, the various species moved in flotillas among the fronds of vegetation. 'Rather fun, these,' he offered. 'They seem quite happy with their lives.'

'No piranhas there,' said Cox. 'They're the villains.'

He paced up and down while Fowler gazed at the fish, and then Isabel came in.

'I'm sorry to keep you waiting,' she said. 'Shall we go into the other room where it's more comfortable?' and she led the way across the hall to the drawing-room.

'Mr Vernon is kindly making some coffee,' said Cox, after introducing himself and his colleague.

'Oh, good,' said Isabel. More brownie points for Douglas. 'He'll find us, when it's ready. Have you got any news about that man? Has anyone seen him?'

'We've had some reported sightings,' said Cox. 'But they may not all have been genuine.'

'He'll know it's murder now,' said Isabel. 'He'll have heard the news.'

'Yes.'

'He might get away with it,' she said. 'People do, don't they?'

'It's more difficult to find them if they can get out of the country,' Cox said. 'But ports and airports have been warned to watch for him. Interpol will cooperate.'

At this point, Douglas came in, with a tray. He'd done well, Isabel noticed, making four mugs of instant coffee, neither mugs nor instant being his preferred style.

'You've had no breakfast,' he said to her. 'I've put some toast in for you.'

'Oh, thank you, Douglas,' she answered. 'But I had a huge breakfast at about two o'clock this morning with PC Darwin at a Little Chef. Some toast would be nice, though,' she added. 'Or biscuits. Maybe you'd like biscuits?' she asked their uninvited guests.

'The coffee's just fine,' said Cox. 'Now, I understand you have some important information about the deceased's identity?'

'Yes.' Isabel glanced at Douglas, who was leaving to attend to the automatic toaster. 'I'd like my husband to hear it, too,' she said. If he heard her telling the police, it would remove the need for her to repeat the story to him later, and they would offer her some protection from his wrath. For angry he would be, when he understood that she had realised for several days that Emily was an imposter.

When Douglas returned, she told her tale briefly and clearly. Recounting it to Darwin had clarified her thoughts, and simplified its repetition. There were so many small things which had been puzzling, and she revealed them, from Emily's appearance – although she had not seen her since she was a small child – to her unfamiliarity with Jane Austen. Then she had kept away from Toby during his visit. Finally, there was the note and the very different handwriting. She did not mention Emily's voice; she'd spoken rather roughly, but then many educated people chose not to articulate clearly nowadays.

Occasionally Detective Inspector Cox asked her a question, and Fowler took notes, but Douglas listened without interrupting once. While she spoke, ignoring her buttered toast, Isabel kept her eyes on Cox; she did not want to look at Douglas, knowing that his silence was due to horror so immense that he was lost for words. She'd hear about it later. Moving to her desk, she retrieved the letter and the note.

'She knew a lot about the real Emily – about the family. About Ginnie – the real Emily's mother. She couldn't just have found the letter somewhere, if Emily – my Emily – had dropped it. She must have spoken to her. Known her, somehow.' Isabel declared. She explained that she had written to the Campbells, having failed to trace their telephone number.

'We can check them out,' said Cox. 'It seems clear that she was a fake, impersonating your goddaughter. We need to know who she really was.'

'I suppose you can prove she wasn't genuine by blood tests, if you can find her brothers, or even her grandparents, if not the real Emily Frost,' said Douglas, speaking at last. The wicked, silly girl, he was thinking. Could she have harmed the original Emily Frost and so taken on her identity? Hiding among a lot of anarchists and living off the land was a good way of escaping justice. He decided not to put this theory into words; the girl was dead, after all, whatever she had done.

Cox pressed Isabel to consider whether Emily could have met Godfrey Sutton before she came to Fordswick.

'She never named the man she was meeting,' Isabel explained. 'He telephoned and asked to speak to her. I never asked her who he was. She simply said, "a friend". I should have shown more interest, I suppose, but I wanted her to feel I trusted her. After all, I did think she was my goddaughter.'

'Rowena Watkinson seems to think his name was Graham, and that's what he called himself at the boarding-house in Northtown where he had a room,' said Cox. 'We're fairly sure it was Sutton who stayed there, though we need corroborative evidence.'

Douglas cleared his throat.

'Might Alice have anything of his? From when he lived at Ford House formerly, I mean?' he asked.

'I doubt if Alice will have kept anything he gave her – if he did give her anything,' she said. 'Except Rowena, of course, and that was unintentional.'

'Or careless,' Douglas remarked. 'He did some painting. There might be old paint tins he might have used. Or brushes. It may be that you could find fingerprints on them.'

In spite of the circumstances, Isabel had time to note his use of *might* and *may*. Perhaps this pedantry of his had been one of his attractions for her. She still respected it.

'We'll ask forensic to have a look,' said Cox. 'There could well be something in the flat, if no one else has used it since.'

'As far as I know, they haven't,' Isabel said.

'Well, that's a step forward,' said Cox. 'But we're no nearer finding out who the dead girl really was. However, now we know about her arrest, we can ask other protestors if they knew Godfrey Sutton. We can trace those that were arrested through the court.'

At this point in their conversation, a call came through on Fowler's personal radio. He left the room to take the message, soon returning to say that the preliminary report on the postmortem had been received.

'The doc thinks she was only about sixteen or seventeen,'

he said. 'Really quite young. Not twenty-three, like the real Emily.'

'And I let her out with a man who killed her,' said Isabel, on a wail.

'Isabel, she pretended to be twenty-three. You weren't responsible for the bogus girl, only for the real one,' said Douglas firmly.

'She'd been around, Mrs Vernon,' said Fowler. 'She'd had a child, and some major surgery within the past year. This may help us trace her background.'

'What did she die of?' Isabel asked faintly.

'Internal haemorrhaging,' he said. 'Her spleen was ruptured, possibly by a blow or kick. And hypothermia. It was a very bitter night.'

23

Godfrey had heard the radio broadcast. So she'd died. Well, by leaving her in that wooded spot, he'd not expected her to be rescued and revived but when he met her, only ten days ago, he'd had no thought of harming her. He'd returned to Fordswick on a whim, and then seen the child's swing, been curious, and come across Emily. One thing had led to another, just as years before, meeting Alice in a bar, he'd embarked on the path that had led him to this moment, fleeing in his van.

He'd thought at first of leaving the country. He had his passport and some money, but the van would be a target; they might be watching out for him at the ports. Those people in the street in Northtown could have described him, and someone might have noted the van's number. Thoughts of catching a ferry from Hull or Newcastle had been in his mind, but even if he got on board without being challenged, he might be stopped before he could disembark at the end of the journey. While he had the van, though, he had shelter and a means of transport; by now he hoped he was out of range of any road blocks that had been set up and if he stuck to minor roads, he'd avoid most police patrol cars. The van was the problem, yet if he abandoned it, because his funds were limited he was helpless. He must disguise it.

During the night it had got warmer and the air was damp. He could use mud to mask the registration number, and lie up while the hunt was on, move when it was dark. He had enough food and water for two or three days, if he could find a place where the van would not attract attention. He'd left Emily in a wood. There would be other wooded, deserted places.

Trying to sell the van would be risky, but if he simply dumped it, it would mean a serious loss of capital, and could he get more transport? Godfrey had not lived an honest life, but stealing cars and robbing banks was not part of his experience. Battening on people was, though he did not think of it in such terms; finding opportunities to further his own ends was his main skill, and he might still do it, if he stayed cool. He'd soon need gas, though; Godfrey still thought in transatlantic terms.

Large service areas probably had closed-circuit television. A smaller, rural filling station might not, but would such a place be open on a Sunday? It wasn't very likely, if Britain operated as it had done when he left five years ago. He was wishing he had not returned, until he remembered that he was also wanted in Toronto, though an arrest there, for fraud, was a better prospect than facing a murder charge in Britain. That stupid Emily: it was her fault that he had been forced into taking violent action. Why couldn't she have gone along with his plan? If she had, they'd have smuggled the child into his rented room, where Emily would have kept her quiet while he drew the ransom, which the Watkinsons would have paid as soon as they knew the kid was missing. He'd have given her a hundred quid or so.

All his life, Godfrey had lived for the moment. At school, after his parents separated he had stayed with his mother, and he had extorted money and sweets from younger children by using threats. He would buy his mother presents, and when she asked how he had paid for them, he pretended to have done jobs for people after school. His mother thought him wonderful. Then she remarried, and he was the outsider. As soon as he was old enough, Godfrey joined the army, which gave him a family and trained him to be tough. During this time he got married but it didn't last. After his discharge – he was not found suitable for re-engagement – he had worked for a builder and married for the second time, but making off with materials from the site he was working on and selling them on the side had landed him in trouble with the law. He'd spent six months in prison, losing contact with his wife, and after that had moved around, picking up casual work or working minor scams, finally moving in with a woman he met in a club. Like his more recent Canadian partner, she had her own business – hers was hairdressing – and for a while he successfully convinced her that he was going daily to an insurance office where he was a departmental manager. In fact, he was working as a maintenance man in a hotel. As the Watkinsons were to discover later, he was a good carpenter and handyman, and while there, with access to guests' rooms, he stole credit cards and money, getting caught eventually. It was not long after his second stint in prison that he met Alice.

Godfrey had driven down a lane, planning to use mud on the van's registration plates, both front and rear. Then he remembered his shoe cleaning kit. Relic from his army days, he liked clean shoes and boots. He used the liquid from a rub-on container to turn a three into an eight, and a C into a G. That was all it needed. He'd buy some spray paint with which to complete the job, making it more permanent, and then, in a quiet glade, he'd spray the entire van.

First, he must trim his hair and shave off his moustache and sideburns. He put the kettle on.

Most of his schemes had worked; it was only when they became too ambitious that things went wrong, like thinking he might marry Alice, and this latest venture which he had embarked on impulsively, because the child and Emily gave him the opening.

He who dares, wins, thought Godfrey as, reluctantly, he removed his moustache and sideburns. Being cleanshaven altered his appearance considerably. He should visit a barber, get a short back and sides haircut, but if he did, the barber might remember him. He clipped round his own head as best he could. A fresh opportunity to change his fortunes might arise; he'd just have to recognise it when it came.

Toby arrived at Elm Lodge as the police were leaving. He said that they'd better hear what he had to say. He had remembered that Emily had brown eyes. The girl he'd seen last weekend had blue ones. It was as simple as that.

'You'd never seen it, had you, Mum?' he asked. 'She was the only one in the family who had them. All the rest were blue. Both parents, and the two boys. At the time, when we were children, that meant nothing to us, but it did to Hugh. He knew he couldn't be her father. You remember – Mendel's theory – roughly speaking, two blue-eyed parents will have blue-eyed children, brown-eyed parents will have brown-eyed sprogs, and a brown and a blue-eyed couple may have either. Emily's brothers teased her about it – they kept calling her eyes deep brown pools, and they made her cry because she thought tadpoles lived in pools. Very likely Hugh caught on in the end and that was why he scarpered.'

'Oh! Are you sure? I'd never really noticed – or at least, if I did then, I hadn't realised its significance and had forgotten about it,' said Isabel. Perhaps this explained some of Ginnie's distress at finding she was pregnant, but who could her lover have been? Not the Spaniard she had later married. 'Well,' she added, 'that's further proof, if any's needed. And she was only about seventeen, Toby, whereas the real Emily must be twenty-three, like you. It's so terrible. The poor girl.' And what about this baby she'd had? What had been its fate? And what was the surgery she'd undergone? There was scarring on her body, it seemed, besides that caused by the injuries she had recently received.

Detective Inspector Cox told them that in an effort to establish the dead girl's true identity, the missing persons register would be consulted, and her photograph would be widely circulated.

'But there isn't one,' said Isabel.

'There may be one among media reports about the protest,' said Cox. Though the dead girl had been photographed from all angles, for forensic records to be used as evidence, such photographs would be useless for identification because of her disfiguring injuries.

The police officers departed, and Douglas, seeing that his wife and son had plenty to discuss, set off on his cycle for a ride.

'Poor Dad,' said Toby, after he had gone.

'Why so?' asked Isabel, surprised.

'Bit out of his depth, isn't he, with all this unmarried mother stuff and demonstrations and what not? Not his scene at all.'

'He was very kind this morning,' said Isabel.

'What? No lecture on being gullible? No sanctimoniousness?'

'You are wicked, Toby,' said Isabel. 'But no. Nothing like that. A cup of tea in bed. He didn't know I'd already had breakfast at a Little Chef with a policeman.'

'He'll want some lunch,' said Toby, reminded of food. 'Shall I make some sandwiches?'

'We'll both make them,' Isabel declared.

While they were in the kitchen, the telephone rang. Toby picked up the cordless instrument to answer it, and Isabel heard the one-sided conversation, which was mainly, on his part, monosyllabic. Eventually, saying, 'You'd better speak to my mother,' he handed the instrument to her.

'It's the grandfather,' he told her, covering the mouthpiece. 'From Scotland. Lives somewhere else now, but he's had your letter.'

The real Emily, it transpired, was at the moment in New Zealand, where she'd been for almost a year, after splitting up with her boyfriend following a miscarriage. Mr Campbell gave Isabel her address.

'We'll pass it on to the inspector,' said Toby, when Isabel had hung up. She had taken note of the grandfather's telephone number and current address. Isabel's letter had been promptly forwarded to him by the people who had bought his former house after his wife's death, and he had received it the previous day. There was no need to tell him that a girl had been posing as his granddaughter; the police would do that soon enough. He had told Isabel that his two grandsons were both overseas. Emily – the false Emily – had been right about that, but how had she known, wondered Isabel as Toby rang Cox to tell him where to find Mr Campbell. Let the police take what steps were necessary next.

Douglas was seldom late for lunch at weekends, but he was still out on his bicycle at one o'clock.

'Let's have a quick bite and then go for a walk, Mum,' said Toby. 'It will do you good to get out for a bit.'

Isabel agreed. She felt like screaming once again. The walk might curb this uncomfortable urge.

Douglas, returning, found the kitchen table laid for him, a pile of ham sandwiches under clingfilm, and a pan of soup ready to warm through. He sighed, turning on the stove. Tomorrow he'd be back at work, predictably ensconced in the ministry, and secure. Alice, however, would not be on the morning train.

What had happened to his safe world?

Isabel and Toby ended their walk at Ford House. She felt the need to check on the household. Toby was not sure if he had ever met the Watkinsons.

'Nice house. I've always thought so,' he said. 'With potential. A bit grim and dark at present.'

'I don't think any part of it's been painted since Godfrey did his worst five years ago,' said Isabel. 'It must have been a sad place until Rowena arrived to brighten things. Alice seems to have been kept well under the parental thumb.'

'Why didn't she rebel?' asked Toby.

'She did, eventually – with dire consequences,' said Isabel. 'But they all love Rowena.'

'Let's hope they don't expect too much from her,' said Toby. 'You know – people invest great hopes in a child and lay a burden on it. Making it justify their existence, in a way.'

'I hope we never did that, Toby,' said Isabel.

'No, Mum. You've been pretty laid back,' said Toby.

'Well, I'm very proud of you both,' said Isabel. 'You're good guys, you two. That's something to have contributed to the human race – produced two sons who are plus people. But no one has a right to have children. They're a privilege – often expensive, sometimes a problem – but not a right.' She and Emily had talked about rights, she recalled. 'I can't imagine not having had you both,' she confessed. 'But you arrived without clinical intervention. How would you feel if you'd come from a test tube?'

'I don't know. I suppose if people want babies very badly, and it's the only way— ' Toby's voice trailed off.

'Some of them want the baby for them, not for it, or because of outside pressures or like needing an heir if you're the king or queen,' she said. 'Though I suppose you'd love it later, for its own sake.'

'Not always,' he said. 'What happens if it's a serious disappointment?'

'What did this man, Godfrey, think about Rowena, when he saw her?' said Isabel. 'He didn't treat her very lovingly, snatching her like that. It wasn't a heartbreak kidnap, as the papers might say, just done for money. But it must have been a shock to find he had a daughter.'

'Is that why he came back here? Because he'd discovered she existed?'

'I don't know. Maybe. Then Emily came on the scene and made it simple for him.'

'Those test-tube dads. Do you think they ever wonder about their kids?' asked Toby. 'They ought to. You shouldn't go scattering it about like that, at random.'

Isabel was glad to hear him say so. She could understand the scientific fascination of creating life, but the moral and sociological ramifications disturbed her.

At Ford House, they learned that the police had been active earlier, with fingerprint experts dusting round in the stable flat and in the kitchen, where according to Rowena, Godfrey had been entertained to lunch. He had also been in the hall. Old paint tins and brushes had been removed from the outbuildings; both there and in the house, various prints were found. So few people came to the house that those legitimately present could be eliminated, though the police had also left theirs around, which, as they put it, contaminated the scene.

'He'll get away,' said Alice. She and Rowena were in the kitchen, where Rowena had been colouring a book about dinosaurs. The elder Watkinsons were sitting by the fire in the drawing-room, reading the Sunday papers. They took several. 'He's the sort of man who always will escape.'

'Even if he does, he won't dare turn up here again,' said Toby. 'He'll always be a wanted man.' Though if caught and prosecuted, he might get away with manslaughter. Better not to mention that possibility.

Alice had made an appointment to see a prospective au pair girl, Cecile, the French one. She would come down by train tomorrow.

'Good,' said Isabel.

She and Toby stayed to tea, and Toby played Snap with Rowena.

'Things will buck up if they get this girl, and if Alice can be persuaded to find something local to do. She might train for something new. She can't be said to have had much of a career, so far,' said Isabel as they walked home. She thought sadly of her plans for Emily to do the same. Now they would never be tested.

'It's not on for her to go to London,' said Toby. 'Not with the fares, and the little girl, and all. Nice little thing, isn't she? Bright, I'd say, not that I know much about children. Pity about the father. Still, environment can overcome heredity, I'm sure.'

'We don't know why he went to the bad,' said Isabel. 'Most families have got a black sheep somewhere or other. And I don't suppose he really meant to murder Emily, only to get rid of her.'

'You can't go hitting people and dumping them just because they're in the way,' said Toby. 'Poor kid, she hadn't had her life.' He was silent for a while, and then he said, 'What if I'd realised sooner that there was something wrong? What if we'd chatted more last weekend, if I'd done the "do you remember" bit? But we were so young there wasn't too much to remember.'

'I was the one who ought to have seen it,' said Isabel. 'If I'd kept properly in touch with her – the real Emily – I'd have known what she was doing and that she was in New Zealand.'

'Mum, you can't be responsible for the whole world,' said Toby. 'You didn't chuck her out, when you had your suspicions.'

'I'd got fond of her,' said Isabel. 'She was a sweet girl, Toby. I wonder if we'll ever find out who she was?'

24

An artist's impression of Emily dominated the tabloids on Monday morning.

In the train, Douglas could see the headlines of other people's papers. His own *Times* was restrained, with a description on an inner page, but across the carriage he read MYSTERY OF ABDUCTED GIRL'S IDENTITY on one, and WHO WAS SHE? on another. Late on Sunday, Isabel and Alice had been whisked into Northtown police station to help a police artist create the likeness. Meanwhile, clips of protestors at the site would be scanned in search of a shot of her as she was in life. Both women would be asked to view the more likely clips.

Douglas missed seeing Alice on the train. Of course she should not have gone to the gallery in the first place; then none of this would have happened. The false Emily would not have been required to work at Ford House and, though still a cuckoo in his domestic nest, she would be alive. He sighed. One made choices and decisions in one's life and some were most unwise. Better to plot your course with care, as he had done, and stick to the design; Isabel knew she could rely on him, and as a servant of the state, his pension was assured. It was typical of her to champion the underdog, as Emily had clearly been; how soon would she have told him of her doubts about the girl's identity?

Surely the pretender's parents would recognise the drawing in the paper? It was accurate; he thought it very good, peering at it across the aisle as it was displayed to him on the front page of the *Daily Mail*. She must have a family somewhere, anxious and concerned. But Douglas had seen the youngsters sleeping in the street; he knew about the unwanted homeless, and those who had run away in search of better lives to find only disillusion. Emily must have been one of them, for why else had she adopted someone else's name and background? He shuddered at the horror of it, but he could see that joining the protestors assured her anonymity, and even friendship. His minister had visited the various sites where demonstrations had taken place and Douglas had gone along on two occasions; he'd had some sympathy for environmentalists wanting to protect rare species and fine vistas, yet safety had to be considered, and the dangers of pollution; weighing up the pros and cons was always difficult and it was impossible to satisfy every interest. He worried about the safety of the planet; mankind would engineer itself out of existence if it could not invent less destructive methods of surviving than some of those now in common use.

In a house in Luton, a woman was reading the newspaper.

Larry had brought it back, as usual, when he came off night shift, and it lay on the kitchen table while he had his breakfast before going up to bed, where she might briefly join him, as she sometimes did, before going to the pub where she worked each weekday. The girl's face looked up at her, round and solemn, one earring hanging from her left ear. It was the earring, really, that told her who she was: the little horse, attached to a tiny ring, though of course hers couldn't be the only one; there must be others like it. She'd had it on that evening, when she came to the house. With her long curling hair shorn off and the fatter face with the blue eyes, the duplicate sat across the table: her father, unaware. He did not know that it was his daughter who had pushed her down the stairs and stolen all her savings; he had not known how much she had, stashed away. She'd said that the thief was a youth, an intruder who had broken in and knocked her over. She'd not been unconscious long, and had soon managed to reach the telephone and call for help. Her expected visitor had sheered off when he saw the ambulance but later he had resumed their regular arrangement, which continued now. She was not badly hurt and had not been kept in hospital. Returning home, she had seen bloodstains in the lavatory pan and a few drops on the floor. So that problem had solved itself.

Larry had glanced at the paper before throwing it aside.

'Terrible what some people do,' he said. 'Fancy snatching a young girl and dumping her in the woods to die. Some sex fiend, I suppose,' he added, turning to his sausages and chips.

He hadn't recognised her from the drawing. She would not enlighten him. If she kept quiet, it would all go away, as it had done before, when the girl came here that night nearly a year ago. She and Larry got on very well without her. He hadn't mentioned her for a long time.

Godfrey had not risked shopping while it was daylight, and with the van stationary he was not using fuel. When dusk fell on Sunday night, he drove on until he reached a main road which eventually led him to a motorway. On most motorways there was heavy traffic as weekenders went home, and tonight he met some of it. Reaching a service area, he drove in, hoping his tactics with the number plates would hold up. He chose an inside pump among other vehicles so that if cameras were operating, he and the van would be surrounded and would not stand out. He filled the tank and his water carriers, and bought a can of black touch-up paint. That would fix the number plates more effectively. Then he drove on, heading north. At a motorway halt south of Carlisle, he stopped for an early breakfast and a wash-up. It was cold and the air was damp; he put on Emily's red woollen cap. As well as keeping the weather off, it was a disguise. Before leaving the service area, he bought the early edition of the *Sun*. There she was staring at him from the front page, with the headline demanding WHO WAS SHE?

Two policemen in a patrol car in the parking area vaguely saw a clean-shaven man wearing a dark jacket and a red cap walking among the vehicles, not loitering nor looking in any way suspicious. The officers knew that a camper van was being sought, and they had a description of the suspect driver, who had shaggy hair, a moustache and sideburns, and had been wearing an olive-green parka jacket at the time the woman was abducted. Two cars drove across their line of vision and they did not notice Godfrey entering a camper van. Back in the van, Godfrey read the piece. So she was a fraud, he thought: the little cow. What was her game? He had seen the police car and drove calmly off. It did not follow him.

Godfrey was running on cash which he had hidden inside the van. He had brought the money out of Canada, changing it at various exchange bureaux; he had not opened any sort of account since he had been back in Britain, because to do so required proof of identity and he was using several different names. His Fordswick trip had been an impetuous diversion which had turned out to be disastrous. He had already used a lot of money on the van, on various other expenses such as food, drink and petrol, and on entertaining Emily. He had about four hundred pounds left, not enough to launch him into business. A pay-off from the Watkinsons would have seen him right; as it was, if he saw a chance, he would try to grab some more.

There was snow on the hills around him. Was it wise to go to Scotland, where the weather would be worse and might mean roads would be closed? His voice would betray him as being English, or even transatlantic – he had acquired some Canadian expressions – so that he would stand out. Godfrey turned about and headed south. All this driving around would be expensive, yet he felt safer on the move. A camper van, seen parked in a lonely lane in winter, was something that would be remembered. If only that girl hadn't got in his way, he was thinking, as he drove on. He'd have found out about the kid without her and he'd have got his money by threatening to claim parental rights. Godfrey was uncertain of the law in Britain but fathers had their rights, and he'd have set about establishing his unless the Watkinsons had made it worth his while to go away again – which they would have done. The girl had come along, and hearing what she had to say, he'd included her in his scheme, which was where he went wrong. Pulling her into the van, he'd hoped to get the kid, too, but she'd escaped. Emily's bulk had stopped him grabbing the kid directly. He should have left them both, cut his losses and cleared off, but he didn't like losing out to anyone, especially a woman. Now he was in real trouble unless he could go to ground somewhere. Today he'd paint the van, really do it, get some cans and turn it blue or green. He'd use masking tape to protect the lights and windows; he'd do a proper job, as was his way.

Pity the kid was so ugly, he reflected; if she'd been a pretty little girl, he might have taken to her.

The traffic was increasing as the working day began. If he were familiar with the district, he'd know where there was a shopping mall which would stock what he wanted. As it was, he'd have to turn off and risk entering a town.

It should be safe enough. He'd continue to wear Emily's red hat; after all, no one on the run would wear anything so conspicuous. Having bought the paint, he'd look for a deserted spot where he could apply it. He'd found plenty of sheltered areas in which to park, and there'd be another. He turned off at the next slip road and was soon crawling along in a line of rush-hour traffic snailing through the outskirts of an industrial area, and then he saw a yellow van ahead of him. On its rear doors, in large black letters, was proclaimed the fact that its owner was a painter and decorator. It just might lead him, not to a customer, but to a supplier, thought Godfrey. And it did.

Further south, the weather had improved and it was a mild and sunny day in Northtown. Isabel went to the shop, where there was a fair amount of sorting out to do after the weekend. Joanna had been busy on Saturday, with several curious customers coming in to find out what had happened the previous afternoon, but she knew few details. Because of her age, Rowena's identity was protected, but the story that the kidnap of a child had been foiled by the missing girl began to emerge. On Monday, a reporter from the local paper called at Gifts Galore to see what she could learn, but Isabel told her nothing. So far, the press had not discovered where Emily had been living, nor that she had been working as a nanny, but that information would soon get out. Once the police started combing through past news clips about the protest site where Emily had been arrested, interest would widen.

Isabel was ready for it when a newspaper rang up offering her, as the abducted girl's godmother, large sums to sell her story. How had they got hold of that? She did not ask, banging down the telephone. Ghouls.

Joanna came in, anxious to hear the news and to help with the accumulated paperwork, and to see a salesman whose imported products – decorative throws for furniture and wall-hangings – she thought they might promote. Isabel was less sure of their appeal to the customers of Gifts Galore, but when she saw the samples, found them attractive. A policy discussion about the development of the business followed, and in the early afternoon Valerie, the fort-holder from Friday afternoon, came to commiserate about Emily and ask how Rowena was. Just as the shop was closing, PC Colin Darwin arrived.

'I got the boss to let me tell you about your real goddaughter,' he said. 'It's CID business now, you see, and I'm uniform, but I am a bit involved. Sometimes we overlap.'

'Well? Have you found her?'

'Yes – and she is well, the real Emily,' said Darwin. 'She's in New Zealand, just as her grandfather said, after first spending time in South America with one brother and in Spain with the other. She's working in a tourist office, and plans to be there for a while. We now know which hospital she was in when she had a miscarriage, and this looks like being the connection with the false Emily. She was in a small ward with a girl who'd also miscarried but who'd been pregnant longer, and had had surgery. She'd got internal problems of some sort which could have caused the miscarriage – insides the wrong way round, or something. The real Emily was only in there three nights; it would have been fewer, but her minor operation was delayed because of other more urgent cases. They were both in a bad state – both upset – and the other girl seemed to like listening to the real Emily chatting about the past – kept asking her questions. The chat stopped the other girl crying – seemed to comfort her. She had no visitors. Your Emily felt very sorry for her. She couldn't remember her name – thought it was Rose – something like that. It should be possible through hospital records to find out who she was. She was very young, only sixteen.'

So if this was the same girl, the postmortem estimate of her age was accurate. It explained a great deal.

'That's dreadful,' said Isabel.

'I know,' said Colin. 'She was all right with you, though. You hang on to that. At the end, she had a good few weeks, even months. I expect she was happy enough on that site.'

'Something awful had happened to her,' said Isabel. 'It must have done.'

'I think so,' he agreed. 'According to your real goddaughter, she had long wavy fair hair and was pretty. This might help in the identification. We've faxed our sketch out to Auckland, and the guys there will add hair at the direction of your Emily, and slim her down a bit. That may help.'

Isabel suddenly began to cry.

'That poor girl. I can't bear it for her,' she said. 'She was lost, wasn't she?'

'Yes, I suppose she was,' he answered.

'We'd have saved her. I'd have saved her, if she hadn't died,' said Isabel. 'I'd have helped her, somehow. Got her sorted, trained, settled. No matter what Douglas said, I'd have done it.'

Colin knew she would have tried, but would her efforts have succeeded? No one, now, would know.

'I'm sure you would,' he said. 'Now, why don't we go along to The Pineapple and have a drink, before you go home? You need one.'

Isabel blew her nose.

'Sorry about this,' she said. 'And I would love a drink, but are you, a policeman, suggesting I should drink and drive?'

'You could always have tonic water laced with angostura,' he suggested. 'It makes a pinkish, sophisticated tipple.'

Isabel laughed.

'All right,' she said. 'I'll try it.'

Over their drinks in the bar of the pub along the road, he told her that the real Emily would be writing to her, faxing the letter to the police station, and that he would personally deliver it. This would be quicker than the post. Then they could ring each other up, bearing in mind the time difference.

'You'll have to get a computer. Have E-mail,' he suggested. 'I bet your New Zealand Emily has access to it.'

'I'd never learn,' said Isabel.

'Of course you would. Do a course. Take Alice along with you. The pair of you could surf the Internet,' he said.

'It might be very good for Alice,' said Isabel. 'I think that's a brilliant idea.'

'The old boy might like it, too,' said Colin.

Isabel thought at first that he meant Douglas; then she realised it was Mr Watkinson he had in mind.

Godfrey had bought his paint. He'd got several colours – blue and red and yellow – deciding that if he made his van conspicuous, with psychedelic designs, it would seem like a young person's vehicle and deflect suspicion. He paid cash. At the big, impersonal retail warehouse, no one paid him much attention. He looked like any other customer, a man in early middle age, wearing a red woollen cap, jeans, and an olive green parka jacket. Then he drove through the town and into the countryside beyond, turning off the main road, seeking a place where he could apply the paint, unseen.

The weather had changed again and was on his side. It was sunny and dry, and though frost was forecast, it was not freezing now. He had to drive a long way before, travelling down a minor road, he found a track leading through farmland. He turned into it; there had been very little traffic on the road he had just left, so if he could find shelter here, he could do the job. He went carefully along the track. The ground was soggy where it had thawed; this was a van, not a four-wheel drive vehicle designed to cope with slippery surfaces, so he must be careful. As he progressed, going down a slight slope, he saw a barn some hundred yards away or more, reached by a rutted path across a field. That was a bit of luck, but it was too much to hope that it would be unlocked so that he could spray the van inside. However, he would be able to park behind it, out of sight of anyone approaching.

As he expected, the barn, stacked with hay, was locked. The farmer took no chances in these times of heedless arson. Godfrey drove round to the rear of it and looked about. In the hollow below him he could see the grey slate roof of the farmhouse, but no windows were visible; he would not be overlooked.

He was so absorbed in spraying angular designs in different colours on the van that when a tractor, towing a trailer coming to load hay, chuntered up the slope towards him, at first he did not hear it. The farmer, seeing him, turned round and drove back down the slope towards his house. A modern man, often out of doors for hours and whose wife was pregnant, he carried a mobile phone to keep in touch. Once he had dropped over the brow of the hill and was out of sight, he dialled 999. He had not seen the paper and he thought the man was probably a robber, possibly armed and with accomplices, seeking to disguise the van. Then he drove his tractor along the track to the road, where he parked it to block the way in case the man finished his task before the police arrived.

A police helicopter was already looking for Godfrey. It had scoured the wrong area the day before; no one realised he had travelled so far north until a customer in a retail warehouse had noticed a man buying masking tape and quantities of paint in spray cans. He had seen the man leave in a white camper van, but had not attached importance to it at the time. Later, learning that the police were looking for a man in such a van, he'd called them, describing the man's clothing, including the red hat. On the computer screen, the officer speaking to him saw the recorded fact that the dead girl's red woollen hat, and her earring, in the form of a small gilt horse, were both missing when she was found.

The helicopter was soon directed to the farm, and Godfrey, hearing its clatter, saw it hovering above him. A voice, as though from God, called down to him, advising him not to resist arrest. But he did. He leapt into the van and set off down the track towards the road, then, seeing the tractor, he turned aside over the grass. He hadn't got far before the van skidded, slithering on the surface thaw, and the engine stalled. All the time, the helicopter was above him. Godfrey flung out of the van and started running; the farmer, now, was in pursuit, in his tractor, and two police cars were coming fast along the road, converging on the scene.

The farmer abandoned his tractor to run after Godfrey, and though he was hampered by his heavy boots, he had the satisfaction of bringing him to the ground in a rugby tackle.

'I'll sue you for assault,' snarled Godfrey, as the farmer held him captive by sitting on him while the helicopter landed reinforcements.

'I don't think so,' said the farmer, very happy. He did not know who his captive was until after the two police cars had arrived and Godfrey had been arrested and cautioned on suspicion of murder. One of the police cars got bogged down in a sticky patch. The farmer towed it free.

News of the arrest was on all the radio and television bulletins. No name was given for the accused man.

Darwin heard it on his personal radio while still in The Pineapple with Isabel, who said she would go home by way of Ford House to make sure they had heard.

'Alice won't have to identify him, will she?' she asked. 'One hears about identification parades. Not nice.'

'No – she hasn't seen him this time round, remember. Nor has the old man. It's the mother who did. She's well able for an identification parade, but I doubt if it will be necessary. There'll be plenty of evidence.'

'What a relief to know he's been caught,' said Isabel. 'Thank goodness. I hope he pays for it.'

A few years inside, thought Colin; that would be the result. A good brief would get him off with manslaughter, and even if he were convicted of murder, with remission he'd be out before Rowena was an adult. Could anyone guarantee that he would stay away from her then? Injunctions could be taken out, but they could be defied. Sutton had the power to inflict great psychological damage on the child. On the other hand, unless there was something in it for him, Godfrey might decide to keep away. In the interval, Rowena's mother must get tough and learn how to protect herself, her child and their inheritance from a man who might seek to make public his connection with the family.

He said none of this to Isabel. There was time enough. Before they left the pub, he called his headquarters back and then said that he would follow her along the road and go with her to see Alice.

'Can you believe it? No one was bothering about letting her know he'd been arrested,' he said. 'This is where police and public relations break down. Victims need to know what's going on. Unless she's required to give evidence, which is unlikely, or her mother is, she may not even know the trial date. You probably will, though,' he told Isabel. 'You may be called as a witness. So you can tell her.'

Isabel stared at him.

'Is that right?' she said. 'About Alice not being told?'

'It's correct, but not right,' he answered. 'They'd have got round to it in the end, I expect. If I do rise up in the hierarchy, I mean to try to alter that.'

'I should hope so,' said Isabel. 'What about Victim Support?'

'They do try,' he admitted. 'They do good work and I'm sure they are a big help in certain cases.'

In convoy, they drove back to Fordswick, where Mr Watkinson had heard the news on the radio. Alice had just returned from taking the au pair girl to the station. Cecile, unhappy in her present post, had liked the idea of three months in the country, after which she planned to return home. She was to come at the weekend, when her notice at her current employers expired.

This would see the Watkinsons through the aftermath of Emily's murder and Muriel's operation.

'Good news all round, then,' said Isabel.

No one said anything, that night, to indicate that the situation was by no means resolved. Godfrey Sutton would be charged, and would not get bail – that was certain. He would be remanded in custody, committed for trial in the High Court, and eventually would face a judge and jury.

'It's ironic,' said Colin, sitting by the fire in the drawing-room at Elm Lodge. He had volunteered to tell Douglas, when he came home, all that was likely to happen, since Isabel feared her explanation would not satisfy him.

'What's ironic?' asked Isabel.

'Sutton's not really a killer. He's a coward who set out to defraud the Watkinsons. He devised a scam which backfired because Emily was gutsy, and when she stood up to him, he freaked. He's probably a man who bullies women. Certainly he doesn't like them.'

'You do, don't you?' said Isabel.

How attractive she was, he thought, but she didn't realise it. Had anyone told her so, recently? That husband of hers, for instance, with his fish and his pergolas and ponds?

'Yes, I do,' he said. 'And just occasionally, men and women can be friends.'

They were sitting comfortably together, one on either side of the fire, when Douglas returned. He had not heard the news; it had come through too late for the evening edition of the *Standard*, which he usually bought at the station. He listened carefully to what they told him, absorbing what was said and also what was implied about future problems, both before and after Godfrey Sutton was sentenced.

He did not mention his visit that day to a café near Alice's art gallery, where he had seen the man whom she had met for lunch. He had bought a sandwich for himself, and coffee, and had approached the man, whose name he did not know.

'May I?' Douglas had said, taking the seat opposite Paul, not waiting for permission.

The man, who was reading the *Independent*, glanced up and nodded, returning to his paper.

'I think you are – or were – a friend of Alice Watkinson's,' said Douglas sternly. 'No doubt your paper refers to the abduction of a young woman and her subsequent death. The young woman was Alice's nanny. Alice's child was abducted, too, but the girl saved her.'

Paul, startled, stared at this stranger with the long thin face and piercing eyes.

'Yes,' he said, cautiously. 'I do know Alice – er – Watkinson.' Now he had learned her surname.

'Have you been in touch? Commiserated?' Douglas asked. He was on the point of telling this pale man with the greying hair that the abductor was Rowena's father – for that made the whole thing more horrific – when his habitual caution stopped him. It was unlikely that this fact would remain undisclosed throughout the trial, unless the defence advised against it, since it made the crime more heinous, but perhaps, to protect the child, it could be suppressed. Though even so, some investigative journalist might pry out the truth and, maintaining the strict letter of the law, expose it subtly.

'What is your interest in this?' Paul asked.

'I am her neighbour. My wife is her friend. The nanny was living in our house,' said Douglas.

'I haven't rung her. I hadn't known her long, and I'm sure she's got enough to deal with, without my adding to her troubles,' Paul said smoothly.

'You were a fair weather friend, then, were you?' Douglas asked. They'd been on kissing terms. How far had things gone between them? Were they lovers? Had they had the opportunity?

His mind switched away from this unprofitable track as Paul said, feebly, 'Possibly.'

'What a shit you are,' Douglas said, in pleasant tones, rose to his feet, and, oh-so-accidentally, tipped his coffee over so that it spilled towards Paul, drenching his sandwiches and dripping on to his lap. 'I wish I'd poured it on your head, but I didn't want to scald you,' Douglas added, and he turned on his heel and walked out, abandoning his own sandwiches.

The episode had attracted almost no attention. Two women at a neighbouring table had overheard Douglas's remark and seen the spill, but after giggling together and muttering something about a lover's quarrel, they continued with their own more interesting conversation. Paul used his napkin and the one Douglas had ignored to do some mopping up. As it was a self-service place, no staff hovered helpfully around. Curiously, he had lost his appetite. He went out to the washroom to try salvaging his clothing, but his pride was seriously dented. He might even have to find another place for lunch, in case the madman returned.

Back in the bookshop, he felt shame, but this was a time when it was best to walk away.

25

There was a frost that Monday night, and on Tuesday morning it was chilly on the station platform as Douglas waited for his train. He felt good about his brush with Alice's boyfriend, or however he should be defined, though if someone had described a similar incident, concerning someone else, he would have been disapproving of such conduct. He could not understand what had made him act so uncharacteristically. Was it Emily's death, or something more? Amended likenesses of the dead girl had been faxed through from Auckland and might be in the morning's papers. Identifying her was important. Someone must have missed her, worried about her; she was someone's daughter.

Just as Rowena was: and Alice was another, kept immured at home. Douglas could see that her parents' demands combined with Alice's own shy disposition had been no preparation for adult life.

Inside his *Times* there was a sketch of a pretty young girl with long wavy hair touching her shoulders, and a much thinner face than Emily's had been.

WAS HER NAME ROSE? asked a headline in someone else's paper, which he could see across the aisle, and where a larger version of the sketch was printed.

All the papers contained reports of the capture of the man wanted in connection with her death. He had been arrested on a farm somewhere in the Midlands; a police helicopter was involved. There were few details. Before reporters could arrive, Godfrey had been removed and the area cordoned off, and once he was charged, which would be today, the case would be *sub judice*.

In Luton, there was no hiding the amended sketch from Larry. His wife had already seen it displayed on the early television news.

She set his plate of eggs and bacon before him as he glanced at the front page of his paper. Colour drained from his face.

'Seen this?' he asked.

She nodded, silent.

'It's our Emily,' he said. For that, not Rose, had been her name; she had shared it with the girl whose identity she had adopted. Perhaps the coincidence was what had triggered her deception.

The woman nodded again.

'Say nothing,' she suggested. She would not tell him that the girl had been here. 'If no one comes forward, they'll let it drop.'

'Someone else will recognise her,' Larry said. 'A teacher. Someone.'

'She hadn't been to school for years,' the woman said. 'We'd have heard, if she had.' There would have been social services coming round, claims for maintenance, all that. 'You haven't seen the papers,' she advised.

He'd get over it. She'd go upstairs with him after breakfast, help him to forget it. There was no point in him feeling responsible.

*   *   *

Among all the other women who saw the artist's sketch that morning, one had a searing shock. Rose saw her daughter's face, looking older than the last time she had seen her, her hair a little longer, staring at her from the page.

Secretly, she had tried to find her, but without success. Her second marriage had brought difficulties. Her new husband was not unlike her first, in that he was possessive and overbearing, and his son and daughter, younger than Emily, manipulated differences between them in such a way as to make every problem apparently her fault. Rose had tried to defend her when she could, but Emily seemed to resent the attention that she gave her stepchildren, and she did not find in Ted the kindly father figure which she longed for. Then Rose and Ted had a daughter of their own, Sandra, whose birth seemed to separate Emily still more from the others, although she was very good with the baby and helped Rose care for her. Ted, however, criticised everything she did and told Rose he feared that, from jealousy, she might harm Sandra. The row which followed prompted Emily's disappearance. Soon afterwards, Ted changed his job and now they lived in a pleasant, modern house in Milton Keynes, not so very far from where Emily had been found abandoned.

Allowing her to stay in care had been a dreadful decision, but the girl herself had thought it would be for the best.

'Ted and the kids don't like me, Mum,' she'd said. 'They like Sandra, though. I don't want to make trouble for you. Maybe things will be better later.'

But there had been no further opportunity. After the move, Rose's visits to the children's home to see her had grown fewer, and although she wrote and sent presents, when Emily was moved to another home, contact ended. Then she absconded, and eventually, Rose had given up her limited efforts at tracing her, though she often thought about her.

Her failure to recognise the shorn-headed girl in the first drawing was understandable; today's paper showed both sketches, and apart from the cropped head, excess weight had padded out Emily's neat features. Rose hadn't noticed the likeness to her father which his new wife had seen instantly.

Rose laid her head on her folded arms at the kitchen table and wept for the daughter she had lost and had betrayed. Ted would have to know about it. This was something she could not avoid. Emily must be identified, and given a proper funeral.

Moving like an old, old woman, she went to the telephone.

After she had called the police, she wondered about the earring depicted in both sketches. Who had given it to Emily? Someone must have cared for her enough to do so.

She didn't have to identify the body. That had already been done by someone with whom Emily had been staying. In any case, it was unrecognisable. One of the interviewing officers, wanting to punish Rose, made that quite clear. A jury would be shown photographs of her injuries at Sutton's trial. There were no reliable dental records, but DNA testing would confirm that this really was her daughter. Rose agreed to give a blood sample to be matched. She told the police she did not know Emily's father's present address, a last attempt at shielding her from him and his vicious wife.

Cooperation between police forces was involved, since Emily had vanished from one area, and had been found in another in whose jurisdiction Godfrey had been charged. A third force had arrested him.

Darwin heard about the identification. He telephoned Isabel

to tell her. Isabel's cleaning lady, whose day it was at Elm Lodge, had felt deprived at missing out on all the excitement but she was one of the first to hear this; she, like all the village residents, had been shocked by what had happened. The matter had been endlessly discussed in The Bull, where it was decided that nothing was too bad for Godfrey Sutton. Joe Pugh achieved distinction because he had seen the van, though not its owner, who, it was said, had eaten in The Stick and Monkey. Some of the more recent arrivals in the village patronised that pub, but did not know the various participants in the drama and were a disappointment to reporters questioning them. They did not get much information from the long-term residents, who clammed up when approached. The Watkinsons had lived in Fordswick for many years and were respected, and the little girl had done nothing to deserve notoriety. Godfrey Sutton, though, was remembered as a fly-by-night. No one was sure he was Rowena's father, though it was suspected, but he had spread his favours elsewhere, too.

There didn't seem to be much of a sex scandal. What there had been was long past and small beer by today's standards. Another, more sensational case soon drove it from the headlines. The story might be big when Godfrey Sutton came to trial, but that would not be for months.

A few fine days were succeeded by very stormy weather, when strong gales blew, and spirits faltered, but while the evidence to be used against Godfrey Sutton was assembled, normal life was resumed in Fordswick. Strangely, no journalist had mentioned Emily's own arrest. The defence knew nothing about it, for Emily had not told Godfrey how she came to be staying at Elm Lodge, beyond the fact that Isabel was her godmother. Colin Darwin, who, much to his satisfaction, had now been switched to CID, hoped they would not find out, since it could be used to present the victim in an unfavourable manner. After Emily's mother had come forward, an inquest had been opened and adjourned until police enquiries were complete. The case was now with the Crown Prosecution Service.

Godfrey, awaiting trial, knew his chances of a manslaughter verdict were good. That might mean as much as seven years, but he would get remission, he told himself, staring at the walls of his cell. He kept quiet about why he had been remanded, and although he was not yet proven guilty, the pressures became inexorably hard to bear. He had found his previous short stretches almost intolerable, and since then had contrived to spend a lot of time out of doors and away from other people. Now he longed to be back in his van, driving around, a master of the road. If he were to be put away for years, as must happen, he thought he would go mad.

After his arrest the van had been examined. The receipt for the paint had been found, and his efforts to change the registration number were exposed. Emily's and the child's prints were inside the vehicle, and several of Rowena's hairs. Emily's blood had stained the red hat Godfrey had been wearing, and her earring, also bearing traces of her blood and skin tissue, had dropped on to the floor of the van and was discovered under the front seat, where she must have kicked it in her struggles, either by accident or on purpose. It would be nice, if fanciful, to think she'd managed to do it deliberately, leaving it as a clue, said Isabel, when Colin Darwin passed on this information. He thought her injuries were too severe to have left her capable of such reasoning. There were also two postcards in the van, bought in Northtown Museum, still in their bag with the receipt dated nine days before the crime.

By now, Godfrey's past record had been discovered and the fact that the police in Canada wanted him for fraud. He'd operated scams for years, it seemed, but in the end had not got away with sufficiently large sums to make him a likely subject for extradition. A Canadian wife was suing for divorce; there was a suspicion that there might be other wives, but even if that turned out to be true, a conviction for bigamy would not attract a heavy sentence.

Isabel received a letter, forwarded by the police, from Rose, who said that she had tried to write several times but had torn up each attempt. She made no effort to excuse her own neglect of Emily, but said she wanted to thank Isabel for looking after her in her final weeks of life. She knew so little about her daughter's last few years: only what the police had told her, which was almost nothing. If Isabel had the time, and did not hate her too unforgivably, would she reply? A stamped addressed envelope was enclosed.

Isabel went to see her. She told Alice, showing her the letter, but no one else. Alice tried to dissuade her.

'You don't want to get any more involved,' she said.

'She's feeling guilty. So she should, I know, but you've had experience of a ruthless man, with Godfrey; we don't know about Rose's domestic life. She parted from Emily's father and is remarried – the letter tells us so – but that's just the tip of the iceberg. I'd like to know a little more, and I can tell her what the real Emily – my Emily – has said.' For Isabel's genuine goddaughter had not only made a detailed statement about her period in hospital and the girl who had been in the next bed, but had talked about it at some length on the telephone to Isabel. 'The mother's going to be haunted by it for the rest of her days,' Isabel continued. 'It's not going to hurt me to go to Milton Keynes. I shan't tell Douglas, by the way,' she added.

'Would he forbid you?' Alice asked, incredulous. She smiled.

'Probably, but I would not obey,' said Isabel.

Alice smiled quite often, these days, Isabel had noticed, and even sometimes laughed. The au pair girl, Cecile, was a big success, willing and cheerful, and having been overloaded with work by her previous employers, found the more reasonable expectations of the Watkinsons a pleasant contrast. She had agreed to extend her stay throughout the summer. Alice was giving her English lessons, and Alice and Cecile spoke French together every day for at least half an hour. Rowena was learning, too. Everyone tried not to think about the trial, which was scheduled for October, and that was surprisingly soon, Douglas told them. He had been looking into sentencing and penal matters. The system needed serious revision, he declared, with fine defaulters cluttering up prisons, which did not pay the fines and cost the taxpayers money; far better set them to work to pay off their debts doing something disagreeable, like cleaning public lavatories. He played chess with Robert Watkinson regularly now, on Sunday afternoons, and they discussed this and other problems over tea after their game. As Douglas was not in the Home Office, he felt able to express his views. Both men thought Godfrey would offend again as soon as he came out of prison.

So did other prisoners. Though not a sexual offender or alleged child molester, the fact that Godfrey had tried to kidnap a child had been discovered through the grapevine, and he was attacked several times. This, however, was not generally known outside the prison. Awaiting trial, desperate to relieve his situation, and though not one of the protagonists, he became involved in a demonstration during which a prison officer was taken hostage. Godfrey had tried to join a roof-top protest, enabling him to get outside the building, but before that happened, the incident turned into a minor riot and Godfrey was among the injured. Later, it was said that other prisoners used his collaboration in the disturbance as an excuse for attacking him again. This time, he ended up in hospital.

On a bright, cold day, Isabel went to Milton Keynes, where she met Rose in a café in the shopping centre, a better plan, both thought, than for Isabel to go to Rose's house; a visit by a stranger might cause curiosity among her neighbours, who knew nothing about Rose's connection with the dead girl. So far, that information had not been made public. It was a touchy subject with her husband, and best avoided.

She tried to explain this to Isabel, who had arrived early and been on a small shopping spree, buying a book for Rowena and a pretty blouse for Alice, whose image, Isabel had decided, needed improvement.

'I don't want things to break up, you see,' said Rose, a small, faded woman, not forty years old, yet looking more than fifty; her hair was an unlikely red, with a frizzy perm and fringe. Was its natural state blonde and wavy, as Emily's once was?

Yes, was the answer, for Rose showed Isabel some snapshots of Emily as a child and herself a pretty, smiling woman, with an elderly couple in the background.

'My grandparents. They had a farm in Suffolk, and me and Em went to stay there, long ago,' she said.

She cried a little, telling Isabel that she had left Emily's father, taking the child, because he was brutal to her and very strict with Emily. Later he had pressed for access, and when she had denied it, had snatched the child away. The woman he was living with, whom he had finally married, had beaten her, and eventually Rose had got Emily back but they never felt safe, and when her present husband came along, a widower in a secure job, with two children of his own, it had seemed the perfect rescue.

'And it was, in a way,' said Rose, weeping into the sandwiches which were all she would order, forcing Isabel, who fancied pasta, to do the same.

Isabel told her what she knew about Emily, all of it favourable, and said she thought Godfrey had treated her properly until that last day, though clearly he was only making use of her. But both women knew that Emily's standards of good treatment might not be very high.

'Who gave her that little earring? Did she say?' asked Rose.

'Yes,' said Isabel. 'I asked her if it was one of a pair, and she said yes, but she'd lost the other on the site. She said a boy called Billy gave them to her, but he had gone away soon afterwards.'

'I suppose we won't ever know what happened, before she went protesting,' Rose said.

'No. I didn't ask her much. I thought she'd tell me if she wanted to,' said Isabel. But Emily must have been pretty desperate to have risked the bluff of calling on her for help. Isabel might so easily have disowned her.

No one but Emily's stepmother ever knew about her visit to her father's house, and he never referred to her again.

'She didn't know where I was living,' said Rose. 'I did try to find her, and I put adverts in the paper where we used to live, and where her dad used to live, but nothing came of it. My husband didn't know,' she added hastily.

'No – well, I can see how difficult it was,' said Isabel. The woman was clearly terrified of this second husband, and, with another child, was dependent on him. She was not capable of standing on her own feet: and nor was Alice, Isabel saw, in a flash of revelation, but there was still hope for her.

'There'll be the funeral,' said Rose.

'Yes,' said Isabel, and waited.

'I've got some money saved,' said Rose. 'I'll see to it.'

'Do you want to have it here?' asked Isabel. Then she added, 'It may attract the press, you know. Do you want to be there?'

'Not really,' said the woman. 'I didn't go to see her. They said I wouldn't recognise her.'

'You wouldn't have,' said Isabel. 'I wouldn't have, except I knew it was her, and she had a little mole on the inside of her right arm.'

'Oh yes!' Rose smiled.

'I was there when she died,' said Isabel. 'I held her hand. I'd like to think she knew I was with her, but the nurse thought she'd been unconscious for hours. So while she was out like that, she couldn't have been suffering or frightened.'

'I'd like to kill that man – that Godfrey Sutton,' said Rose, suddenly showing spirit. 'What was she to him? Just a girl who got in the way.'

'I wish I could have stopped her seeing him,' said Isabel. 'And I would have done, but you see, the real Emily Frost, my goddaughter, is much older. She's twenty-three. And I thought he was a friend from the past – perhaps from the site where she'd been living. They seem to be a friendly lot, these demonstrators,' she added. 'Different camps of them, in tunnels and up trees, all looking out for one another.'

'They're drop-outs, aren't they? Good for nothing else,' said Rose. 'Hippies, like.'

'Well – yes, I suppose a lot of them are,' said Isabel. 'But some are convinced and passionate. Emily didn't talk about it much. She was embarrassed at being arrested. I think she just got swept up with the rest of the crowd. She wouldn't have been intentionally violent. She was lovely with Rowena,' she added. 'And Rowena loved her.' Then she said, 'When all this is over, I'm sure the police will let you have the earring. They may need it for the trial, as evidence, but not afterwards. I'll ask about it, shall I?'

'Oh yes, please.' Rose's eyes filled with tears. 'Thank you for thinking of it.'

'Would you like us to see to the funeral?' Isabel asked her. 'We could arrange it quietly, though I expect you'd have to give your official consent. And I'd be there, and Alice Watkinson, Rowena's mother. We were both her friends. I'd tell you about it, later. There was a policeman who was there, too, when she died. He'd come. I think they will allow her to be buried soon, if you apply.' The defence were not going to require another postmortem, as sometimes happened. 'Or cremated,' she added. Graves needed tending.

'Cremated,' said Rose. 'And if they sent me the ashes, I could put them in the garden, and plant a bush above them,' she said. 'No one else would have to know.'

'That's a lovely idea,' said Isabel. 'I'll collect them, and bring them to you. We can meet here again.'

'You're so kind,' said Rose.

'She liked singing hymns,' said Isabel. 'And she was a good cook. She said she'd helped her mother. None of that fitted with the Emily I knew, and her mother.'

'I'm glad she remembered,' said Rose.

*　　*　　*

Douglas was very good about it; he arranged it all, and paid for it.

'That unhappy woman needs her savings,' he said.

The cremation took place in Northtown early on a beautiful spring day, with the cherry trees in the crematorium garden covered in blossom. It was a weepy affair, with Isabel and Alice both mopping their eyes. Only they, Douglas and Colin Darwin were present, but the vicar – Fordswick's own, who agreed at once when Douglas asked him to take the service – read the Twenty-third Psalm and the piece from Revelation about a new heaven and a new earth, and some prayers, after which they trooped sadly out into the sunshine. The real Emily Frost had sent flowers. She was staying on in New Zealand for the present. Douglas, astonishingly, had suggested that he and Isabel might take a trip there after the trial, instead of having a summer holiday.

It was the end of the chapter, until the next one opened with the trial, but the memory and the consequences would last for ever.

A week later they heard that Godfrey, as a result of the hostage incident in his prison and subsequent rioting, had had a heart attack and died. At the inquiry which followed, it was alleged that he had seemed to invite the violence he attracted, almost like an involuntary suicide. A verdict of accidental death was pronounced.

Perhaps Rowena need never learn who her father had been.

Isabel, meeting Rose, with the ashes in their container, which she had parcelled up in a plain green bag so that the woman could take it home without its attracting any attention, was able to give her the earring. She had had it cleaned, and put it in a small box in a nest of cotton wool. There was also a photograph of Emily, taken at the site but not during the disturbance, in happy mood. Isabel had obtained it from a freelance photographer whom Colin Darwin had tracked down. Rose went away, sad but reconciled.

Colin dropped into Gifts Galore occasionally. He and his wife had parted two years ago, reasonably amicably, and he often saw his sons, who visited him in his small terraced house in Northtown. His former wife lived four streets away and they shared the children in a cooperative manner which Isabel, when she heard about it, admired. She wished Colin would take an interest in Alice, who could do with the support of a strong man like him, but though Colin went up to Ford House from time to time, and was pleased that Alice seemed to be more confident, he did not fall in with Isabel's romantic plans for him, which she mentioned one evening in The Pineapple.

Colin grinned.

'She's not my type,' he said. 'You are,' he added, holding her gaze.

'I'm married,' Isabel replied.

'So?'

'So, thanks, but no,' she answered.

Inside her head, she felt like screaming once again, this time in words: 'Why not?'

Why not, indeed?

'On second thoughts,' she said, 'perhaps.'

Larry met the man in a pub not far from the prison from which he'd been released that morning. He handed the man a pack of cigarettes. The released prisoner took one, lit up, and, without speaking, pocketed the pack.

'You all right, then?' Larry asked.

'Well enough,' said the man, a small, wiry fellow with a fluff of ginger hair around a bald crown. He grinned, then drew on his cigarette, inhaling deeply. 'Went well,' he added. 'Didn't think he'd snuff it, though. The riot gave us the chance. Mind you, he asked for it. Stuck his neck out, looking for trouble. Got roughed up a good few times.'

'Thanks anyway.' Larry gave him a fat envelope. He'd put in hours of overtime and extra jobs to fill it. 'It's all there,' he said, adding, 'You did well.'

'Did right, mate. Can't have that – kidnapping and beating up young girls,' said the man, a practised burglar, putting the envelope in his jacket pocket. 'Glad to oblige.'

ACT OF VIOLENCE

Margaret Yorke

The quiet market town of Mickleburgh knows very little serious crime, and local solicitor Oliver Foxton's days are occupied with wills, conveyancing, and the occasional drunk and disorderly. The outlying villages of Winbury, where he lives with his wife Sarah, and Deerton, home of their friends the Stewarts, seem like rural havens.

So when four local schoolboys go on the rampage in Deerton and commit an astonishingly needless act of violence, the lives of the Foxtons and the Stewarts are shattered. Attempting to come to terms with what has happened to his friends, Oliver immerses himself in the renovation of an old dolls' house belonging to his friend Prudence Wilmot, a local author, but finds that the doll inhabitants increasingly become a symbol of his own troubled marriage and the tensions the tragedy has sparked within it.

Meanwhile, the schoolboys who merely witnessed the violence come under pressure from their parents and the police to name the guilty party, and they must wrestle with both their misguided loyalty and fear of reprisals, as gradually the police build their case. And all the time another hidden menace lurks in the background, as a released murderer, living near by, is enthralled by the crime – and practising as a counsellor, stands poised to offer help . . .

Unblinkingly addressing the issues of today, Margaret Yorke has written a novel of chilling realism and once more proved herself the mistress of suspense.

'The mistress of the skillfully spun suspense novel . . . her quiet, unemphatic style of narrative makes the story a compelling read'
Sunday Telegraph

THE SMOOTH FACE OF EVIL

Margaret Yorke

Alice Armitage is an elderly, and lonely, widow. An unwelcome guest in the large house she helped pay for, she endures the cold, vicious sniping of her son's ambitious wife, who makes it clear she'd rather Alice was conveniently tucked away in an old people's home.

So when the charming and obliging Terry Brett appears on the scene, Alice is happy to believe that she has found herself a new friend who will liven up her solitary existence. For a while that seems to be the case, but Terry is a conman, and when he joins forces with Alice's scheming neighbour, Sue, their greed takes them further than they'd planned . . .

'A genuine slow-burner running efficiently on greed, lust and desolation'
Observer

'As plausible as it is readable, which is saying a lot'
Punch

Other bestselling Warner titles available by mail:

The prices shown above are correct at time of going to press, however the publishers reserve the right to increase prices on covers from those previously advertised, without further notice.

WARNER BOOKS

WARNER BOOKS
Cash Sales Department, P.O. Box 11, Falmouth, Cornwall, TR10 9EN
Tel: +44 (0) 1326 372400, Fax: +44 (0) 1326 374888
Email: books@barni.avel.co.uk.

POST AND PACKING
Payments can be made as follows: cheque, postal order (payable to Warner Books) or by credit cards. Do not send cash or currency.

All U.K. Orders	**FREE OF CHARGE**
E.E.C. 7 Overseas	25% of order value

Name (Block Letters) _____

Address _____

_____

Post/zip code: _____

☐ Please keep me in touch with future Warner publications
☐ I enclose my remittance £_____
☐ I wish to pay by Visa/Access/Mastercard/Eurocard   Expiry date